A successful playwright, Valerie Maskell grew up in Kent, then attended RADA. She now teaches drama in Newbury, Berkshire. Her remarkable debut novel, FANCY WOMAN, won the TSB/Peninsula Prize for fiction. THE WORKBOX is her second novel.

THE WORKBOX

Valerie Maskell

This first hardcover edition published in Great Britain 1995 by
SEVERN HOUSE PUBLISHERS LTD of
9–15 High Street, Sutton, Surrey SM1 1DF.
by arrangement with Warner Books
a Division of Little Brown and Co. (UK) Ltd

British Library Cataloguing in Publication Data
Maskell, Valerie
  Workbox. – New ed
  I. Title
  823.914 [F]

  ISBN 0-7278-4872-0

Typeset by Hewer Text Composition Services, Edinburgh.
Printed and bound in Great Britain by
T. J. Press (Padstow) Ltd, Padstow, Cornwall.

THE
WORKBOX

CHAPTER 1

MONDAY

Instead of leaving her car when she had drawn up in front of the imposing Georgian portico of Easton Court, Dorothy remained in the driving seat. Just the moment for a cigarette. She imagined feeling in the glove compartment, finding a left-over packet, lighting up and drawing in the first sweet, relaxing puffs. She did not feel in the glove compartment because she had given up smoking six months before. In any case they would be stale.

Four twenty-five. Half an hour with Mum, and she could still reach home in time to persuade Angela into the bathroom with the baby and tidy up the sitting room a bit before dashing out to meet Frank at the station.

There never seemed to be enough room for everyone these days, even with Mum in here. When they had bought Jasmine Villa it was just the right size,

and what an interesting coincidence that it had been
built nearly eighty years ago by her own grandfather. Then when Angie had gone to university it
had seemed too big, but before there was time to
do anything about moving, there she was, home
again with a baby boy whose father she didn't want
to marry. Fortunately she got on quite well with
her grandmother because before Timothy was six
months old, Dorothy's mother was also installed at
Jasmine Villa, having become too frail to live alone
any longer. And then the fact that Jasmine Villa was
once the home of the Clarke family had turned out
to be a disadvantage, adding to the old lady's con-
fusion, and making her critical of the alterations
they were having done. It was a relief, really, when
she needed more nursing care than they could give
and she moved, with surprising docility, into
Easton Court.

Four times a week Dorothy visited. On Mondays
and Wednesdays after school, on Saturday mornings and on Sunday afternoons. Now she sat in the
car, nerving herself to be bright and affectionate.
Poor old Mum! She'd been so smart and successful
and sure of herself, going up to London every week
to buy for her three elegant shops, being wined and
dined by sales managers, and coming home tired
but happy after her busy, interesting day, and now
all that business acumen and sense of style were
gone, and the tall, slim body they had inhabited
had become hunched and gnarled and was huddled
in an incongruous pastel-coloured garment in the

one-time drawing room of this eighteenth-century mansion.

How would she find her today? Sometimes she would be up, sitting in an easy chair, with her hair done, and wearing her rings. But on bad days she would be in bed, sleepy and muddled. Most of the time she seemed unhappy. Who wouldn't be, Dorothy thought, knowing they had come here to die? Presumably patients did sometimes improve and leave Easton Court for somewhere other than the Chapel of Rest; but Dorothy had not heard of this happening.

She crossed the well-kept gravel drive and entered the small entrance hall which led into an oval inner hall of considerable magnificence. It had a gallery at ceiling height, beyond which you could look up to a glass dome in the roof. The furniture was antique, of the same period as the house, and there were great vases filled with chrysanthemums, making splashes of warm colour against the panelled walls. But Dorothy could take no pleasure in these surroundings, assaulted as she was by the overwhelming smell of urine. Most of the aged patients were incontinent, and not even the latest hygienic appliances could obviate this reminder of the failing flesh.

She approached the double doors of the old drawing room. No screen barred her way. Its absence indicated that she was permitted to enter. Today, she saw at once, was one of her mother's better days. She was propped up in a chair. Dorothy crossed the room quickly and sat down beside her, taking her hand.

'Hallo, Mum darling, how are things today?'

'Awful, of course, how else could they be?'

Yes, it was one of her good days.

'What did you have for lunch?'

'I don't know. I don't live to eat.'

'I see old Miss Stanbrook's up and about again.'

'She's dotty.'

'Where's that nice nurse, the one you like?'

'She's off today. It's the other one. The fat one. She's horrible.'

'How is she horrible?'

'She makes us all cry.'

'Oh, Mum, surely not.'

'She does. She hurts us.'

'Oh dear.' Dorothy was distressed. 'How does she hurt you?'

'It's these catheter things.' The old lady moved her dressing gown, disclosing a plastic container on the floor by her feet, with a tube running into it. 'I don't need it. I can control myself. It's just that it's easier for them.' Dorothy did not know what to say. Was it easier for them? 'And it hurts. Makes me feel as though I want to pass water all the time. If it wasn't for that, I wouldn't be too bad, apart from being bored stiff.'

Time for a different approach, Dorothy decided. 'We'll be getting more space at school soon. They're letting us have a terrapin. That's an extra classroom. We shall put the third years in there, they need a bit of peace and quiet sometimes. Miss Fielding's been nagging them for years about it.'

'You wanted to be a teacher.'

'I still do.'

'You're always complaining.'

'I don't think I am. I like my work.'

'No money in it.'

'That's not everything.'

'It's nearly everything. You'll find that out, one of these days, when you're old and ill and nobody wants you. Money's the only thing that can do you any good.'

'I expect you're right. I'm sure money is important. Or what you can buy with it is.'

'That's your trouble. Buying things. Always has been. Wasting money.'

The injustice of this almost brought tears to her daughter's eyes, exhausted as she was with her long day at school, the tension at home, and the emotional effort of visiting the nursing home. She was a careful spender; not even her mother had accused her of extravagance for years and years. Indeed, Angela's not always unwarranted cry was that she was stingy.

She decided that it was hopeless to try and talk, but it was too soon to leave. She looked round the room. The floor was polished, there were flower printed curtains, and toning bedspreads in various colours. The beds were not hospital beds, except for one, at the far end. There was a group of easy chairs where she sat with her mother, and an arrangement of dried leaves and flowers on the table. Apart from the beds, and their ancient occupants, it was more like a hotel lounge than a nursing home.

A woman, round-shouldered and frail, shuffled along the ward and stopped beside Dorothy.

'I just thought I'd say goodbye,' she said, smiling.

'Oh, are you going home? How nice.' Someone was leaving the place alive! Dorothy felt considerably cheered.

'Yes, my son's coming to fetch me in a few minutes. I'm going to live with him. He's been trying to persuade me for so long, I thought I would.'

'How lovely.' And what a good son. He had not fallen short as she, Dorothy, had fallen short. Would it work? What about his wife?

'Yes, it's very nice here, but there's no place like home, I always say, with your own flesh and blood.'

'No, indeed.'

'There are the grandchildren too. They're looking forward to having me, I know.'

'They must be.' Perhaps so, if they were small children. But what if they were teenagers?

'It's a very nice house. Plenty of room.'

'Is it near here?'

'No, it's a long way off. I must go and get ready. I mustn't keep him waiting.'

'You certainly mustn't.'

The woman resumed her shaky progress down the ward, and after one or two attempts to find something to say that would enable them to part on a note of friendliness, Dorothy kissed her mother's forehead gently and said goodbye.

In the hall she saw the old lady sitting in a chair, watching the door. A nurse approached.

'Now come on Miss Molyneux, you mustn't sit there in the draught, dear, come back into the ward.'

Protesting a little, she allowed the nurse to help her to rise and now supporting herself with a walking frame, she set off slowly in the direction from which she had come. The nurse smiled at Dorothy.

'Always thinks her son's coming to fetch her,' she said.

'And . . . and . . . isn't he?'

'Oh no. She hasn't got a son. She's never been married even. They get these funny ideas. You found your mother alright?'

No, thought Dorothy, *since you've asked me, I didn't. There's a fat nurse that makes her cry. Why daren't I say that? Because you might be the fat nurse, for all I know, you might be offended. Well, of course, you would be and then you'd take it out on her in some way. No, if I'm to say anything about that, it can't be to you.*

'Yes, though she seems rather confused.'

'They get like that. So long as she's happy.'

'Oh, yes, I think she's quite happy.'

'You'll be in again soon?'

'Oh, yes.'

'That's right. She likes to see you.'

For a long moment Dorothy stood there. Through the double doors she could see Miss Molyneux slowly plodding down the ward towards her bed. Then she went out into the autumn afternoon and drove home faster than usual.

WEDNESDAY

Down the steep, chalk-walled slope to the sea ran Addie, her feet in their black boots gathering speed, so that she was halfway across the stretch of firm sand that bordered the shore before she could stop. The tide was on the way out and the sands, deserted on this grey November afternoon, were damply brown and strewn with whitish stones and black seaweed. On her right the view was bounded by the chalky headland and on her left by the grey asphalt rise of the lower promenade. Addie put her hands to her mouth and shouted with all her might.

'Jay! Charlie!'

Her voice faded away hopelessly on the east wind. The boys could be hiding in the bathing machines that were drawn up close together against the cliffs. These were no longer dragged to the sea by horses, but still served as changing cabins in the summer. Painted white, each had a little balcony in front and wooden steps down to the sand. Addie ran up the flight of the nearest machine, two steps at a time. The balcony being empty, she tried the door. It was locked. Heaving herself up into a sitting position on the wooden barrier, she swung her long legs over onto the next machine. Empty again. She tried the door, and so she went on down the line of twelve bathing machines, and soon she was enjoying the rhythmic exercise for its own sake. Heave up, legs over, jump down, and rattle. Heave up, legs over, jump down and rattle. She was only a little impeded by her petticoat, her box-pleated maroon dress, her white starched pinafore and her brown coat. Her tam-o-shanter, cleverly made by her mother from left-over dress material, slipped back and she crammed it down over her ears. Breathless, she arrived at the last balcony and remembered she was looking for her brothers. How she wished they would not come down to the sands in winter! She had often found them as dusk gathered, fishing from the breakwater or scrambling over the rocks, in imminent danger, it seemed to her, of drowning or being cut off by the tide. She jumped down the last little flight of steps and ran along the sands and up the slope onto the lower promenade. Climbing on its ornate railings, she surveyed the beach, calling again.

'Jay! Charlie! Where are you?'

The sea off the Kent coast was a thick, unfriendly grey, though to the west an edge of pale gold outlined the clouds. A dark figure stood far out on the breakwater. Was it one of the boys? Whoever it was evidently saw her because he began to walk back towards the sands. When he reached dry land and jumped down she saw he was far too tall for Jay or Charlie. He was shouting something; and then Addie recognized him as Nitty Havergal, a grubby, slow-witted creature who was a byword in the town for dirt and stupidity. Unwanted by any relative, too limited mentally to do even the simplest work, he roamed about, lost and useless.

Once, to Addie's horror, he had exposed himself in front of her; and she was all the more appalled because she did not know then that he was constantly in trouble for indulging in this habit. Instead she held a guilty belief that she was partly responsible. Had she not, out of pity, smiled at him? Had she not, when he'd asked her, given him a sweet? After that she ignored him, running home or to school as fast as she could.

Now she was frightened, for there was no one else in sight. She turned, and ran back along the promenade towards the gap. But there was a stretch of sand to cross before she could reach it. That was where he might catch her. He had broken into a shambling trot, shouting wordlessly. Breathless, terrified, and only a few yards ahead, she reached the bottom of the slope, but it was steep and endless. Her heart pounded, her chest hurt, her head was bursting. She was climbing through red mists and someone was reaching down to her. Someone with a kind voice, who said, 'You'll soon feel better, Mrs Castle. Just relax, just relax.'

With relief she realized that she was safe in bed; ill, obviously, but safe. Not being pursued. Her eyelids fluttered weakly as she tried to convey her gratitude to whoever was there. And then she remembered that she was eighty-four years old.

It was some time before she got it all straight in her mind again. She kept losing herself at different

places in her long past. They had gone back, of
course, that was it. They had gone back to Jasmine
Villa to live. She and Holly. But where were Mother
and Dad, and Jay and Charlie? And Bella? No, wait.
It was a different family. It was Dorothy her daughter, and Frank, and Angela. Angela, who was not
Holly, though so like her.

She must remember that. She knew she often
called her Holly, but Holly was her elder sister, and
Angela was her granddaughter. Jasmine Villa! The
house had lived up to its name. It was a villa and
there was jasmine. The name was engraved on a
glass fanlight over the door. It had been built by
Addie's father, a builder by trade, on a piece of land
he had bought at a bargain price because it was an
odd shape, and at the back of the town.

Would the jasmine have been in bloom that day
when she arrived home, sweating and exhausted,
as dusk fell, her feet sore with pounding the grey
pavements? She entered by the back way. Her
anxiety for her brothers had returned when she left
Nitty Havergal behind and she waited at the kitchen
door, wanting to hear their voices before she
opened it.

The scullery, where she stood, was dark, and
smelt damply of yellow soap and scouring powder.
There was a duckboard on the stone floor in front
of the shallow sink. The walls were dark green and
the window was of frosted glass. Under the sink
was a noisome space where Addie's mother, Nellie
Clarke, kept a zinc bucket and a scrubbing brush.

But the little room was a haven now to breathless

Addie. Her hand was slippery on the brass door-knob as she listened for the boy's voices. It was her mother's she heard, calling out of the opposite door.

'Jay. Charlie. Come along, tea's ready.'

Thankfully, she entered the kitchen.

In contrast to the bleakness of the scullery, it was warm and homely. In the middle was the big scrubbed deal table, now spread with a white cloth, but the main feature was the kitchen range, gleaming with black lead, friendly with the glow of fire behind its bars. It was set into a recess, below a high, wide mantelshelf on which stood a clock, with some letters stuffed behind it; a pair of twisted brass candlesticks; and a drawing of an elephant done by Charlie at school. The walls here were dark green too, except for a wainscot of embossed shiny brown paper which protected the bottom three feet or so, but most of one wall was covered by the dresser. This splendid piece of furniture had been built by Addie's father, and with its cupboards, shelves, hooks and drawers, it played an important part in the Clarkes' family life. The willow-pattern plates were set out on the shelves, and the Coronation mugs along the top, and when anything was lost or misplaced in Jasmine Villa, whether hairbrush or ruler or gloves or loose change, it would sooner or later be found on the dresser.

This room, like the rest of the ground floor, was lit by gas. The shaded white globes mounted on metal brackets at each end of the mantelpiece were already glowing and by their thin yellow light Nellie was making the tea. She looked round sharply.

'Where have you been?'

'Playing with Lily Foster.'

Addie often lied to her parents, as did her brothers and sisters. The boys lied about playing on the deserted sands, and Addie, unable to tell tales even in her anxiety for them, went on her own to look for them. Then she lied about wherever she had been. Holly's lies were simply to get herself out of trouble or avoid questioning, and Bella lied all the time from force of habit.

'Hurry up,' said Nellie. 'Go and take your things off. And call Holly.'

Jay stared blandly at Addie. She knew that he guessed where she had been and was thinking 'more fool you'. He sat down, poking Bella with his elbow as he did so, and the resulting scuffle was briskly quelled by their mother.

When they were finally all seated Addie looked round the table with satisfaction. Her mother she considered beautiful. Her soft, fluffy hair pinned into a high bun was a pale gold, less red than Addie's own. She sat at the head of the table with her back to the range. Opposite Addie were cherubic Charlie, podgy little Bella and dark haired glowering Jay. Beside her sat Holly, sixteen years old and a pupil teacher. But not grown-up yet, surely, though she looked grown-up, with her brown hair done in the same style as her mother's and her high-collared blouse.

There they were. All at home, safe and happy. Addie smiled at her mother. 'Shouldn't we wait for Dad?' she said.

'He's busy in the office, doing some accounts. When you've had your tea, you can go over and help with the bills, if you like.'

Addie, who enjoyed arithmetic and loved her father, said she would. But it was not Dad she had missed, or Mother. No, it was her brothers and sisters; Jay, Charlie, and even Bella, but most of all, Holly. What happy times they had all had together. Yet she could not think of Holly with joy. Why not, when Holly was so gay, so lively, with her piled up brown hair and her full lips that laughed so often and pouted so sulkily?

Because of the Terrible Time.

She must not think of it, must not remember. For years it had scarcely entered her mind, why brood on it now she was old and ill? But still it would come back. And she, Addie, must do everything. There was no one else. She heard someone moaning and tried to raise herself. At once there was somebody in a white cap. Nurse. But Holly hadn't wanted the nurse. No, she had gone to hospital after all and then there was Timothy. Or was that Angela? But Angela was Holly and Holly was Angela and she had pushed down the bedclothes so that her shoulders were cold and it was starting all over again.

Waking in the night, uncovered. Rising slowly out of a deep sleep to find Holly sitting up, clasping her knees, with the bedclothes hunched around her.

'Holl,' whispered Addie, 'what's the matter?'

'You sleep heavily,' said Holly, accusing her.

'What is it, Holl? Shall I light the candle?'

'No.'

'Have you got a pain? You must tell me.'

'I can't.'

'You always do, Holly. You always tell me everything.'

This was true. Holly, nearly three years older, always told Addie everything. Fears, guilts and hopes, she loaded them all onto her younger sister, and then turned away unburdened, while Addie feared, hoped and agonized in her stead.

So it was on this unforgettable night.

Holly told . . . 'I've done something awful. With a man. You know.'

But Addie didn't know. She had suspected and she had feared, but she didn't know. So Holly told her. Made crude by lack of vocabulary and her own youth and desperation, Holly told.

'I don't believe that,' said Addie. 'No one would ever do that.'

'Well, I have, you little idiot.'

'But the horrible stuff . . . it didn't come inside you, did it Holl?'

'Of course it did.'

'But it must have been awful!' Addie moved away a little in the bed. A great many things that had puzzled and worried her were becoming clear. 'Holly, suppose you have a baby? You might.'

'Well, I don't know yet, do I, stupid?'

'You'll have to tell Mum.'

'Tell Mum! Are you mad, Addie Clarke?'

'But if . . . '

'I'll run away, or perhaps I'll kill myself.'

'Couldn't you get married? Then it wouldn't matter, even if you . . . '

To her surprise, Holly gave a harsh sob. 'No, I can't get married. And you're not to ask me who it was because I shan't tell you, ever. So shut up.'

'I wasn't going to,' Addie replied truthfully. More knowledge, she felt, could only make her feel worse. She could see her sister clearly now, with the thin curtains letting in the moonlight. The room was small, nearly filled by the black painted iron bedstead with its brass knobs. Holly was sitting with her knees drawn up, the white sheet and rough, pale blankets held up to her neck. The dark bulk of the chest of drawers faced them. On it were a small swing mirror and the two identical work-boxes of light coloured wood, the lids inlaid with mother of pearl. These had been Christmas presents from their mother, too obviously chosen in the hope that the girls would thereby be encouraged to take up needlework. They both had to accomplish a certain amount of plain sewing and mending but beyond this neither of them was interested.

In the divided trays that rested inside the boxes they each kept different things. In Holly's were her hairpins and such small trinkets as she possessed, while Addie's contained her treasures, including her favourite seashells, a skeleton leaf, and a golden curl of hair that she had managed to keep after she and her mother had taken Charlie for his first haircut. Underneath these trays the spaces that should have been occupied by dainty pieces of work in progress were stuffed with what Addie called their 'muddles': lengths of darning wool; sewing cotton; embroidery thread; bits of lace edging and ribbon; tape and knicker elastic inextricably tangled into a sort of ball. But the muddles were quite useful. Close examination would usually reveal a thread or end of the required colour and material and you could usually draw out almost as much as you needed before the tangle reasserted itself and refused to give up any more. Fortunately Nellie's regular inspections of her daughters' bedroom did not extend to opening their workboxes.

Addie fixed her eyes on hers now, so as not to look at her sister. 'I don't see how you could do it, Holl. It must be horrible.'

'It's alright.'

'Well, I never shall, anyway.'

Addie curled up, trying unsuccessfully to take possession of her share of the bedclothes. But Holly had the last word. 'Perhaps you'll never get the chance.' She giggled suddenly. 'Except for Nitty Havergal.' She lay down, turned her back to her sister, and slept.

Addie stayed awake, the horror if it all over-whelming her. So that was what he'd meant, that was what he'd wanted. And she hadn't understood, not till now, and understanding brought with it a black cloud of guilt and shame that she felt would never leave her. It would never leave her because somewhere, deep down, her sister's words had awakened a trace of excitement. Unwanted, instantly denied, but excitement, nevertheless. So

Holly slept, but it was dawn before Addie fell into a troubled doze.

For the next few months Holly went her usual apparently carefree way. Only with Addie in private was she irritable or taciturn. And Addie, sharing the bedroom, sleeping in the same bed, could not help knowing when her sister was menstruating, and therefore could not help knowing when she was not. Her carefully thought out, desperately tactful enquiries elicited only accusations of nosiness and spying.

'Just you mind your own business, Addie Clarke. You've got babies on the brain,' and Holly, turning over after the candle was blown out, and dragging the bedclothes away from Addie as she did so, would fall asleep immediately while her sister lay awake, worrying and making plans.

It was Addie, pale and without her usual healthy appetite, who was forced to parry their mother's anxious enquiries, and to swallow laxatives she did not need. Even climbing scaffolding or walking round the top of the six-foot-high garden wall was not the fun it had been, though tomboyish games offered some distraction. Those, and the music evenings.

May Kingston, whom the Clarke children called Auntie May, was Nellie's old school friend who had, as Nellie said, done well for herself by marrying Tom Kingston. Musical evenings at their house were rather special occasions. Their daughter Bridget was a good pianist, but Addie preferred

Holly's Strauss waltzes, played with dash and vigour and a good many wrong notes, to Bridget's classical pieces. Holly had a pleasant soprano voice, too, but Addie and her mother were the real singers. Bella was quite a good fiddler, and sometimes Jay could be persuaded to take his flute. Though young, he was a competent flautist, but the spindly chairs and thin china cups made him feel clumsy and awkward. To Addie's sorrow her father never went to Cornwall Lodge with them. He said the Kingstons were a different class and he believed in sticking to his own station in life. Nellie said this was silly, and that a builder was just as good as a chemist any day. Addie thought privately that her father disliked Mr Kingston, which was hard to understand. Tom Kingston being handsome, friendly and not a bit proud, for all his three shops.

So though Addie enjoyed putting on her best velveteen dress with the lace collar, and going round to the Kingstons' nearly as much as Holly did, it was the music evenings at home that gave her the most pleasure. These were not arranged, they just happened. Somebody would start playing the piano in the front room. Mother would go in and say, 'If you're going to be in here I may as well put a match to the fire.' Then the others would follow and they'd be there for the rest of the evening.

Anything from 'Silent Worship' to 'Three Little Maids From School', from Mendelssohn's 'Spring Song' to 'When Father Painted the Parlour', all were performed with equal gusto. Only Charlie was absent on these occasions. He preferred to stay in the kitchen, playing his mysterious games with lead soldiers, moving them about on the table and whispering to himself. Addie missed his pink-cheeked face and choirboy's voice, but still she was happy and absorbed. After a music evening she would fall asleep quickly, and sometimes sleep till morning. But if she was unlucky enough to wake in the night, all her anxieties would come flooding inescapably back.

She put out a hand, under the bedclothes. No Holly. And the bed was strangely narrow. Opening her eyes, she saw with a shock the high, ornate ceiling, much too far away. Then she realized with her usual sensations of horror and relief that she was not thirteen, that it had all happened long ago, and that Holly was dead.

No wonder she had roused. In her half-dream she had been drawing dangerously near to the Terrible Time, and she did not want to think about that, not yet. Some day or night, quite soon perhaps, she would feel strong enough to go over it all again, but just now she did not feel up to it. And in any case it seemed to be tea-time, and teas at Easton Court were really excellent, with little savoury sandwiches, and pieces of very light sponge cake.

CHAPTER 2

'Come along, dear. You don't want to miss your tea, do you?' Addie struggled to raise herself. The nurse put her arms round her and heaved her up. 'Up we come then, oops-a daisy.'

Fool of a woman, why did she put on this idiotic voice, as though she was speaking to a retarded child?

'Your daughter rang up, dear. She was sorry she couldn't come today after all. Something cropped up at school, she had to stay on.'

So it must have been Dorothy's day for coming to see her. Addie tried to look as if she had known this all the time. 'You didn't tell me,' she said crossly.

'Well, you were asleep, dear. It wasn't worth disturbing you just to tell you that, now was it?'

'I wasn't asleep.'

'You looked as though you were. Now, shall I help you with your tea?'

'I can manage.'

Addie took a sandwich with a shaky hand. 'You'd better see to her,' she said. She nodded towards a little skinny woman, who was sitting in the middle of the ward, wearing only a skimpy vest. Oblivious of her near nakedness, she was drinking noisily out of a plastic cup.

'Miss Stanbrook?' said the nurse. 'Oh, don't you bother about her. She's as happy as a sandboy.'

'Can't you get her a dressing-gown?'

The nurse looked offended. 'She'll only take it straight off again. She's alright while there aren't any visitors. Now supposing you get on with your tea and stop worrying about other people.'

But Addie had lost interest in her tea. She'd known Ruth Stanbrook for years. Her family had owned the big ironmonger's on the Parade. Her father, a widower, had been Mayor once, and Ruth had been Mayoress when she was just eighteen. That year she had presented the prizes at the Music Festival in the Winter Gardens, wearing a lace-trimmed dress, and a hat with pink roses. Now here she was, eighty-seven, half naked, and happy as a sandboy. It didn't seem worth it.

And she missed Dorothy. It wasn't like her not to come on her usual day. She was so wrapped up in that school, as if they couldn't do without her. A pity Angela couldn't have come. She could have brought the baby and held him up outside the window like she did sometimes. That made Addie feel rather proud and special. Angela wasn't married. It didn't seem to matter nowadays. That was a good thing, people not having to hide so much. The Terrible Time would never have happened if it had been now, instead of then. Holly would have told Mother, and Mother would have told Dad, and they would have kept the baby like she and Ronnie had kept this one of Dorothy's. No, no that was wrong. It was Dorothy and her husband Frank who had kept this baby, which belonged to . . . who did it belong to? Dorothy had had a baby of course, but then she'd been married. What a job it was to keep things straight when so much had happened in your life. And it wasn't that your brain was going, just that there was so much to remember. And these girls here treated you as if you didn't know anything. She looked at poor old Ruth who was sitting at the table in the middle of the ward, now decently covered by a red dressing-gown. She was cramming bread and butter into her mouth as though she was starving, poking it in with her forefinger. The nurse went up to her and said, in her jolly voice, 'Now then, Miss Stanbrook dear, that's not a very nice way to eat, is it? There's plenty of time.'

Addie remembered Ruth's boy, Harold Smith, who hadn't had plenty of time, because he'd been killed on the Somme, poor lad, when he was twenty-four. Perhaps he'd had the best of it.

I'm getting morbid, she thought. *Mustn't brood. Doesn't do. I've done enough brooding. What I did, I did for Holly. I must have said that to myself about a hundred thousand times. Think about something nice. Weddings. Dorothy and Frank had a nice wedding. No, that was*

*Dorothy and Kenneth. Dorothy and Frank got married in
a Registry Office. Not so bad as you'd think.*

Holly's wedding. What a beautiful day they'd had
for that. April, 1915.

It had to be a quiet wedding, because it was wartime, so no veil or orange-blossom, but still, Holly
wore a cream georgette dress, ankle length, and a
brimmed hat made of the same material, stretched
over a wire frame. Addie and Bella were bridesmaids, in cream serge skirts, with white lace
blouses. Very useful afterwards. They wore straw
hats trimmed with the georgette.

Holly at twenty-seven was beautiful, her soft,
dark hair pinned up in a loose roll, and always
smiling and lively. Well, nearly always. Teddy
Kingston had wanted to marry her for years. It
made Mother furious the way Holly messed about.
Of course she was pretty and popular, but you
couldn't go on for ever being the leading light of the
Operatic Society and the Tennis Club. Supposing
Teddy married someone else? Where would the
musical evenings be then? She and Teddy had been
on the point of announcing their engagement three
years before, then Teddy's mother had been rushed
into hospital for an emergency operation. Holly had
called it off at once, saying it wasn't a proper time,
which was funny, because Holly did not usually
bother about the proper time for anything. May
Kingston was ill for a year during which Holly was
cross whenever Teddy or getting married was mentioned, though Teddy said his mother didn't want
them to change their plans on her account. How-

ever, after a year she began to improve and now you would never know there had been anything wrong with her, so the wedding was on again.

Now here they were. Holly had handed her small bouquet to Addie and the wedding proceeded. The ceremony was long, because, the Kingstons being Catholics, it took place at St Austin's. Holly was taking instruction.

'It's awful rubbish,' she said to Addie, 'but there'll be such a fuss if I don't do it, and as I don't believe in God anyway . . . '

This frankness appalled her sister, who half expected the bride to drop dead in front of her, but nothing happened, and she admired her courage.

The nuptial Mass went on and on. It was very cold in the church. Holly's arms showed mauve through the cream georgette. Father Christopher and his assistant seemed to have a lot to do, passing briskly back and forth in front of the altar, murmuring prayers. Bella heaved a sigh, shifting from one foot to the other, and Addie frowned at her and shook her head. But Dad smiled encouragingly. Bella was his pet. Dick Kingston, the best man, caught Addie's eye. She allowed herself to smile slightly without actually looking at him. Seeing him so smart in his dark suit, it was hard to believe that he and she had once climbed trees together. Long ago, of course, before the Terrible Time. She knew he had liked her, in spite of the wire-rimmed spectacles she had worn since she was seven. And once he'd touched her hair, before she could toss it away behind her back, and told her it was the only really

gold hair he'd ever seen, and that she must never
do it up in a bun, even when she was grown up.
He was looking at her thoughtfully. Perhaps he
intended to ask her out. Well, she wasn't much
interested in young men, not like Bella, but she
thought she might as well go if he asked her.

There were just thirty people at the wedding
breakfast at Price's hotel. Addie and her mother
were both anxious that everything should be alright.
They were well aware that the Clarkes were socially
inferior to the Kingstons; but the long table covered
with stiff white damask, the shining glass, the silver
vases of pink and white carnations and the meal of
soup, roast chicken and ice cream were all perfect.
The speeches were witty and serious and sentimental, especially Ted's father's. Strictly speaking he
should not have been called upon to speak, but
being well used to public life, it was natural that he
should. He told Ted that if he wished to change his
mind about being married to Holly, he, Tom would
gladly change places. There was only the difference
of two letters between Tom and Ted, he said, and
Holly might not even notice. This caused a roar of
laughter, in which, Addie noticed, Holly did not
join, and Auntie May Kingston was naturally rather
less than whole-hearted.

Nellie leaned across to Addie and said, 'Would
you like to sing again, dear? I'm sure Dick would
accompany you.' Addie had sung 'Oh Divine
Redeemer' in church.

Holly looked up. 'Let her off this time, Mum,'
she said. 'She's supposed to be enjoying herself.'

Addie, realizing that Holly did not want to relinquish her position as the centre of attraction pleaded a sore throat, though in fact she would have enjoyed singing more than talking. She never knew how to take Dick's jokes. He couldn't really mean he wanted to go climbing trees with her again. Still, he was very nice.

There! She had thought about the wedding, and it had cheered her up. It was so easy to remember. Lying back with her eyes closed, she could hear the buzz of conversation, the spurts of laughter and the music of the Langley Trio; the glasses sparkled for her under the pink-shaded lights, there was the spicy scent of carnations, and Holly smiling at her when she'd refused to sing.

Why then, was there something wrong? Something pressed down, not admitted; a voice waiting to whisper evil, to spoil everything. Was it the thought of what was awaiting Holly that night, in her honeymoon bed with Teddy? That awful something that was inextricably mixed up with Nitty Havergal and the Terrible Time? No, it was not. That hadn't worried Holly at all.

No, it was that moment when Holly was ready to leave, wearing her going-away costume of maroon cloth, trimmed with braid.

Nellie said, 'It's time you were thinking about going, dear. Mustn't miss your train.'

'Well, Ted, I know you'll look after her.' That was Dad.

'There's plenty of time; I must say one or two special goodbyes.'

Holly came over to where Addie was standing and kissed her cheek, then squeezed her hand. 'I'll want to see you every day, Ad.' Addie began to cry but Holly had moved away and was speaking to Bridget, her old friend and new sister-in-law, who was already married with two children. Then she went on, pausing in front of Father Christopher, the jolly old priest, who must have made a joke because Holly was laughing as she left him and started across the huge room to where Tom Kingston, tall, thin and handsome, but looking very middle-aged and unusually serious, stood alone between the two great windows, his back to the mirror. So Addie could see Holly's face change as she approached him. They stood there, not smiling, not touching. Then Holly turned and walked away down the room and Addie knew.

She'd known ever since, in her heart, though she'd tried for years to unknow. She stopped going to the musical evenings for a time, because just being in the same room as Holly and her father-in-law made her feel sick; but they'd all kept on at her and she'd given in after a few weeks. What was it Holly had said? 'I shan't tell you ever'? But she hadn't bargained on Addie guessing the unlikely truth.

How could she be so carefree, standing by the piano with Ted's arm around her waist, singing a duet from *The Yeoman of the Guard*? Addie could see her now in her russet velvet dress, with the gold locket. In fact she could see the whole room, the Kingstons' drawing room: the firelight glittering on the brass fender; the pink and green pattern of the carpet; the potted ferns on the other side of the glass doors that led to the conservatory; the grand piano – it was all still there in her mind. There was Mother, looking so dignified, in her navy blue crêpe de chine, and Mrs Kingston in lace. Before the war they had always enjoyed dressing up for these evenings. They had given up doing so for a while, but then it began to seem stupid to make things drearier than they had to be, and the best frocks had come out again. Ted looked very spruce in the black jacket and striped trousers he wore for business, but Tom Kingston had changed into a smoking jacket, which gave him an air of rather dissipated elegance.

'Come on Dad, you repeat that bit, then it's back to the beginning and da Capo.'

Ted's father leaned forward, studying the music, and Holly did the same, her hand casually on his shoulder. Dick was not there. He had enlisted soon after Addie had refused his offer of marriage. That scene was not so clear.

They had been walking along the promenade one Sunday as they quite frequently did after Addie started going to the musical evenings again. After they had bemoaned the fact that the band no longer played and told each other that the war would be over in six months, Dick had suddenly said, 'Well, Ad, isn't it time we named the day?'

Instead of feeling joy at these unromantic words Addie had turned cold with horror. Not because she disliked Dick; indeed she was quite fond of him in a sisterly way, but because she had made up her mind that whoever she married would have to be told about the Terrible Time. And now the impossibility of ever telling Dick swept over her, so instead of behaving with dignity and saying either yes or no in a quiet, sensible way, she broke from him and ran like a schoolgirl all along the front to the gap where she went slipping and sliding down the slope to the sands and hid weeping behind the bathing machines.

Nobody had understood. After all, Dick was a nice boy, and the Kingstons and the Clarkes were already linked by ties of friendship as well as marriage. She hadn't seen much of Holly around that time; she was so busy with rehearsals for *Iolanthe*.

Then Dick had gone away, the rumpus had died down, and once more she and her mother were walking round to Dorset Gardens on Saturday evenings. Addie was glad Dick was a qualified pharmacist. He'd be fairly safe at a military hospital.

She missed his pleasant tenor voice. It wasn't so much fun singing with Ted, and there'd been the belonging feeling that Dick's presence had given her. But what else could she have done? She sighed.

'Cheer up, Addie, do.' Her mother came over and sat down beside her on the couch. 'What's the matter with you?'

'Nothing,' said Addie. 'I'm just tired, that's all.' She stared down at her lap, feeling her mother's anxious eyes on her face. She knew what she was thinking. That she missed Dick, was regretting having turned him down, and that she might offend the Kingstons, sitting there looking glum and refusing to sing.

Nellie patted her hand. 'We'll go home soon,' she said.

Bella had just finished her usual inaccurate rendering of Dvořák's Humoresque on her violin. 'Oh, Mum,' she wailed when Nellie called her. 'We haven't done "Three Little Maids" yet. Come on Addie, don't sit there looking like a dying duck.'

'Addie's tired,' said Nellie. 'She's had a hard day.'

Terry Keenan, a young man of Bella's age who lived next door to Cornwall Lodge, seized his chance eagerly. 'I'll walk home with Bella, Mrs Clarke.'

'Well, I'd rather she came with us.'

'Oh, don't be silly, Mum, she'll be alright with Terry. You go on home if you want to.'

Holly seemed eager for them to go, so Addie and Nellie went up to the big, cold bedroom with its heavy mahogany furniture and put on their coats and hats.

Auntie May accompanied them to the front door. 'I shall be going to bed soon,' she said. 'I suppose they'll be singing away till midnight as usual.'

They set off briskly up the road. The Kingstons' house was in a pleasant, prosperous residential area between the sea-front and the main shopping street. The cold wind from the North Sea chased them along. They held onto their hats, hugging their coats around them.

'It'll be better when we get to the corner,' Nellie assured Addie.

There was quite a number of people about, returning from choir practice, or whist drives, or just going home from work. They said 'good evening' half a dozen times before they reached Southdown Road. The chemist's shop on the corner was owned by the Kingstons. Ted and Holly lived in the flat over it, and Ted managed the business. They had nice big rooms, but no garden.

There was another Kingston's the Chemists further down the road and still another near the harbour. A dim light showed from the interior of this one, which meant the dispenser was still there. Through the glass door you could see how well the shop was fitted up, with its mahogany counters and glass-fronted cupboards and little drawers. It was all dark wood, very serious as befitted a chemist's which was really more of a profession than a trade. High up in the windows the great glass flasks of jewel-coloured liquid glowed darkly red and blue and green, giving the shop a religious look. It was too cold to stop on the corner, but they glanced in as they passed, feeling proud of Holly's connection with the place.

Further along, on the opposite side of the road and out of the wind, they paused to peer into the unlit window of the hat shop where Addie worked. The hats were displayed on stands of various heights, so that it looked like a gloomy forest, misty with veiling, crowded with flowers and exotic birds.

'That's nice,' said Nellie. Near the front of the

window was a black velour hat, trimmed with feathers.

'Come in tomorrow and try it on.'

'It's too young for me.'

Nellie was wearing what was known in the trade as a 'matron's hat' – heavy-looking and trimmed with sober loops of ribbon. Addie did not try to persuade her but said instead, 'I dressed the window. It looks nice in daylight.'

'You'll have to set up on your own, one of these days.'

'What about Miss Jones?'

'You could go down the other end. You wouldn't interfere with her there.'

'I wouldn't want to be down there. I like the good class trade.'

'Well, then, I shouldn't worry too much about Miss Jones. She's had her money's worth out of you. You have to think of yourself. You have to make the best life you can.'

I must, thought Addie. *I must make the best life I can.* But did her mother not expect her to marry? That somehow was rather a blow, though she had turned Dick down, and was hardly likely to get a better offer. Supposing she had to settle for the single life, then a business of her own would be some consolation. And she had plenty to enjoy as things were: her singing; her work; their family life. And after all, Mum had needed her, needed someone to turn to when Dad had his operation, and when they didn't hear from Jay who was in France or Charlie who had recently enlisted. And she liked to have plenty to do and think about, because that kept the Terrible Time at bay, though every now and again some chance remark would send her back onto the old treadmill.

I did it for Holly – it wasn't my fault. Holly told me to do it. But I needn't have. You don't always have to do what other people tell you. And it was wrong. Wicked and wrong and perhaps even cruel as well.

Then why was it she, not her sister, who struggled to bear this burden? Sometimes, when Holly was still at home, Addie would whisper into the darkness of their bedroom. 'Holly, I can't help thinking about . . . you know what . . . '

She always received the same reply: 'Shut up and go to sleep, Ad. I've forgotten it, why can't you?'

But Addie often lay awake, wretchedly aware of the single workbox that stood on the white embroidered runner on top of the chest of drawers. Sometimes she pretended to herself that in the morning she would open her eyes and see the two boxes side by side and know that the whole thing had been a dream. Then, raising her head as the greyness of early light filtered into the room she would discern the oblong shape, menacingly alone.

Yet Holly, apparently forgetting it all, had certainly made the best life she could. She had married Ted, and they seemed perfectly happy together, laughing at their secret jokes, sitting on the couch holding hands, even when they'd been married for months. And Tom Kingston treated her just as he treated anyone else. With the same casual gaiety with which he put his arm round Addie's waist

as they sang a duet, he'd kiss Holly's hand and
congratulate her on her voice and acting. You
couldn't really mind. Addie felt she ought to shrug
away, tell him she didn't like that kind of thing, but
after all she would only succeed in looking absurd.
Yet how wicked he had been to seduce young Holly.
Addie could not help wondering where and how it
had all happened. Had he told her that he loved
her, had he wanted her to run away with him?
Surely it must have been like that. But if so, why
hadn't they gone off together, like Mr Hewett, who
taught the piano at Argyll House two doors from
Jasmine Villa, and Dolly Williams, one of his pupils?

Dolly was eighteen and Mr Hewett over forty,
but one Sunday morning Mrs Hewett had run hat-
less up the front path and banged wildly at the
door. When Bella opened it she pushed past her
calling for Nellie, and then collapsed in tears on the
front-room sofa. Nellie had stayed shut in with her
for nearly an hour, only coming out to tell the others
to get on with their dinner. They'd eaten silently
that day, wondering what was going on. When
their father left the room, Holly had said, 'He's gone
off. That's what it is, I bet you. He's gone off with
that Dolly Williams. Silly idiots.'

'Poor Mrs Hewett.'

'You mean poor Dolly.'

And Holly had been right. Mrs Hewett had bat-
tled on for a while with her three children, and then
died suddenly, no one quite knew how, and he had
come home to look after the family. Dolly had gone
back to her father and mother. The whole town

had blamed her. She was spoken of as 'that Dolly Williams' or 'that Williams girl' and people told their daughters not to speak to her.

Well, Holly had done better than that. She had a pleasant home, was loved and admired, and had the prospect of wealth when Ted inherited the business in which he was already a partner. Yes, Holly had made herself a good life, and she, Addie, must try to do the same.

As soon as she had made this resolve fate seemed to aid and abet her. Miss Jones promoted her to manageress, announcing that she was going to stay with her sister in Harrogate for a few months, so Addie would have things all her own way. And about the same time, she decided to take singing lessons, and met Miss Marion.

The war dragged on, the blackout was enforced, meat was rationed as well as sugar and tea, and Jay came home from France on leave. He wandered quietly about, resisting all attempts to cheer him up, making the whole family anxious and depressed; and while all these things were going on, Addie sang – at charity concerts, and troop concerts, in the choir of the Catholic Church to please the Kingstons, and walking along the sands to please herself. It was Tom Kingston who told her that she should have lessons, that she was wasting a great gift and her father who found out about Miss Marion.

She was one of two maiden ladies, Miss Frederick and Miss Marion Frederick, who had recently come to Culvergate. Miss Frederick, it appeared, had a weak chest, and it was hoped that the bracing air of the South-East would do her good. Miss Marion was a professional singer who had given up her career, temporarily at least, to look after her sister. She had been a member of the D'Oyley Carte opera company, but now let it be known that she was not averse to singing locally, or even doing a little teaching. Addie went over to Foreland Bay by tram on early closing day.

She enjoyed the ride through the mile or so of countryside that separated Culvergate from Foreland Bay. As they passed the lodge and ornate iron gates that marked the entrance to Easton Court, the home of the local gentry, she peered eagerly up the drive through the smeared window of the tram, hoping to glimpse the house. She'd seen it once, years earlier, when the whole family had spent a memorable Saturday afternoon at a charity fête in the grounds. Then she and Holly had pressed their faces against the long windows to gaze at the splendours within: the huge high-ceilinged rooms; the chandeliers; the great gilt-framed pictures. Nellie had been shocked at their bad manners and dragged them away. Holly, of course, had said, 'I'm going to live here one day,' and Addie had announced her intention of doing the same. Nellie had told them not to talk nonsense.

Updown Close was hard to find. Even when Addie knew she was in the right road she walked past the gate twice, because it was not like an ordinary front gate but was set in a high wall, with no name or number visible. Pausing uncertainly, she saw Updown Close painted on a board fixed to a wall, almost concealed by ivy.

Entering, she found herself in a little square garden, quite unlike any other garden she had ever seen. It was laid out in a pattern with miniature hedges, and a lot of crazy paving. The house was on her right, not facing the road, like most houses, and it was joined to the garden wall at one side. On her left the view was bounded by a high, dark hedge. The whole place had a secret, impenetrable look. Addie went into the little porch and knocked at the door. The brass knocker had an impish face that leered nastily at her, and she felt such an attack of shyness and anxiety that she was on the point of running away. She took herself firmly in hand. After all, she was twenty-five, a business woman and well known locally as a singer and winner of music festivals, even though untrained. Why on earth should she be nervous of meeting strangers? Had they heard her knock? She looked for a bell pull, but there was none. A cool breeze whisked round the little garden, shaking the daffodils that grew below the hedge, and scattering the crazy paving with cherry blossom. It had been a dull, cold day, with no feeling of spring in the air; indeed, the acrid smell of an untimely bonfire somewhere nearby made it seem more like autumn.

Addie shivered in her thin jacket. She had dressed herself in her best spring outfit for this interview and felt cold. She knocked again, suddenly impatient. Did this unknown woman want pupils or didn't she? If she did, it would be better not to let them freeze in the porch for half an hour while she made up her mind to come to the door. In a moment she would appear and say, 'I'm so sorry to have kept you waiting,' expecting Addie to say politely that it did not matter, but why should she be so polite when she was shivering with cold? Addie was mentally composing a reply that should be at once courteous, reproachful and faintly tinged with annoyance when the door opened and a uniformed maidservant stood in front of her. She was momentarily taken aback, having expected to see Miss Marion herself. The Clarkes had never had a maid, indeed, the previous generation of Clarkes and Wellsteads had supplied domestic staff to the prosperous families of the town. Nowadays Nellie had a charwoman two mornings a week for the rough, but that was all. The Kingstons however had an ancient cook called Lily who ruled the kitchen unseen by any but the family, a greasy-haired house-parlourmaid called Ivy, and a man for the garden and odd jobs, with a woman in daily as well, so Addie was not entirely unused to servants. Yet her mental picture of two spinster sisters slightly down on their luck had not included anything like this well-starched person who stared at her without a word.

'I . . . Miss Frederick . . . Miss Marion Frederick is expecting me,' she said, falling over her words nervously.

She was admitted into a narrow but well-carpeted hall and the maid opened a door immediately on

her right. 'In here,' she said coldly. 'Miss Marion
will not be long.'

Once again Addie was surprised. She had certainly expected her prospective teacher to be sitting
waiting for her when she did not greet her at the
door, but the room was empty. As empty, that is,
as a room crowded with furniture can be.

A bright fire burned in the grate, and it was very
warm. There were plants, flowers, bowls of fruit
and books scattered around the room, and a brilliantly coloured Spanish shawl was draped over the
piano. There were photographs everywhere, many
of them in silver frames. Some seemed to be of
actors or singers. These were signed with effusive
scrawling messages like 'To dearest Jessie from your
own Billy'.

This last was scribbled on a picture of a girl with
fluffy hair and a simpering smile, holding up a tam-
bourine. She was dressed in gypsy clothes but
looked exceedingly ungypsylike. Another showed
a man in eighteenth-century costume leaning
elegantly on a pedestal as though incapable of
standing unsupported, and was signed 'In memory
of a wonderful season, Eddie Best'.

Realizing that she was guilty of curiosity, Addie
sat down on the chaise-longue that was drawn up
to the fire. That in itself seemed an indulgence. At
home they had chairs each side of the fire and what
they called the couch in the window, so that you
couldn't put your feet up and be warm at the same
time. Here you could do both, though with such a

blaze the farthest corner of the room could not be chilly.

Addie sat still and waited. Five minutes passed. For something to do she rose and went to the window. She looked out at the bleak, secluded little garden. Nothing else was to be seen for the wall was six feet high, and the dense hedge on the other two sides even higher. A curious sense of unreality swept over her. A piece of coal shifted in the grate, otherwise the silence was unbroken. She looked at the little watch she wore on a chain round her neck. It was two minutes past five. Beatie, her assistant who was also her friend, would be locking up the shop. For this important occasion she had come away a whole hour before the Thursday closing time of five o'clock. On other nights they closed at eight. She had been a few minutes early, but still, when you weren't certain how to find a place you had to allow plenty of time. The air in the room was heavy with the scent of flowers. Addie looked at herself in the gilt-framed mirror over the fireplace. She thought she looked quite smart in her spring costume, and her hat with its turned back brim was new and fashionable. Her face was puddingy, though, and she wished she didn't have to wear pince-nez. Still, Dick had wanted to marry her in spite of those things.

For a few moments she thought of Dick in his army uniform as she had last seen him. He'd come to Jasmine Villa while on leave and they'd had a long and painful interview in the front room. There were of course two rooms at the front of the house, it being double fronted. Their first family home in a terrace had only one front room, which was always referred to by that name, so the room to the right of the front door at Jasmine Villa was still The Front Room, although it was actually the sitting room, and the one on the opposite side of the hall was The Dining Room. This was seldom used, meals being taken in the kitchen except at Christmas.

For three months Addie had felt guilty about leading Dick up the garden, as her mother put it. Her father had been kinder, though naturally he could not understand why she should refuse to marry someone whom she obviously liked. Father was always kind. Kind and quiet, yet humorous too. Sometimes Addie was near to telling him the truth. If the truth had not concerned Holly she would certainly have done so, but there was no way round that. Then another restraining thought occurred to her, which was that she might not be believed. After all, who, looking at the lively, competent young matron that her sister had become and the genial, successful Justice of the Peace whose son she had married, would imagine them capable of possessing such a shameful secret? Easier to believe that she, Addie, had gone off her head, through jealousy, or some mysterious cause.

Bother Miss Marion Frederick! Why didn't she come? Vacant moments like this were something to be avoided, affording as they did a chance for the enemy to take possession.

Think about something else! Supposing she were asked to sing, what should it be? She opened her music case and took out a selection of songs and scores. Musetta's Song, perhaps, or something from an oratorio, like 'He shall Feed His Flock'. What would please this unknown woman? If she were to be accepted as a pupil that would mean coming here every week, getting to know this strange room. The woman whom she had not even seen yet would become familiar, perhaps a friend. There were brisk footsteps on the stairs and the door opened.

Marion Frederick was as tall as Addie. She had masses of dark brown hair that was neither fluffy nor sleek. Her eyebrows too were dark and thick, and her eyes were deep-set and hooded, smudged underneath with dark shadows.

Addie stood up. To her annoyance she heard herself say, 'I'm afraid I was rather early.'

'Hardly at all, my dear, hardly at all.'

Miss Marion spoke graciously, though she made no apology for keeping her waiting. She came up to Addie and held out her hand. Accepting it uncertainly, Addie felt her own hand warmly clasped between both of the other woman's. They stood like this for what seemed an extraordinarily long time. Addie wanted to move away but did not know how to do so without being clumsy. Suddenly she was released and the teacher went quickly to the piano, which was already open.

Sitting down, she removed several rings and a bracelet which she placed beside the keyboard. Then she rubbed her hands, clenching and flexing her fingers while she surveyed the instrument in front of her as if it was something new and fascinating. She struck a fierce chord, afterwards launching into an elaborate, apparently impromptu cadenza, finishing with a flourish. This was just the kind of behaviour that Addie loathed. Holly, who was only a fair pianist, often went through this sort of showy ritual before starting to play. To her Addie could say, 'I do wish you wouldn't do that. Why do you?' To which Holly would reply. 'Because I like to,' and do it even more.

The cadenza over, Miss Marion became the teacher. 'Sing me a scale,' she commanded.

Addie sang several, in major and minor keys, and then 'He shall Feed His Flock', after which she produced the 'Jewel Song' from Faust.

'But that's a contralto song.'

'I can sing it.'

And she did. She knew that she had an unusually wide range, and she wanted to show it off.

At the end she stood smiling, expecting praise, but Miss Marion to her surprise looked serious. Had she been wrong, misguided about the quality of her voice? Surely not. Once more her hands were being enfolded in the strong, dry hands of the other woman.

'My dear, you have a great gift. To help you use it as it should be used will be a great privilege. Can you trust me?'

The low voice seemed to throb with emotion. Addie felt desperately ill at ease. Because of her height her arms were being pulled slightly downward by the clasping hands, which resulted in her being forced to bend a little. This was tiring and awkward and must, she felt, look foolish. Also, with nervous tension and the heat of the room her palms were sticky with sweat. She herself would have hated the touch of sweaty skin, but the other woman seemed to experience no such revulsion. Embarrassment made her even hotter, and the heat from her flushed face caused her pince-nez to mist over so that she could hardly see. It felt like a long time before she was free and could remove them and polish them with her handkerchief.

'Do you always wear your glasses when singing?'

'Oh yes, always.'

'A pity. The eyes can be so expressive.'

'I can't see without them.'

It was nearly true. The room had become a blur, full of fiery flickerings and grey-blue shadows, with Miss Marion a pale enthroned statue. As quickly as she could, Addie replaced them, feeling their reassuring pinch at the sides of her nose, but conscious at the same time that her green eyes dwindled behind the thick lenses.

'Well, thank you, Miss Frederick,' she said, for something to say.

'Oh, Miss Marion, please. I was known as Jessie Marion all my years in the theatre, so I am used to that name.'

'Miss Marion.'

'And you are Miss Clarke, I know. But since we are to be teacher and pupil, I think I shall call you Adelaide.'

There was a light tap at the door. Instead of saying 'Come in' Miss Marion rose and went to open it. Holding it slightly ajar, she conversed briefly with whoever stood outside, then turned and said, 'I shall have to ask you to excuse me . . . my sister . . . not so well today . . . '

'Of course, I quite understand.'

Briskly, lessons were arranged, fees touched upon, and Addie had collected her music and was being ushered into the passage and so out of the house. Dusk was falling in the square, secret little garden. As she reached the gate in the wall she looked back, but the front door was already shut. Never mind. This time next week she would be back.

'You left your biscuits, Mrs Castle. Don't you like that kind?' The nurse's voice broke in, recalling her sharply to the unwelcome present. Why couldn't they leave you alone?

'I'm not very keen on biscuits.'

Actually she did not dislike them, but Mother had always said they dried up the blood. It seemed unlikely, but there was often some kind of twisted truth in these old sayings. She never ate many, just in case.

'Doreen should have taken them away when she took your tray. I expect she thought you might want them. Never mind. Now, a little wash, eh? And we'll get you nicely tidied up before dinner.'

'Tidied up' was a euphemism for several not very enjoyable attentions, but Addie bore them with what patience she could. It was better to get it all over before supper, or dinner as the nurses called it, though such a light meal scarcely qualified for that title. It was usually very appetising, though, and attractively served on good china and silver. That was part of what you paid for at Easton Court. They had delicious grilled plaice on Fridays, and the lamb cutlets were always tender. English, of course.

It was awful to think so much about food, something that had once interested her so little. Still, what else was there? Nothing nice could ever happen again, except in her mind. Plenty of nice things could happen again there, and plenty of nasty things too. That was the trouble with reliving the past. You couldn't choose.

Yet apart from the Terrible Time she had very little to worry about. She could honestly say to herself that she had never really hurt anyone. She'd been a careful, competent wife to Ronnie, and made a good deal of money which he had enjoyed spending. Dorothy had always had everything a child could wish for, had never gone without sweets or toys or pretty frocks, even in the hard times. What a pity she hadn't been more talented. It would have been such a joy to lavish money and opportunities on a really musical daughter. If only she had inherited Addie's voice, they could have done so much. Proper training, in Italy perhaps, with no need to earn her living, until she was really ready.

Money or the lack of it, had been an insurmountable obstacle for Addie herself. She remembered going to the Royal College of Music with Miss Marion for an audition. The great teacher had been visibly impressed by the beauty and range of her mezzo-soprano, but when he understood that she would have to support herself and could only study and practise in her leisure hours, he told her that the whole thing was a waste of time. Miss Marion had tried so hard to think of a way round the problem, and it had been a disappointment. But still, it would have meant giving up her job and living away from home and secretly she was glad that she would not be forced to do either of these things.

Poor Miss Marion had been more upset than Addie herself, not realizing how much relief there was behind Addie's suitably wistful expression. On the way home in the train she had held her hand, comfortingly and embarrassingly, for much of the journey.

So the wide world never had the opportunity of hearing Addie sing, but the environs of Culvergate continued to enjoy her increasingly frequent public appearances. Nellie suggested that it was a waste of money having lessons; you didn't need to go on learning for ever, did you? Addie said yes, you did. Without lessons you would get into bad habits.

'Then what,' enquired Nellie, 'is to stop *her* getting into bad habits? She doesn't have lessons, does she?'

'Oh, Mum,' sighed Addie, 'it's different.'

'Well, I don't see how.'

Addie did not answer.

They were sitting in the kitchen, early one Thursday evening. Addie had just come in from work and would soon be off to catch the tram for Foreland

Bay and Updown Close. She'd been going there for
over a year now, and every time she felt this strange
mixture of excitement and apprehension. Sometimes Miss Marion really made you feel quite
uncomfortable. She didn't seem to have any
ordinary reticence. Perhaps it was being on the
stage that did it. On that day in 1917 Addie was
almost happy. Certainly as happy as she could be
with Jay in France, and Charlie going there any day.
They were expecting him home on embarkation
leave. Looking back in later years she realized that,
like many other people at that time, she had completely failed to understand what war was really
like. Young men were eagerly enlisting, falsifying
their ages to do so, being photographed in uniform
and singing songs with words like 'Good Byeee,
goddbyeee, wipe a tear, baby dear, from your eyeee'
and Addie herself sang 'We don't want to lose you,
but we think you ought to go'.

In after years she was ashamed of this, but as she
left the tram and walked down Updown Close she
thought only of her coming singing lesson, and of
her teacher.

When Elsie, the maid, showed her into the sitting
room Miss Marion was already seated at the piano,
trying out a new song. She was very up to date,
keeping abreast of all the new shows in London.
Though oratorio and opera were not beyond her
she was happiest with musical comedy. She nodded
to Addie who took off her hat and sat down on the
couch by the fire. As usual the room was warm,
scented, and subtly lit. Outside the evening sky was

shot with red and violet. The plush draped window showed only the garden and the sky; the high walls and the hedge screened alike the next house and the road. They could have been miles from anywhere. Addie succumbed to the luxury of it all and leaned back listening.

She thought *I could sit here like this for ever* and she wished she could say the words aloud. 'I could sit here like this for ever.'

The Clarkes, with the exception of Holly, did not express their feelings easily or often. It was Holly who laughed and hugged and kissed. If she had been more like Holly . . . Jessie Marion finished her song, brushed aside her pupil's shy expression of appreciation, and then at once plunged into scales, arpeggios and exercises.

'Breathe!' she cried. 'It must come from the diaphragm. BREATHE!' Addie breathed. 'Expand your ribs! More!' She rose suddenly, took Addie's hands and pressed them against her own ribs. 'Feel,' she commanded. 'Feel the expansion.' Her hands over Addie's held them against her knitted silk blouse. She wore no corsets. Addie could feel her warmth through the thick silk. She stood there with her head a little bent, otherwise she would have been gazing into the dark-ringed eyes at very close quarters indeed. At last she was released and they went on with the lesson. Miss Marion was hard to please that day.

'Get above the note,' she insisted irritably. 'Come on, you can do it,' as her pupil braced herself to reach high C, no mean feat for a mezzo. She sang the note through a gathering mist and clutched the piano for support. The final chord was triumphantly crashed out and Miss Marion swung round on her stool just in time to see the singer crumple to the floor.

It was not really a faint, in fact it was little more than an attack of dizziness brought on by the hot room and the continued deep breathing. After a moment Addie was able to stumble to the chaise-longue. Left alone, a strange feeling of well-being possessed her. There was a velvet cushion under her head, her shoes had gone, and so had her glasses. The thought of her teacher's hands making her comfortable was a pleasurable one. She lay still.

Miss Marion was soon back. She brought a small glass containing a very little brandy. She held it while Addie sipped, but it was at the wrong angle. It would have seemed rude to take the glass herself, so she put her hand over Miss Marion's to tilt it and they stayed like that, while Addie slowly finished the brandy. Somehow it seemed to mean something. *But it didn't mean anything*, she thought, *I don't want her to think I'm soppy*.

Bella and her friends were often soppy, wandering about with their arms around each other and being best friends. Dressing alike, sometimes, even. Addie sat up and said she felt better and would go home.

'Elsie will put you on the tram. You cannot possibly go alone.'

'Oh no. I'll be quite alright, really, I will.'

The idea of being accompanied to the tram by the

forbidding Elsie was dreadful. But she still felt weak and wondered that Miss Marion had not offered to come herself. Or had she come herself? She thought she could remember walking up the lane with her. No, that was imagination. So hard to distinguish fact from fantasy. It would have been nice if she had.

But on that far off day there had at least been several more singing lessons to come, and Addie looked forward to Thursday every week.

Business was quiet and people did not like to spend too much on hats in wartime; but every now and again there was a wedding, which was good for trade, or an order for black which was almost as good, though sadder.

There were letters from Jay and Charlie, which were amusing and affectionate, while telling them very little, and there were the musical evenings at Cornwall Lodge. Addie often thought how lovely it would be if Miss Marion could come to those. How she would be admired, what a nice change it would be for her, shut up in that little house with her ailing sister. How she would like Holly, whose liveliness would certainly appeal to such a theatrical personality. She would probably want Holly to become a pupil. Addie rather went off the idea.

In any case she could not really imagine Miss Marion in any surroundings but her own.

Sometimes, on the tram to Foreland Bay, she would imagine Miss Marion inviting her to stay to supper. She would see the dining room, perhaps even the bedroom. She wondered if the legendary

Miss Frederick was like her sister. It didn't surprise her that a career should have been abandoned for the sake of this unseen invalid. She would have done the same for Holly.

For some weeks visits to Updown Close were uneventful, though not unexciting. Then something rather uncomfortable happened. One Thursday Addie arrived a little early. Shown into the sitting room by Elsie, she took off her hat and coat, fluffed out her hair with a quick glance in the mirror and went to the piano. She began a scale and heard the door open. Turning, she saw to her surprise that the maid had re-entered and was looking at her enquiringly, waiting for her to stop singing. Had she some message? Was Miss Marion ill, the lesson cancelled? But surely she must have known this sooner, could have told her when she arrived. But no, the woman was not delivering a message, she was saying something on her own account. She came closer.

'I'm sorry to bother you, Miss, but I felt it was time I said something.'

'Yes?'

'You mustn't come here any more.'

'What do you mean? I have to come. For my lessons. What's the matter?'

'You can get lessons off somebody else. It isn't right, Miss. A nice young lady like you.'

'Why are you saying this? Supposing I were to tell Miss Marion?'

'Her!'

Such scorn in her tone – scorn for her employer,

whom Addie admired and respected more than
anyone she knew. The flat, quiet voice went on
insistently. 'Take my word for it, Miss. Don't come
any more. I've seen what I've seen, and I've heard
what I've heard, and I know. I'm giving in my
notice.'

They stared at each other. The servant's face was
doughy and expressionless as ever, the eyes blank.
Then she left the room.

Addie sat down shakily on the piano stool. Of
course, she was crazy, that was it. Really, she ought
to have been warned. Should she say anything
about it?

Then in came Miss Marion, charmingly dressed
as usual, the masses of brown hair becomingly
arranged, the dark eyes glowing affectionately.
With the accustomed gesture she grasped the pupil
by the shoulders, told her she looked pale, must
not work so hard. Seating herself at the piano, she
ran her hands up and down the keys, then came to
a stop and said, 'Well, what have you got for me
today?'

The lesson proceeded. As always, Addie was
bullied, praised, encouraged and castigated,
reduced almost to tears, and then uplifted by the
achievement of a note or phrase she had thought
beyond her. An hour later she left the house.

Closing the gate, she remembered Elsie. Firmly
she turned her thoughts to something else, putting
the strange conversation out of her mind. Of course
the silly creature had been reading too much trashy
rubbish, talking as though Updown Close sheltered

some kind of criminal activity. Absolutely ridiculous.

The following week, however, she was a little nervous about facing the maid again. Would she even admit her to the house? How should she be treated? Addie need not have worried. Miss Marion came to the door herself.

'I had to part with Elsie,' she said cheerfully. 'I really couldn't stand that sinister creature about me another moment. Quite a good worker, in an unimaginative way, but oh, that blank face of hers, totally without expression. She was only the maid, I know, but when someone lives in your house and you have to see them morning, noon and night, some slight degree of rapport is a great help.'

'She certainly was rather expressionless,' said Addie, feeling her way carefully. 'It makes you wonder what people are thinking, when they are as blank as that.'

'Absolutely nothing, in her case, I promise you that!'

Miss Marion spoke with a vehemence one might have thought unnecessary had one not been familiar with her manner.

Elsie's replacement, a pale, quiet girl called Doris, seemed to find the work beyond her. Addie would be kept waiting at the front door for several minutes before the new maid arrived, slightly breathless, to admit her. Her caps and aprons were less white and stiff than Elsie's and the sitting room, still the only room that Addie had seen, took on a rather dingy appearance. Often the hearth needed sweeping, the silver frames were tarnished, and a film of dust lay on top of the piano. The window panes no longer gleamed, but showed smeared and grubby in the setting sun.

The atmosphere changed too. One day Addie told her teacher that she had accepted an engagement to sing in the lounge of a local hotel at tea-time, on Sunday. Business being far from brisk at the shop, she was glad of the money. In any case she was looking forward to it, but Miss Marion was outraged. That such a gift should be so wickedly squandered! That a pupil of hers whom the great Benotti had accepted should sing in a tea-room, while idiots clattered their cups and saucers, and insulted her by talking!

'It's with the Langley Trio,' said Addie mildly. 'They're very good.'

'The Langley Trio! Three down-at-heel women in dusty black frocks scraping and strumming on third-rate instruments. I doubt even if the piano is in tune.'

'Of course it is.' Addie began to feel cross. They were going to give her two guineas for the two groups of songs. It was quite a lot of money.

'Well, I suppose you will please yourself. Now we had better do some work.'

Miss Marion was impossibly hard to please that day. At the end of the lesson she closed the piano and sat staring sombrely at the sheet of music that faced her.

'You should be preparing to tour the capital cities

of the world, not singing in tea-shops. What has happened to all our plans?'

'It's not a tea-shop. It's a hotel.'

'Oh, of course, that makes a world of difference.'

Addie was not used to sarcasm. Her hands trembled as she pushed the long hatpin into her smart hat. Pulling on her gloves she said, 'I'm sorry,' though she did not know what she ought to be sorry for.

'Take no notice of me. Life is never what it ought to be, we must remember that. I have my difficulties.'

If only she would say what those difficulties were, but she did not. Sadly, Addie went home.

The week passed slowly. She felt desperately anxious to go back to Updown Close. She woke up in the night, alone and lonely in the big bed she had once shared with Holly, and thought about Miss Marion's difficulties. Did she need money? She could lend her some; she had her savings. Certainly they needed a better maid. How could she help her to find one? She remembered Elsie. Was it all something to do with what she had said? The unseen invalid sister, was she mad? Or a criminal? What kind of criminal? It was all so worrying and frightening. Addie had heard of people who couldn't help stealing. Perhaps she had been let out of prison on condition that she never left home, or saw anyone. 'I have my troubles.' Well, of course, everyone had troubles of some kind. It was no good expecting life to go smoothly for long, because it never did.

For a moment Addie contemplated the lack of smoothness in her own past, and Holly's, then firmly, she turned her thoughts back to the inhabitants of Updown Close – 'No place for a nice young lady like you'. Well, of course, if Miss Frederick was a thief, or mad and dangerous like the wife in Jane Eyre, that would account for Elsie's strange behaviour. But it didn't quite fit. At this point Addie fell asleep.

After a few months Miss Marion's new maid managed to raise her standards a little, though this was probably because there was a good deal less to do in summer – no grates to clean, no fires to be laid and lit, washing soon dry instead of hanging damply round the kitchen. So Doris found time to dust and polish, and Miss Marion took heart and tended the garden and brought flowers into the house. This was Addie's second summer of music lessons, and though she still admired the room which was often filled with sunshine in the early evening, she preferred it in its winter guise, full of warmth and softness, with sharp gleams of reflected light, and soft, mysterious shadows.

CHAPTER 3

Between lessons, Addie frequently sang at the Winter Gardens, as well as with the Langley Trio. Culvergate boasted a very competent Municipal Orchestra, whose Sunday afternoon concerts were immensely popular. When Addie was engaged to give a group of songs during the second half they were literally crowded out. Accompanied by the pianist while the other players remained in their places, Addie sang sentimental ballads, or well-known songs from operettas such as *Veronique* or *The Vagabond King*. On alternate Sundays she would join the ladies of the Langley Trio at the Koh-i-noor Tea-rooms on the front. Recently reopened, this superior establishment had closed at the beginning of the war, but was now flourishing again. The better-off among the visitors and the more socially minded residents liked to take their afternoon tea in its elegant surroundings while enjoying some light music.

The Koh-i-noor was a curved white room overlooking a lawn with fountains. Gilt chairs; many
potted palm-trees; waitresses in neat black dresses
with frilled white aprons and matching caps; the
discreet clatter of cups and saucers and the faint
aroma of tea made the place inviting on a summer
afternoon. People wore their best clothes to go to
the Koh-i-noor; the cream cakes were wonderful
and the ices, served in dishes that were silver-col-
oured, if not silver, and embellished with crisp
wafer biscuits, were the best for miles around.
When Addie sang the waitresses tried not to make
a noise, and she was always rewarded with enthusiastic applause. She was generous with encores until
she realized that the Trio became slightly resentful
if kept too long in the background.

On this late August Sunday, she tidied her hair
before the inadequate mirror in the cupboard that
the management grandly called the Artistes' Room,
and took a handful of sheet music out of her music
case. After so many performances she was almost
casual about appearing in public, often not deciding
what she would sing until the last minute, and Miss
Doris Langley was a good accompanist. Now Addie
adjusted the draped skirt of her black velvet dress
that had cost her the fees from three Sunday concerts and went out into the tea-room. As she
approached the small platform in the centre of the
long side wall that faced the tall windows a spon-
taneous burst of applause astonished her. She knew
she was popular with audiences, but before she had
even sung a note! This was a real accolade. She

handed her music to the pianist, and after a brief discussion launched into a ballad concerning a little girl, a little boy, and a lilac tree. It was one of her favourites, though Miss Marion had said that she did not know whether to laugh or cry at her pupil's taste in music. But the Koh-i-noor regulars seemed to approve of the song, so Addie had kept it in her repertoire.

As she sang, her eyes roved over the audience, noting people she recognized, and the gratifying lack of empty tables. The waitresses leaned against the wall, listening, and no one dreamt of trying to attract their attention. She smiled at Holly and Ted seated nearby, and Beatrice with her aunt some distance away. A rare treat for Beatie, on her shop assistant's wage. Addie decided to sing something specially for her.

A moment later she forgot about Beatie, because she saw Miss Marion, resplendent in bottle-green georgette with amber beads, and a smart hat, sitting at a table near a pillar. Evidently she was not alone, for she appeared to be whispering to someone, but her companion was concealed by a bulky man at a nearby table who had turned his chair the better to see the singer.

Addie, whose mind was frequently elsewhere when she sang her most often repeated numbers, began to revise the programme she had somewhat vaguely planned. Why had she decided on this particular song, which her teacher so despised? What could she choose next, that would meet with her approval, and also please the habitués of the Koh-i-noor? Before the now thoroughly embarrassing little boy had tied apples on the lilac tree she had made up her mind. Gilbert and Sullivan, yes, that was the answer. And one of the more difficult songs with which she could show off a bit. She would sing 'Poor Wandering One'. Mabel's song from *The Pirates of Penzance*. Miss Marion had appeared as Mabel for the D'Oyley Carte. She had not brought the sheet music, but that did not worry her. She knew it well, and Miss Langley, a Gilbert and Sullivan fan, would be able to manage an adequate accompaniment.

It was a relief to finish with the wretched lilac tree, and after a whispered conference, and some opening chords, she began again,

'Poor wandering one,
Thou hast surely strayed,'

reminding herself, after a glance at Miss Marion whose companion was still invisible, that she was supposed to be entertaining the whole room, and must not look only in one direction.

The song went well, and by the time she reached

'Poor wandering one, if such poor love as mine
Can help thee find true peace of mind,'

she was thoroughly enjoying herself, singing, she thought, her very best. A small commotion arose a few yards away on her right. Someone scraped a chair, there were protesting voices. With her eyes on the other half of the room Addie ignored it, thinking that her teacher would be angry at the disturbance and hoping that she would not reprimand those responsible, which she was quite capable of doing. After a moment, still singing, Addie looked round and saw that the table by the pillar was empty. Then she noticed that a waitress had opened the double glass doors at the end of the room and a small woman in a pale flowered dress was passing through, followed by someone tall in dark green. Miss Marion leaving while she was singing! It must be of course that she, or the small woman who was presumably her sister, had become ill, felt faint perhaps, because of the warm, crowded room. And Addie had meant to go over and speak to them when she had an opportunity. Without faltering she finished the song, and acknowledged the applause. Then she descended from the little platform and went to have a word with Holly and Ted, as they would expect. Holly said, 'Did you see those awful women? Crashing out like that in the middle of your song? Spoilt it completely.'

'I didn't really notice them.'

'Well, I did. I think they had a quarrel, the little one seemed to be nagging on all the time.'

'I don't notice people when I'm singing, unless I know them.'

Addie left them after a moment, thankful that she had the excuse of wishing to speak to Beatie. When she returned to the platform she sang two songs by Guy D'Hardilot, just the kind of thing Miss Marion deplored. But the tea-drinkers at the Koh-i-noor liked them, so what did it matter?

Addie thought much about this incident during the next two days, but on the Wednesday she and her mother had arranged to make the long, complicated journey to see Charlie, in a military hospital, and after that it didn't seem quite so important.

Charlie, serious curly-haired Charlie, had been gassed and expected to be 'invalided out' of the Army. Nellie and Addie were both thankful for this, but after they had seen him they were less sure that he was one of the lucky ones. The sound of his rasping breath had stayed with them all the silent way home, but still, they had seen the MO and he thought that Lance Corporal Clarke would be discharged to a convalescent home in two or three weeks' time.

On the following day, as Addie walked up the lane to her regular Thursday lesson, she was thinking, not of her teacher's strange behaviour but of her two soldier brothers, for Jay was still in France and they hadn't heard from him for two weeks. Owing to his eyesight he was in the Pay Corps, so not in the trenches, but still in hourly danger. She remembered how she had followed them both down to the sands as a child, and how their mother had devised rules for their safety, forbidding not only the sands in winter, but tree-climbing and getting their feet wet and going without a proper dinner and dawdling on the way home from school. And it had come to this.

Opening the gate in the wall, Addie wondered if

she would be capable of singing that day. Every time she thought of Charlie, staring at them with wild eyes as though he hardly knew who they were, using all his mind and energy for the difficult act of breathing, she felt like crying.

Miss Marion was not already at the piano, as she nearly always was on Thursdays. Addie took off her hat and sat down on the couch. Too dispirited to try her voice, she stayed there with her music on her lap, waiting. She could hear voices overhead. It was the first time she had heard a sound from any other room. They seemed to be arguing, subdued but bitter. A door banged, there was the sound of running footsteps, and then a crash as of breaking glass. The voices were rising, no longer subdued but screaming indistinguishably; and there were thuds, almost as though people were fighting.

Addie went to the door, opened it quietly and looked out into the passage. Doris was standing uncertainly at the foot of the stairs. They looked at each other, frightened and anxious, saying nothing. There was a heavier thud and a kind of tinkling clatter as though someone had overturned a dressing table, followed by silence. Thick, slow, silence that was much more terrifying than the awful noises. Bravely, Doris started up the stairs, while Addie hesitated at the bottom.

Obviously the Jane Eyre theory was the right one. What would Doris find? Had murder been done up there? Addie leaned against the wall, shaking, believing herself to be ill-starred, a bringer of bad luck to herself and others. Should she have let little

Doris go up there alone? She mounted a few steps, and stopped to listen. There were voices again now, and the sound of stifled weeping. Suddenly the farthest door opened, and Addie retreated. In a moment Doris was coming downstairs towards her. Halfway down she whispered, 'It's alright,' and then in her normal voice added, 'Miss Marion's so sorry about your lesson, Miss, but she says to say she's not so well today, and I'm to make you a cup of tea before you go, if you'd like one.'

And then she winked, hugely, closing one eye and squeezing it shut, while keeping the rest of her face perfectly straight, as if to say, 'She may want to pretend nothing's happened, but we know, don't we?'

Addie looked at her coldly. 'I won't have any tea, thank you. There'll be a tram soon, if I go now. Tell Miss Marion I quite understand.'

Doris, feeling perhaps she had gone too far said, 'Yes, Miss' politely and without expression.

'Do you know if . . . I suppose it's next week as usual?'

'Oh yes, Miss, she said to tell you that.'

Addie returned to the sitting room and hurriedly prepared to leave. A moment later the front door closed behind her and Doris's footsteps sounded along the passage to the kitchen. All was quiet. Crossing the little garden Addie looked up curiously at the bedroom windows, and saw her teacher standing, half concealed by the curtain, looking down. She moved away quickly. Addie stared at the place where she had been for some seconds willing her to reappear, but she did not.

She caught the tram, but did not go straight home. The thought of Nellie's questions was unbearable. Her mother had become more and more disapproving of her visits to Foreland Bay, appearing to resent the time and money involved. If she were to tell her she had gone all that way for nothing she would become even more insistent on her giving up the lessons.

She thought of going to the flat above the chemist's to see Holly. But Teddy would be upstairs, having his tea with her, and she could not describe what had happened with him there. Not that her sister was much good as a confidante anyway. She would say 'How extraordinary' and giggle a bit and soon turn the conversation to her own affairs. Then she considered going to the shop. She had the key on her, as she usually had. She could do some paper work, take her mind off things and soothe her troubled spirit that way, but she didn't feel like checking orders, or doing accounts, so in the end she went down to the sea.

The day had been bright, but now the sun was setting and a cool breeze had sprung up. In peacetime the place would have been crowded with visitors, but now there were only a few people about. She crossed the green and leaned on the iron railings that were set within a few feet of the cliff edge.

Looking out towards the horizon, feeling the air cool on her face, she thought of nothing. She had been feeling sick ever since she left Updown Close.

Why? Wasn't it perfectly normal for sisters to have rows? She and Holly did. At least, they had done when they lived in the same house. Yes, but they'd never fought, never broken things, and anyway, they'd only been girls. And Miss Marion had known she was coming for her lesson. It was not to be understood. She turned away. This time the sea would not bring her peace, as it often did.

Somebody stood beside her. A twangy cockney voice said, "Scuse me, Miss, 'av'n't I seen you somewhere before?'

He was a soldier, young, thin, perky and smiling hopefully. Addie felt herself blush. 'No, I don't think you have,' she said curtly, and, almost elbowing him aside, she briskly crossed the promenade and ran across the green to the road.

His voice came after her, injured, aggrieved. 'Sorry, I'm sure. Anyone can make a mistake.'

She hurried towards home. Nothing mattered now but getting there. Did she look like that kind of girl? The kind that could be 'got off with' in a public place? Her clothes, what was wrong with them? They were fashionable, but not cheap, and quiet enough, surely? Just because she had been standing alone. It didn't occur to her then that he might have been attracted by the red-gold hair showing beneath her hat, that he might himself have been taken aback by the sad severity of her expression, not to say the pince-nez.

She had a miserable week. When she wasn't puzzling over the situation at Foreland Bay she was a prey to remorse about the soldier. He had been young, he hadn't meant any harm. He could be in France any day. Perhaps he would be killed. She could at least have been polite to him. What was she doing for the war effort after all? A bit of singing, and some knitting, and writing letters to her brothers. Other women were nurses, or worked in munitions factories. And she couldn't even treat a young soldier with common politeness. Perhaps he had been on embarkation leave.

Again and again she returned to the question of her singing lessons. Could she go back? Wouldn't it be dreadfully embarrassing? She could not go back. She would write instead. For an hour she would cling to that decision, but the thought of never going there again; never seeing Miss Marion; never hearing her praise or suffering her strictures; never seeing the luminous dark eyes gazing at her; never again trying to match the expansion of that splendid ribcage . . . no!

It was all ridiculous, nothing to do with her, just a quarrel between the sisters, of course she would go. So she went on all that week, sharing her thoughts with no one. Bella said, 'Addie's in a mood, isn't she, Mum? Addie, you aren't half in a mood.'

But Nellie only said, 'Of course she's worried, we all are, and Heaven knows we've got plenty to worry about. Have you written to Charlie this week?' and Addie felt guilty because she had scarcely thought of her brothers for days.

On Wednesday night she slept little. Having made up her mind that she was certainly going to

Updown Close as usual, she longed for the difficult first moments of the meeting to be over. Then everything would be back to normal. Perhaps there would be no difficult moments, after all, the whole thing had obviously become exaggerated in her mind.

She felt sick again as she left the tram and walked down the lane. She had been practising hard and was determined to earn praise. Would Miss Marion be there at the piano when she entered the room? She would stop playing and singing and would take her hand – 'My dear, I know I need not explain to you. Life is not easy, but one does one's best' – and this time Addie would not be embarrassed, would not withdraw her hand but would return the affectionate pressure, saying something like 'Explanations are not necessary between friends'.

The daylight was beginning to fade, and a cool autumnal breeze fluttered the leaves as she pushed open the gate, and closed it behind her, feeling that she entered a private world. A piece of white paper fluttered across in front of her feet, which struck her as unusual. Miss Marion was not the kind of person to allow litter to spoil her garden, which was still colourful with Michaelmas daisies and late roses. Addie considered picking up the scrap of paper but there was nowhere to put it and to take it into the house and give it to Doris might look as though she were being critical. So she left it where it was and knocked at the door. Doris was often slow in answering her knock and she waited patiently in the porch with considerably more than

her usual sense of anticipation. Thursday had come.
She was here. Would Miss Marion refer to last
week's missed lesson? Would she refer, even
obliquely, to her difficulties? Addie renewed her
determination to offer help, if the opportunity
arose. If she could do nothing, well, at least Miss
Marion would know she was on her side. 'If there's
ever anything I can do . . .' she imagined her own
voice trailing off, and then the reply, 'My dear, how
like you to say that. I promise . . . '

Coming out of her daydream she realized that
this was an extra long delay, even for Doris. It
would look as though she were late, unless Miss
Marion had seen her pass the window. She knocked
again, loudly, and waited once more, but no Doris
appeared. Something must be wrong. She moved
to the sitting room window. If there was anyone in
the room she would tap on the glass. Not very
polite, but if no one let her in . . . The dark blue
curtains were drawn across. Strange she hadn't
noticed earlier, but her attention had been caught
by the little piece of white paper that had now come
to rest at the edge of the crazy paving. Stepping
back, she looked at the upper storey. All the curtains were drawn. The windows were blank, blind,
secret. Trembling now, she returned to the porch
and knocked at the door again, banging the brass
knocker hard and repeatedly. Nothing happened.
Shamelessly, she tried the handle. It turned but the
door being locked did not give. Leaving her music
case she went to the far side of the garden and
down the narrow passage between the wall of the

house and the high, thick hedge. There was no garden at the back, just a little yard with a dustbin and a clothes-line, and one or two outbuildings. This side of the house was less private than the front, being overlooked by the one next door which was only a few feet away. On her right was a door, and two windows, one with frosted glass, the other set higher in the wall and partly obscured by a net curtain hanging from a rod halfway up.

Addie knocked on the door with her knuckles until they hurt. Perhaps they were all ill, all lying upstairs in darkened rooms, too weak even to call out. Somehow she would have to break in, call a doctor, stay and look after them. She saw herself carrying beef tea to a pale Miss Marion, who lay back on a huge pillow with her hair in plaits. Standing on an upturned bucket she was just able to see over the top of the curtain, into the kitchen. Except for a deal table and one upright chair, it was quite empty. The range was black and cold; the shelves were bare. No crockery, kettle or saucepans. Nothing. The door stood ajar, and beyond, without any possible shadow of doubt, lay the rest of the house, bleak and deserted and silent. Then she heard a voice. An upstairs window next door had been opened and an untidy woman in an overall was leaning out.

'You looking for Miss Frederick?'

'Yes, but I think they must be out.'

'They've gone. Done a flit. Day before yesterday.'

'You don't happen to . . . have their address?'

'No. Never had anything to do with them. Funny lot. One of her pupils, were you?'

So there had been others.

'Yes, yes, I was . . . '

'Fancy going off without saying. Still, they were a funny lot. Kept themselves to themselves.'

'Well, I'll be going. Thank you.'

'No trouble, ta-ta.'

At the front of the house she collected her music case, and then saw the piece of paper still there. She picked it up. It was a little grey snapshot of two women standing together in front of a brick wall. One was Jessie Marion. She had her arm round a small, thinner woman, and they were both smiling. Addie could just make out that the small woman wore pince-nez like herself. She had fair, fluffy hair and a fragile look. Addie smoothed out the photograph, dusted it carefully, wrapped it in her handkerchief and put it in her music case, and then for the last time she went out into the lane.

She had gone straight home that day, and up to the room she had once shared with Holly. Thank goodness there was no one in the house, no one to comment on her early return, no mother to be solicitous about a pretended headache, no tiresomely curious Bella to probe for the real reasons. She had left her music case downstairs in its usual place but the little photograph she took with her. Without even taking off her hat she lit the candle that stood on the chest of drawers, unwrapped the picture and stared at it as though it could tell her some truth, give her some reason. Was the other woman the mysterious older sister? But this one looked younger, if anything. They were both smiling and happy, and now they were somewhere else. Perhaps still smiling, still happy, because still together. Miss Marion had not lost her sister as she had lost Holly. She looked and looked at the faded snapshot, which after all told her so very little, then she put it away in her top drawer, among her handkerchieves and lace collars. She did not want to tell Nellie that the sisters had left the district, but of course she would have to. Her mother would undoubtedly be very pleased, though it was hard to understand why.

She did tell her, when she came in from having tea with Holly, and had to bear her derogatory remarks, and her assumption that they had left unpaid bills. She supposed that Addie had seen the error of her ways, persisting with lessons in the face of disapproval.

'But you knew nothing about them,' burst out Addie at last, and then realized that of course this was the whole trouble. Nellie still feared the unknown for her children, even if it was only a tram ride away.

She went to bed early, and woke in the night. She had dreamed that she was the fragile woman in the snapshot, that Miss Marion's arm had enclosed her own shoulders, and that she had stood in the sun with her, to have her picture taken.

She could not understand the desolation which engulfed her as she slowly realized the true state of things. After all, Miss Marion was a woman, and you couldn't fall in love with another woman, could you?

Moving in bed, Addie felt a spasm of pain shoot through the lower part of her body. Why couldn't Ronnie leave her alone? He knew she couldn't stand that sort of thing these days. Opening her eyes, she saw the big, softly lit room, with the row of beds facing her, each one containing an old woman. Some were propped up with pillows and had started their dinner; a nurse was helping one of them; and a wardmaid with a tray was approaching her own bed. She realized that the pain had been occasioned by the permanently inserted catheter, and felt even angrier than before.

The nurse opposite said loudly, 'You'll have to help Mrs Castle, Luisa.'

Crossly Addie grabbed the spoon, but she spilt the soup and had to let the Spanish girl feed her. Humiliation on humiliation. She opened her mouth to say 'I don't want any' but the wretched girl took the opportunity to jam the spoon into her mouth. Well, the soup was good, that was something. By the time it was finished Addie's temper had improved a little. She even attempted a joke. 'Worse than a baby!' she murmured.

'Never mind,' said Luisa, smiling as she removed the messy tray, 'it doesn't matter.'

They were very kind here, almost all of them, and that was really the most important thing. Well, she'd been kind, hadn't she, so she had earned kindness at the end of her life. Kind to her brothers and her sisters and her parents, and to Ronnie. Surely she had been kind to Ronnie. He'd enjoyed the money, the cars and the holidays abroad. He'd been able to buy himself expensive clothes. Yes, she'd been very kind to Ronnie. Why then had he left her? Left her alone just when she needed him? Left her alone in that big house and moved into a flat. He'd never taken up with anyone else, there'd been no divorce. And Dorothy seemed not to blame him, to see his point of view, even.

She began to think morbidly about people whom she thought had disliked her. There was Winnie, Charlie's wife, for one. She'd never got on with her, somehow. She'd been so possessive, wanting to separate him from the family, and keep him to herself. And then Maud. That was a long story, but she had no time for Maud, running Jay's life the way she had. But she'd been polite to both of them, never done them any harm. In fact of late years she'd seen quite a lot of good in Winnie.

That terrible little house they'd lived in though; not Charlie's fault, poor Charlie, he'd been ill so much, but she'd always felt so out of place there and that awful time when Winnie had invited them at Christmas, and afterwards when she tried to make it up Charlie had been so rude and they hadn't spoken for weeks and weeks. Might never have spoken again if she hadn't been determined. She couldn't bear the thought of losing Charlie for always, but he was so loyal.

And Ronnie, well Ronnie had not disliked her, in

fact she sometimes thought he still loved her. And yet he had gone away.

Luisa was returning with her main course. It was mince. They thought it would be easier for her to manage. Well, that was true, but if you were paying Dover sole prices you didn't expect to be fobbed off with mince.

She ate a little, with assistance, but couldn't be bothered to finish her meal. Perhaps they had drugged her without her knowing. She said firmly, 'It ought not to be allowed,' but whether she meant the mince or the sleeping pills she did not really know. Soon after the trays were cleared away she was asleep.

CHAPTER 4

THURSDAY

Waking in the early hours, Addie remembered where she was quite quickly. Turning her head, she could see the night nurse sitting at the desk at the end of the ward, knitting by the light of a shaded lamp. Between the curtains opposite the first grey light of dawn filtered in. She wondered if they would be getting her up that day. No point in it really, she was so weak and shaky that she was much more comfortable in bed. They told her she was improving, but of course you didn't expect to improve at eighty-four. In any case, what was the point of hanging about after they'd all gone? Holly and Ted, Win and Charlie, Maud and Jay, the names of the married couples, forever linked, ran through her mind. Percy and Bella, Addie and Ron . . . but they were not forever linked, he had left her and in any case he was still alive. He and she, the last of their generation, though not the youngest. Well, she had never wanted this, to out-live them all. Though at least she need have no fears for them now, that was one thing. Her brothers and sisters! What a worry they'd all been. Determined to make fools of themselves, to make wrong decisions, marry people who weren't right for them. All those weeks when Charlie, her own beloved curly-haired little Charlie, had refused to have anything to do with her. All Winnie's doing, of course. She'd never forgiven her, but she'd had to pretend forgiveness, or she'd never have seen Charlie again. Except by chance, like that time he'd passed her on his bicycle going down Dane Hill, and she'd called out and run after him, but he'd gone straight on, freewheel-ing down the hill at a reckless speed, home to his dear little wife.

She hadn't taken to Winnie from the first. They'd been expecting Charlie home for Christmas, that winter of 1917. He'd been moved from the military hospital to a Red Cross convalescent home at Fore-land Bay. They all visited him, as often as they could. Addie always averted her eyes when they passed the end of Updown Lane; she didn't want to be reminded.

The convalescent home was a cheerful enough place. Almost all the patients were up and about in their hospital blues, with white shirts and red cotton ties, and there was a lot of laughter and joking, though many of them had lost limbs and were still in pain, some were shellshocked and others had been gassed like Charlie, and would never be really well again.

They could sit with Charlie in the chintzy day-room which had once been the drawing room of this substantial house on the clifftop, looking out over the sea, and talking to him about what they would do when he came home, and how they were saving their rations up for Christmas. Addie and Holly were there together one Sunday afternoon when he introduced them to Winnie.

A young woman in the uniform of a VAD nurse, sweet and smiling and as fresh as a daisy in her white cap and apron, was handing out thick mugs of tea. Charlie called to her, 'Win! Winnie! Here a minute.' The girl approached uncertainly. 'Don't be shy. Holly, Ad, this is Winnie. These two are my sisters. You'd better like each other because . . . because . . . '

Here a fit of coughing overcame him. When it was over he sank back exhausted, unable to speak, and Holly dragged Addie away, ignoring her protests.

'It looks as though Charlie's clicked,' said Holly on the tram.

'Oh, surely he won't think of getting married, will he?' said Addie. 'It wouldn't be fair, to her, I mean.'

Her heart sank. Was Charlie to be taken away from her just when she was about to get him back? He must come home. He would need careful looking after. He was to be invalided out, a frightening phrase but almost worth it to have him safe, never to go away again.

'What did you think of her?' Holly was saying.

'I didn't notice her.'

'Rather sweet, I thought. A sweet little thing. I can imagine Charlie liking a sweet little thing. So different from us.'

'He'll need someone strong, to take care of him,' said Addie. 'I doubt whether he'll be able to earn a living, in any case.'

'Sweet little things are often amazingly strong,' said Holly. 'Anyway, you wouldn't want him not to get married, would you?'

'She doesn't look the right sort to me.'

'The trouble with you is that you're too possessive. You want to hang on to us all.'

'No, I don't. But well, it's a pity to break up the family.'

'Who's going to break up the family? Silly old Ad! You didn't lose me when I got married, did you? I see you nearly every day.'

'It's different with brothers,' answered Addie. 'Anyway . . .'

'Anyway what? . . . Oh, look!' Holly pointed excitedly as the tram passed a turning. 'Isn't that the road where your music teacher lived? The one that did a bunk?'

Addie ignored this. 'When he's home,' she said, 'he'll probably forget all about her.'

'Don't you believe it,' said Holly.

That was the last time they went together to visit Charlie, because Ted joined the RAMC and was soon commissioned, and Holly took over the management of the shop, with the help of an elderly man called out of retirement to do the dispensing. It was an anxious time, with the constant fear for Jay who was still in France, and Charlie's terrifying attacks of asthma. They had kept him in the convalescent home over Christmas, and really he hadn't seemed to mind at all – he was obviously quite happy there with Winnie.

Almost every day they heard of the death in action of someone they had known. Bella's young man, Terry Keenan, was killed on the Somme and Addie wept as she packed up the black hats ordered by his mother and sister, thinking of how he'd enjoyed the musical evenings and walked home with Bella afterwards. She wrote to Dick, and knitted scarves and balaclavas for him. Her letters were amusing and rambling, detailing the lives of the people around her, joking about the queues for food, and telling how her mother had tried to make a Christmas pudding using carrots instead of dried fruit from a recipe in a women's paper and similar stories. Then in one letter he repeated his proposal of marriage and spoilt the whole thing.

Poor Dick. He had quite misunderstood Addie's motives in writing the friendly, entertaining letters. He thought she was regretting her refusal and waited quite happily for her acceptance. Addie was desperate. How could she make more wretched a young man who already had the miseries of the trenches to contend with? She thought and thought. All her original reasons for not wanting to marry him were still just as powerful. In the end she wrote an equivocating reply, suggesting that they wait until he came home and they could decide how they felt then. Dick wrote back as soon as he could, saying he knew how he felt already, and asking for a photograph. Addie sent one in which she looked particularly pudding-faced and hoped it would put him off. As usual, there was no one in whom she could confide. Obviously not Holly, who had married Ted without feeling the least need to confess to him, and there was no one else.

The whole dilemma brought back the Terrible Time with appalling clarity to Addie's mind. For months she was on the old treadmill of guilt and shame. Her only comfort was the sight of Holly, happy and efficient in the corner shop, respected by all as young Mrs Kingston, of Kingston's the Chemists. It was worth it, she told herself, for what sort of life would her sister have had if the secret had come out? Clearly *her* conscience did not bother her in the least. It seemed to Addie, however, only right that someone should suffer for so dreadful a deed. She tried to be glad that it was herself. During this time she formed the habit of taking solitary walks along the sands, when she would sing at the top of her voice, and the sound would be swept away on the wind so that she could scarcely hear it. Then the physical exhaustion gave a sort of peace for an hour. She became thinner, and lost her appetite. She knew her mother was worried about her because she tried to feed her up, making her drink glasses of milk mixed with beaten egg, a revolting mixture, and buying little jars of Valentines Meat Juice.

It was none of these things that helped Addie back to a healthier frame of mind, but after months of misery, when the war had ended, Charlie was out of hospital and Jay back from France, there was so much to do and so much to distract her, that the old formula 'I did it for Holly' finally regained its magic. Charlie became engaged to Winnie and Holly confided that there would be\ an addition to the Kingston family in the autumn. Even then, though often alone with Addie, she did not refer to her past experience. Addie longed for her to do so, feeling that what might after all have been a bond between them had become a barrier. However, there was not much time to spare, what with the shop, helping to look after Charlie, and more and more singing. She still sang in the choir of St Austin's with Holly and Ted and the rest of the Kingstons. With the exception of Dick they were still the mainstays of their church. It had been a relief to Addie when immediately after his demobilization he told her he had decided to become a doctor. The long training, he said, made it impossible to ask her to wait for him, but if when it was over . . . He didn't want her to feel he was letting her down. Addie told him she didn't feel like that at all and sincerely wished him luck. She enjoyed the choir more without him gazing at her soulfully over his music. It was enough that sometimes Tom Kingston would smile across at her as they sang away together. And then she would smile back. What else could she do?

Slowly the town returned to life. Empty shops were stocked with goods, and dark hotels took down their shutters, put up new curtains and opened their doors. Summer visitors returned and the Kingstons held a garden party in aid of the church funds. Cornwall Lodge was set in a large L-shaped garden, with smooth lawns, flower-beds, and a great mulberry tree under which Mrs Kingston stood with Father Christopher and other important people to open the proceedings.

There were stalls and raffles and hoop-la and teas and entertainment by the pupils of a local dancing school, after which Holly and Ted and Addie had sung a selection from Gilbert and Sullivan. Father Christopher had personally thanked Addie, saying how much he appreciated her generosity in giving her time, when she was after all a busy professional singer, and what a pleasure it was to hear the celebrated Miss Adelaide Clarke. Addie thought for the first time, 'I am Adelaide Clarke, the well-known singer' and felt very pleased with herself. Then suddenly she remembered Miss Marion saying, 'You should be preparing to tour the capital cities of the world,' and her little bit of local fame seemed unimportant, and not worth bothering about. But soon other people came up and said how much they had enjoyed listening to her and they hoped she would be singing at the Winter Gardens again before long, and really it was very pleasant. Addie went over to where some of the Catholic ladies were serving teas and sat down at a little table.

It was a pretty, summery scene, despite the

sprinkling of black among the light dresses. Addie's own was green and white voile, long-waisted, and much shorter than the styles of pre-war days. Some of the other dresses came from the shop which Addie still managed for Miss Jones, for she had just branched out into ready-made clothes, but for the most part they had been run up by their owners or by local dressmakers. Mrs Keenan was still in black for Terry, and she glanced reproachfully at Bella who was larking about, as usual. Addie called to her. 'Bella, come and have some tea. I'm just going to.'

Bella came over, accompanied by a slim, short, smiling young man. And that was the first time she spoke to Ronnie.

He'd been such a good husband in so many ways, and he'd really loved her. Well, she hadn't wanted him to go away. It had all started with the twin beds, she could see that now, but never mind, think about the good times, the picnics on the sands with all the family sitting in a half-circle of hired deck-chairs, and later on when they had their own hut on the lower promenade. That had been nice and convenient with fresh tea instead of thermos flasks, except of course Charlie and Winnie stopped coming. Just because they hadn't a hut of their own, and she wouldn't let them bring their own tea. Still Winnie was always difficult, sweet as anything to your face and then going on to Charlie afterwards. Of course he always tried to please her, even if it meant giving up the family picnics which Addie knew he enjoyed. And it was probably the one time in the week when he got a decent piece of cake.

Winnie was a hopeless cook, but it was no good saying anything to Charlie. Of course he had to keep on the right side of her, she was so quick to take offence. Ever since that awful Christmas. Well, she had to think about it, go over it again, see if she had been at fault herself. Let's see, when would it have been? Charlie was married in 1921, but of course they hadn't got a house straight away; they'd lived with Winnie's parents over the newsagent's in the High Street, right down at the harbour end, where you got all the drunks in the evening.

But still, they'd thought the world of Charlie, as well they might. Though how he had put up with it, she couldn't imagine. She knew they had the milk bottle on the table and didn't always bother about saucers because Mrs Smith had taken one out of the cupboard specially when she offered her a cup of tea in the room behind the shop one afternoon. Of course, it was all clean and tidy, you had to admit that, and Mrs Smith had taken her upstairs specially to show her Winnie's old bedroom; with its pink rose wallpaper and carpet on the floor and a pretty dressing table with lots of white lace and pink ribbon, it looked fit for a princess. You could see they doted on Winnie, they must be glad she'd made such a good catch. She'd raised herself a lot by marrying into the Clarke family who were connected with the Kingstons. But Winnie didn't use this room any longer. Mrs Smith took Addie to the spare bedroom, now shared by the young couple, and there was Charlie's Sunday jacket on the back of a chair with a petticoat of his wife's carelessly thrown on top, and Charlie's dressing-gown hanging behind the door, with Winnie's pink one, and a white china chamberpot with pink roses on it clearly visible under the bed. The whole thing had made her feel rather sick. She'd looked round rather quickly and said, 'yes, very nice,' and gone downstairs.

She felt sorry for her youngest brother. How could he possibly be happy in that cramped flat after the comparative spaciousness of Jasmine Villa? Well, of course they hadn't stayed there long, they'd got one of the first council houses, with a little bit of garden, quite enough for poor Charlie, but surely council houses weren't meant for their sort?

She'd always felt conspicuous visiting them, knowing herself to be elegantly and expensively dressed, once the shop was doing well and Miss Jones started paying her commission. The gate was so little, the front path so short, and the door so narrow.

Yes, it would have been Christmas 1922, after she and Ronnie became engaged, and little Jimmy was three years old and his baby sister Gillian just over a year. Such sweet, attractive children, and they really adored their Auntie Addie, you could see that. Absurd, really, how she'd dreaded having to go and see Holly after Jimmy was born. Nellie, returning from an early visit, had told her that the baby was beautiful and Holly blooming, but still Addie delayed. When she had run out of reasonable excuses she went nervously to the flat over the chemist's where Holly lay in bed attended by a professional nurse, and was reassured by the pink, healthy infant and his smiling mother. The events of long ago obviously cast no shadow over Holly's present joy; even to think about the past here seemed sacrilegious.

Addie smiled to herself, remembering the children, and might have gone back to sleep with cheerful thoughts in her mind if it hadn't been for Miss Stanbrook trying to get out of bed and the nurse persuading her back. The disturbance roused her again and after she remembered where she was and why she was there, the thought of that awful Christmas tea at Winnie's came into her mind and there was nothing to do but think it through and try to decide where she had gone wrong.

Christmas 1922. She and Ronnie had been engaged for almost a year. Their shops, or rather those they managed, hers for Miss Jones, his for a jeweller with several branches, had remained open till late on Christmas Eve – too late for Ronnie to catch a train to London and on to Bromley where his mother and sisters lived, so of course he would spend the holiday with the Clarkes. He lived in a boarding house, closed for the winter except for one or two permanent lodgers. The owners had been disappointed when he announced his plans, for Ronnie was a lively young man and they had been relying on him to cheer up their own Christmas.

The day itself was pleasant. They went to St Austin's in the morning because Addie was singing a solo. Ronnie had a low opinion of religion and said the whole thing was a lot of humbug, but as Addie's beautiful voice soared alone from the choir gallery he was filled with pride and when many people thanked her for her singing as they left the church he held her arm so that everybody should know that he was her fiancé.

The dinner was perfectly cooked. They ate in the rarely used dining room, with all the best china and linen, and the whole family was there. Mum and Dad, Jay and Charlie, Bella and Holly, Ted of course, and the babies, and Winnie. She and Charlie, married for nearly two years, had at last moved into their own house. Beatrice, Addie's assistant, was there too. She was a bright, jolly girl, alone in the world since her aunt had died of influenza. She was fond of music and devoted to Addie, who had actually invited her for the day. However, she was sitting next to Jay. He had always liked her and before he was ensnared by Maud they had been for several walks together. Such a pity it had come to nothing. Beatrice, being an orphan, wouldn't have wanted to take Jay away from the family. Dinner over, the party split up; Nellie to rest after her arduous work in the kitchen, the others to wash the dishes and then to set out for a digestion-aiding stroll. Holly and her husband and children would be going to Cornwall Lodge for tea, and Charlie and Winnie were spending the rest of the day with her parents. Bella disappeared, no one knew where.

'Off after some boy, I suppose,' said Addie bitterly. 'People ought to stay with their families at Christmas.' It was bad enough that Charlie and Holly would not be there. Still, she put a good face on things, and Jay and Ronnie fooled about and made her laugh and Bella came in soon after tea, so although Jay had to visit his fiancée in the evening, the rest of the day was really very pleasant. It was on Boxing Day that everything went completely wrong.

If only Winnie hadn't insisted on them all going to tea at College Road. There just wasn't room for a start. And Addie really didn't want to take Ronnie – supposing he got the idea that council houses were alright? He'd already said that he thought Charlie was lucky to get one, considering the housing shortage. Addie did not tell him that Winnie's uncle was on the council. Winnie's mother often talked about him.

The house was at the end of a little terrace. It had the distinction of having the front door at the side. The short path went down steeply because the houses had been built in a hollow. The tiny front garden was neatly dug, but nothing grew in it as yet. Before Nellie, who was leading the party, had time to knock, the door was flung open by Charlie. He was smiling and happy. Winnie, looking nervous, was standing behind him in the small square lobby. Just one door led out of it, and the steep, narrow stairs.

'Come straight in,' said Charlie, leading them into the living room. 'Let me take your coats.'

'Oh, do come upstairs.' Winnie was so pathetically anxious to do the right thing. 'They'll want to take their coats off in the bedroom.'

It was all a crowd and a fuss and people getting in each other's way until finally the hostess led Addie, Mother, Bella and Holly, who was carrying the baby, back into the lobby and up to the spare bedroom. It was sparsely furnished and bitterly cold, but Addie was glad they were shown into this room rather than the marital bedroom next door.

Nellie had seen the house on previous occasions, and so had Bella, who liked to poke her nose in everywhere, but Addie, occupied with the shop, her singing and Ronnie, had not done so, though Winnie and Charlie had moved in several weeks earlier. Now they filed out of the door and back down the stairs. The men's coats were hung on pegs in the lobby and they had to push past them to get into the room. Being the only one, it was always crowded with furniture, and now with people. A door to the left led to the kitchen. It could be opened without coming into contact with the square of carpet which covered the middle of the floor, with a wide surround of linoleum in a parquet pattern. Two brown upholstered armchairs with wooden arms faced each other beside the fire, which was burning brightly in the small grate. On the dark wood mantelshelf stood a wedding photograph of the happy couple, and a smaller one of Winnie's parents. Winnie had worked a great many cushions and chairbacks for her bottom drawer and these were generously strewn about. The gateleg table, ornamented by a beige crash table runner, heavily embroidered in orange and green, was drawn up to the window. There were books, knitting and cards from friends strewn about the room, and a new calendar was pinned up. Four upright chairs stood against the walls.

Charlie urged his father and mother to take the best seats by the fire, Bella perched on the cretonne-covered pouffe and the rest sat where they could. There was a great deal of 'Do come and sit here' and 'No, no, this is quite alright' and bringing more chairs from upstairs until they were eventually all seated and then no one seemed to know what to say. Little Jimmy sat on his grandfather's knee and was easily entertained by his massive old pocket watch, but Gillian, who could not be allowed to crawl about because there was no fireguard, soon became peevish and wriggled frantically, waving her arms. Addie tried to take her but the struggling infant somehow hit her in the face, knocking the pince-nez, which bit into her nose painfully, bringing tears to her eyes.

Holly said, 'It's your fault, you always think you can manage them better than anyone else,' and Ted took Gillian and started throwing her up in the air, which made her laugh and Holly became crosser than ever. Winnie decided that it was time for tea, early as it was, and there was a general reshuffle and business as the table was moved into the centre of the room, a distance of about three feet, and the chairs rearranged around it.

Winnie disappeared into the kitchen, and Bella, directed by her mother to help, got up reluctantly from where she had been huddling up to the fire and left the room. Jay, who was very thin, was desperately cold after the walk so he immediately took possession of the pouffe. At once Bella, having found her assistance unwanted, returned, and tried to push him off. He laughed and clung on, but Bella was not in the mood for romping and sat down sulkily on the far side of the table, saying she was freezing. After that, of course, Jay offered her the seat, but she said no, it was too late. What idiotic nonsense, and at their age, for Bella was twenty-six, and Jay nearly thirty.

The cloth was laid, and tea brought in: plates of bread and butter, both brown and white; two kinds of jam; plain cake; Christmas cake; a pink blanc-mange, rather unsuccessfully turned out; and finally the tea things on a wedding-present tray. With every chair and stool in the house brought into service, nine of the party were able to squeeze round the table, with the babies on their parents' knees, placing a good deal of crockery in grave danger. Addie's father was encouraged to retain his position by the fire. He thought little of this honour, saying it made him feel like a grandfather.

'But you are a grandfather, Dad,' said Holly, giving the baby a piece of bread and butter which she happily squeezed into a pulp before putting it more or less into her mouth.

Everyone relaxed a little, Winnie poured the tea, and the cups were passed along the table.

'Charlie, Charlie dear,' said Winnie, 'will you go and put the kettle on for some hot water?'

Charlie did so.

A moment later: 'Charlie, Charlie dear, you did put the kettle on, didn't you? Do you think it's boiling yet?'

'Poor old Charlie,' said Addie. 'Let him sit down for a minute.' Her mother looked at her warningly.

'It's alright, Ad,' Charlie spoke soothingly. 'Win just wants to look after our guests.'

Guests! That showed how far away he had become. She'd been his sister, living in the same house, loving him, worrying about his cough, part of the same family. Now she was a guest. Her nose still hurt at the sides; she was wedged in at the edge of the table between her mother and Holly and her unpredictable daughter; she was full up with cold turkey; and now Charlie was placing a repulsive helping of pink blancmange in front of her. Couldn't he even remember she hated blancmange?

She ate what she could, like everyone else, but there was far too much very ordinary food and no one was hungry. Dad said, 'Your wife makes a good cup of tea, Charlie,' and asked for a third cup just when the hot water had run out, so Charlie was sent out to the kitchen to put the kettle on the gas stove again. Nellie wondered aloud whether gas would do Charlie any harm; would it have been better to have a range? Winnie had to admit they weren't given the choice.

Then just when Charlie had sat down again there was the sound of the gate, a knock at the door, and it was Winnie's parents, squeezing into the crowded

room, taking off their coats and being greeted unen-
thusiastically by Winnie.

'I said she wasn't expecting us,' said Winnie's
father, a thin, grey man.

'I told him, if you can't go and see your daughter
without an invitation, who can you? Didn't I, Dad?'

His wife was a plump little woman whose clothes
looked too tight.

'It's very nice to see you,' said Nellie politely. 'It's
been quite a while, hasn't it?'

'I don't suppose you come down our way very
often,' said Mrs Smith, giving her hat to Winnie,
and sitting down in Charlie's place. 'I was saying
to Dad, we should ask you round one evening.
We're all one family now, and families should stick
together, shouldn't they?'

Mr Smith leaned over the table towards Gillian
and poked her in the stomach with a long forefinger, saying, 'Who's a pretty girl, then?' The
corner of his jacket dragged in Addie's blancmange.

When tea could decently be said to be over clearing it away was achieved with difficulty and the
table pushed back. It seemed as though something
was about to begin – but nothing was. Nellie said,
'You're very quiet, Addie,' which was annoying, as
though she usually made a good deal of noise, and
then Jay chipped in: 'That's because she's jealous.
She doesn't like the birds fleeing the nest, do you,
Ad?'

Mrs Smith tried to be tactful. 'Who's going to be
next, then? You'll have another one gone by this
time next year, Mrs Clarke.'

Jay, newly engaged to Maud, looked sheepish. Mr Smith said something facetious to Bella about her not being left on the shelf for very long, and Nellie introduced Ronnie, rather quickly. Mr Smith seemed surprised and then excused himself by saying he'd always understood Miss Clarke was a business lady, as well as being very musical.

'She still needs a husband, though, don't you Ad?' Ronnie laughed, laying his arm round her shoulders, and all the men sniggered unpleasantly. After that there was a long moment's silence, and Mrs Smith said, 'Angels passing over' and still the silence went on.

'Well, what shall we do?' asked Charlie, with bright desperation.

'I'll help you wash up if you like,' said Addie to Winnie. Anything to get out of that room. But Winnie had her best dress on, dark brown velvet with lace collar and cuffs, and said no, Charlie would wash up later. So Addie stayed where she was. How on earth could they go on sitting there?

Holly announced that she and Ted must go home, because of the baby. Their departure filled the next ten minutes, but after that the evening stretched interminably ahead.

'Pity there's no piano,' said Mrs Smith. 'Addie could give us a song.' Addie! Mrs Smith was calling her Addie when she hardly knew her at all!

Bella, who had returned to her seat close to the fire, and was looking thoroughly glum, cheered up a little at this suggestion. 'She doesn't need an accompaniment. Come on, Ad, sing something.'

Addie felt her face grow hot. The capital cities of the world! But she said nothing.

Mr Smith said, 'Not here, Mother. You'll have to go to the Winter Gardens to hear Miss Clarke. You can't expect her to sing just for us.'

He hadn't said 'for nothing'. Perhaps he hadn't even thought it. If only she had stood up, sung something cheerful from Gilbert and Sullivan, made them join in the chorus. Why hadn't she? Was it because she was what Ronnie called 'too big'? She didn't think so. It was just that she felt uncomfortable, out of place, embarrassed. So she made the mistake that had brought her so much unhappiness.

'Well,' she said, 'couldn't we all go home and have some music? That's what we generally do.'

Nellie demurred, but Mrs Smith seemed eager. Bella, who had plans of her own, rushed upstairs and came down again with an armful of coats. It seemed to be generally agreed that a musical evening at Jasmine Villa would be a good way to end Christmas. It was dark as they set off briskly up the road. Under the lamppost Nellie paused.

'Where's Charlie? Where's Winnie? They were coming, weren't they?'

Mrs Smith answered, 'Oh yes, I'm sure they were. I expect Winnie's just tidying up.'

Addie and her mother looked at one another. 'Just pop back and see what's happening, dear. You can catch us up.'

Nellie and the others went on, except for Ronnie, who waited under the lamppost. Addie ran back and knocked at the door. It was several moments before Charlie opened it. Waiting there, she remembered standing at the front door of Updown Close, which had never opened agáin. Then Charlie was there, his once chubby face white. He was wheezing.

'What do you want?'

'Well, aren't you coming . . . you and Winnie?'

'No, why should we?'

'I thought . . . we were going to have some music.'

'We invited you to come here, for tea and supper. I'm sorry we can't provide a piano. I should have thought you could have done without one for once.' It was cold on the step. Charlie half closed the door.

'We didn't mean to offend you.'

'Well, you have. Winnie's crying.'

'Oh, how silly. Look, Charlie . . . let me come in.'

'You've been damn rude to Win . . . and to me. If you're going to start calling her silly as well, you'd better go home. And you needn't lower yourself to come here again.'

'I didn't mean that. Charlie . . . please . . . '

So he let her in. The living room was empty.

'She's gone upstairs. I'll see if I can get her to come down.'

He was gone a long time. Addie waited, quite forgetting Ronnie, freezing under the lamppost. Eventually she decided to have a look in the kitchen. The used tea-things were piled on the table, beside mounds of uneaten blancmange, and big cakes with only a slice or two missing. More pathetic still, she saw, set out on the little dresser, a pork pie, sliced beetroot, biscuits and cheese, and a bottle of Winnie's mother's home-made wine.

A second clean table-cloth was folded ready to hand. Winnie had done her best, but in Addie's opinion this best was not nearly good enough for Charlie. Oh, what an awful mistake he had made. And now they were saddled with Mr and Mrs Smith for the rest of the evening. Surely Winnie's own mother ought to have realized she'd expected them to stay for supper, but no, of course she and her husband had just dropped in uninvited.

Charlie found her in the kitchen. 'She won't come down.'

'I didn't realize you expected us to stay to supper.'

'We did at Holly's last year.'

Yes, of course they had stayed to supper at Holly's, in the big corner room above the chemist's, where most of the delicious food had come from the kitchen at Cornwall Lodge because Holly was too busy with the baby to do a lot of cooking. Tom Kingston had provided the wine and naturally there was a piano.

'Well, that was different,' said Addie, stupidly.

'Yes, it was. You're a snob, that's your trouble, Addie Clarke, and if my wife isn't good enough for you, it's your loss.'

She knew what Holly would have done. She would have burst into tears, flung her arms round Charlie and everything would have been forgotten, but though she was trembling inside, though her throat ached with love, and tears pricked her eyes, she said in quite a calm voice, 'I think I'd better go.'

Outside she was surprised to see Ronnie walking towards her. 'What the hell have you been doing? It's bloody freezing out here.'

'Don't speak to me like that.'

If he was going to swear at her now, while they were engaged, what sort of monster would he turn into after they were married? They continued up the road, side by side, a space between them. After a moment or two she said crossly, 'You needn't have waited.'

'Of course I waited. What's happening? Are they coming, or not?'

'No, they're not. They've taken offence. We were expected to stay to supper.'

'Well, it's not my fault. It was your idea we came away. Anyhow, we couldn't have sat there looking at one another the whole evening. Tell you what, let's go down to Holly's – she'll be pleased to see us. We could have a bit of a sing-song there.'

'Mum's expecting us. I'm going home anyway. You can do what you like.'

'What d'you mean, I can do what I like? We're engaged, aren't we? Surely we can agree on where to spend the evening?'

'Being engaged doesn't mean we have to spend every minute together.'

'Now look here, Ad . . . '

'Don't call me Ad.'

'I shall call you what I flaming well like . . . '

'Don't swear at me.'

He stopped and caught her by the arm, but she shook him off angrily, and strode away along the pavement at top speed.

'Don't expect me to come running after you, because I shan't,' he shouted.

A couple standing at the gate of one of the council houses turned to look at them, and the youth called out, 'Better run for it while you've got time, mate. She looks a bit of a tartar to me.'

Addie stopped at the corner, trembling with rage and humiliation. He had made a public show of her, to be sneered at by Winnie's common neighbours. Ronnie, smiling now, having made some facetious response to the young man, caught up with her, and tried to put his arm round her waist. He wanted to prove to the interested onlookers that she wasn't such a tartar after all.

'Don't come near me,' she hissed. 'Don't come near ever again.'

Ronnie withdrew his arm, and his face changed. His bright blue eyes seemed to glitter angrily. He spoke loudly, not caring who could hear. 'Right you are then. I've had enough. You can walk home on your own. Only don't come crawling to me in the morning. Because it's all off. Understand?'

'I never crawl to anyone,' answered Addie truthfully. 'Do what you like.'

Unfortunately, even if Ronnie went straight back to where he lived, their paths still lay in the same direction. He crossed to the other side of the road, and each walked briskly along on opposite sides for a quarter of a mile.

CHAPTER 5

Rising slowly out of sleep, Addie remembered only that Ronnie had left her. Had crossed the road and walked away and left her; to spinsterhood, maiden-auntishness, and a lonely old age. She was over thirty, on the shelf. No one else would come along now. And he'd had such a nice smile, such piercingly brilliant blue eyes, and he went everywhere with her, to every singing engagement. It was much better than going on your own. She lay feeling alone, utterly bereft. Why did families have to break up? They'd all been so happy and now Holly was gone, Charlie was gone, and soon no one would want her.

But presently, as her mind cleared, it began to come back to her. They had made it up. He hadn't left her because Bella had appeared round the next corner. They had reached the end of College Road and turned into a more prosperous avenue of red-brick Edwardian villas. Lights showed in all of them, because Boxing Day was a day for the front rooms to be used. And Bella had come flying along, nearly knocking her over, calling to Ronnie, teasing them for having had a lovers' tiff, and Addie prayed that he wouldn't let her down, that he wouldn't continue the quarrel in front of her sister. He came across.

Bella said, 'What have you been doing? Mum made me come back and see what was happening. Are they coming?'

'No, Winnie's upset. She'd got supper ready.'

'Oh, how soppy of her. They can eat it tomorrow. I'll go and persuade them,' and she was off down the road, holding onto her hat, her scarf flying. Addie and Ronnie walked on together.

A year later they'd been married: four years after their first meeting at the garden party. Though they had actually set eyes on each other before that. After four wartime years in the navy and a brief period of employment in a London department store, Ronnie had come to manage Pringle's, the jeweller's shop next-door to Miss Jones's dress and hat shop, now elegant and successful under Addie's management. Although he had said good morning several times, raising his smart trilby hat as they approached their respective establishments, Addie had not, as she put it to herself, fallen over him. It was Bella, of course, who recognizing him at the garden party had introduced herself and then Addie.

She remembered his immaculate suit and neat bow tie, and how he'd said, 'I heard you sing last night. At the Winter Gardens. Fancy you managing a shop as well. Your sister tells me you'll be singing in Ramsgate next week. I'd like to come if you'll tell me where the place is.' Admiration shone out of his eyes. It occurred to Addie that she was becoming less fat-faced, and that the green and white of her dress and hat complemented her gorgeous hair and the green of her eyes. He hadn't wanted lively, talkative Bella, even though she had tried her best. It was obvious that in an admiring, hopeful and thoroughly respectful way, he wanted her.

The following week he had escorted her to Ramsgate on the tram and sat proudly in the front row at the concert, and taken her home in a taxi that cost him far more than he could afford. Soon they were going everywhere together and he was accepted at Jasmine Villa as 'Addie's young man'. And at twenty-seven she had to take him seriously.

She was glad that Jay liked him, though he didn't seem to mind that she spent time with Ronnie which once the brother and sister would have spent together. He had a life of his own outside the family now. He had Maud.

Beatrice was the one he wanted, of course. Plump, cheerful Beatrice, Addie's slave in the shop, and handmaiden whenever she was needed. She could sing quite tunefully, and play the piano reasonably well, and was a practical, happy girl, despite her gloomy home life with an aunt after her parents died. She wasn't pretty, in fact, she was rather plain, but her face was so lively and her smile so frequent that no one had time to notice this.

Beatie would have made an ideal sister-in-law and
they would have had a family, which was what Jay
wanted. But he'd married Maud.

She was one of four strictly brought up daughters
of a local tailor. They were all tall and thin and
beaky-nosed, with nothing to say for themselves.
They had one spoilt brother, Frank, and it was
through him that Jay met Maud. He had asked her
to go for a walk with him the next Sunday afternoon
simply because he couldn't think of anything else
to say. He spent the rest of the week asking Addie
how he could get out of it, and being too kind to
take her advice. Beatrice, who had hopes, and
indeed had already had a few Sunday afternoon
walks as well, was desolate, but tried mistakenly
not to show it. If she had done so perhaps Jay's
kind heart would have led him to disappoint Maud
after all. But she was brave, which Addie admired
her for, though she could see it was a mistake.

Straightaway Maud had invited him back to tea.
He'd told Addie all about it, feeling trapped and
terrified.

The family, with the exception of the tailor, were
seated round the table in the dining room. The tea
was rather plain, with seed-cake. The four girls were
almost silent. Frank chatted naturally, teased his
sisters and cheeked his mother, who seemed to
enjoy it. When tea was over, Mrs Barrett had said,
'Take Mr Clarke to see your father, Frank. He's in
the other room.'

Jay said, 'Oh well, I'd better be going . . . um . . .'

but Maud, giving utterance for almost the first time, said firmly, 'Dad wants to see you.'

So Jay, a lamb to the slaughter, was led into the drawing room which was scarcely used by anyone other than Mr Barrett.

The room, overlooking the garden and facing west, was for these reasons, and no others, brighter than the dining room. It seemed to be entirely furnished in dark red plush, and had a pruny sort of smell. Whether this came from Mr Barrett or the furnishings, Jay did not know.

Knowing that Maud's father was a tailor, Jay had imagined a thin little man, used to sitting cross-legged, and sewing. Instead he was large, grey-bearded and very dignified. He invited Jay to sit down, then asked Frank to remove the tray of tea-things – there had been fruit-cake, Jay noticed – and rose to his feet.

Of course Addie had not been there, but Jay had not only described the incident, but had drawn a little picture of it in her autograph book with himself very tiny and frightened on the horsehair couch, and the enormous Mr Barrett towering over him and saying, 'You have dared to walk out with my daughter, the beauteous Maud?' A few weeks later he tore the drawing out, spoiling the book.

Addie did get to know the room later, but only on formal occasions like going to see the presents, and then the wedding itself. Mrs Barrett saw no point in spending money on hotel receptions. So she could picture the scene, and it made her angry. How stupid and weak of Jay. On leaving the house he had accepted an invitation for the following Sunday and then expected Addie to help him wriggle out of it.

After a good deal of consultation they'd decided that the best way was for him simply not to go. A note was hard to write, to call round would be fatal, whereas merely staying away would perhaps convince them that he was a vague and unreliable young man.

On the Sunday afternoon in question Addie was going for a walk with Beatrice. She and Ronnie were not yet at the stage where he came to tea every Sunday as a matter of course. Afraid that Jay would weaken at the last moment, she persuaded him to come too. It was very pleasant indeed, with Jay full of jokes, as usual, linking arms with both girls and running them down the slope to the sea in a most undignified way, especially for a Sunday. You could see he was really relieved to be free of Maud. Beatrice shrieked with laughter, overdoing it a bit, Addie thought, but still she would tone down in time. Naturally their walk had led them away from the town, in the opposite direction to the Barretts' house, which was a small Victorian villa in one of the roads that led from the main shopping street down to the sea-front. It was an inferior house, but in a grander position than Jasmine Villa. The spread of the town had not caught up with the odd-shaped plot of land belonging to the Clarkes, and the walk back home was long and boring.

Tiredness quietened Beatrice, and the three were in a harmonious mood as they turned the last corner

but one. And at the final turning that led home-
wards a tall, thin figure waited. A female figure,
sombrely dressed in a grey tailored costume of
slightly dated cut, and a heavy looking felt hat.
Maud!

'Oh, crikey!' moaned Jay, running his hand
through his dark curly hair, and then tugging at
his starched white collar. They approached, Addie
elegant in wine velveteen, Beatrice small and lively
in brown, one on each side of Jay, tall and thin in
his navy blue suit.

Maud waited, standing quite still in the middle
of the pavement.

'Hello Maud,' said Jay. 'This is my sister Addie,
and her friend Beatrice.'

Her friend! Really, she could have kicked him.
What was he so afraid of?

Maud ignored the girls. Looking straight at Jay
she said, 'We shall be late for tea.'

Her words and her voice were confident, if quiet,
but her pale grey eyes gazed at Jay anxiously. Her
beaky nose was very pink, and she looked as if she
had been standing there a long time.

Jay said, 'See you later then,' to Addie and
Beatrice, and walked back down the road with
Maud. He simply gave up, as Addie told him later.
Afterwards he had tea with the Barrett family every
Sunday until he and Maud were married four years
later. He only brought her home on rare occasions.
She was shy, he told them.

Once Addie said to him, 'You're only marrying
Maud because you're too soft to get out of it.'

Jay was defensive. 'She'll liven up when we're on our own,' he said. 'You'll see. You don't know her. She's alright really.'

But Maud had never really livened up. Indeed, the list of things that Maud could not or would not do had grown, over the years, until they seldom went out, but Jay had never ceased to consider her and care for her, and only Addie knew that he had never really loved her.

Sounds of activity around her brought Addie back to the present day. She opened her eyes and looked round the ward that had once been the blue drawing room. Sister Rowles bustled up. Her mother had once been daily help at Witney Gardens and she was always very pleasant. She accorded Addie some dignity, calling her Mrs Castle, instead of dear, and sometimes talked about how lovely the shops had been, with Madame Adelaide in gold handwriting over the door, and real flowers in the windows. So unlike those awful chain stores which only kept small sizes and rows and rows of dresses all alike.

Addie said good morning to Sister Rowles with marked politeness, to show she didn't despise her for being the daughter of her daily help.

When she was washed and made ready for the day she was surprised to find she felt much better. 'Is it Wednesday?' she asked.

'No, Thursday.'

No Dorothy today, then. Wednesday and Saturday and Sunday were her days. She hadn't expected to feel as strong and clear-headed as this ever again. Must have had some sort of a turn, and now she was getting over it. If she went on like this they'd be sending her home. Well, home was pleasant enough but still she'd get back to the shop as soon as she could. Even Ronnie was not really to be relied on, going to the bank and not coming back for hours. And the staff never knew where they were with him, fooling about one minute, and the next being over-critical and hard to please.

The customers liked to see her, too. It was such a personal business; you simply had to be there all the time or they strayed across the road to Terry's, and never came back. Addie regarded the town's one department store as the only competition worth bothering about, though she knew she had never had very much to fear. Their clothes were over-priced and badly displayed. No one there had Ronnie's flair for window-dressing, let alone Addie's own elegance. And she really cared about making her customers look their best. She smiled to herself, thinking how tactfully she had steered an outsize customer away from ivory tulle, and into a dignified black velvet. She could easily have ordered the tulle in the right size, though heaven knows what the manufacturers would have thought, but it would have been against her principles, even if it meant losing the sale altogether. Mrs Mainwaring had come in specially to tell her what a success she had been at the Masonic Ladies' night in the black velvet and then spoilt it by saying, just as she left the shop, 'I did love the white net, though, but you wouldn't let me have it, would you? I shall always wish I'd at least tried it on.'

Tried it on! Good Heavens! Stupid fool of a woman. She wouldn't have got it over her head, let alone zipped it up. Next time she could go to Terry's where the girls would do anything for a sale, and if she wanted scarlet satin they'd let her have it and end up looking like a saveloy.

She'd said that to Ronnie and he'd laughed and repeated it, rather unwisely, to several people. She didn't make many jokes, though when she did, they were much better than his.

But wait. The shop wasn't there any more. Madame Adelaide's two elegant little windows had been replaced by a brash chromium bordered square, and the space was filled by the very same mass-produced garments that she and Ronnie had so despised. Why had Terry's bought it as a going concern, with extra payment for what was called goodwill, and then thrown it all away like that? Just to prevent anyone else getting in, she supposed. It had hurt to see the demolition of the old shop-front. Dorothy had steered her across the road while it was going on, so that she shouldn't be upset by the sight of the Regency striped wallpaper hanging in strips and the fascia-board with Madame Adelaide on it in gold leaf being used as a footbridge over a mysterious hole in the floor.

Funny how you could forget for a minute that all that had happened. Well, she was too tired for it now, anyway. Eighty-four was a good age. She did feel a bit better today. Perhaps they had been right, and she would go home again, after all. Though where was home? Not the flat, no. That had been part of the shop for ages. The Regency Room. Madame Adelaide's Regency Room for Exclusive Evening and Bridal Gowns.

Where then? The house in Witney Gardens. She didn't think so. There had been somewhere else after that. She would have to find out, though you felt such a fool asking the nurses things like that, things you really ought to remember. And they often gave you such silly, meaningless answers. One thing, she knew she didn't live here. She wasn't that much of a fool, unlike Mrs Arden Woolley, who had been one of her best customers and now occupied a bed opposite her, convinced that Easton Court was her own house and the nurses were her maids.

The night staff had tidied the ward and gone off and the day staff were taking over. The junior nurse pushed the breakfast trolley in through the double doors. It was quite bright outside, and inside there was a cheerful bustle. Miss Houghton, in the next bed to Addie, leaned over a little and said loudly, 'Good morning. You're looking better today.'

'What? What did you say?'

'I said, you're looking better today.'

'I'm quite alright, thanks.'

'Had one of your little turns, didn't you? Still, you'll be back to normal again soon.'

So that was it. That was why she'd been feeling so groggy. She'd had one of her little turns, whatever they were. If only they'd tell her.

'When?'

'The day before yesterday. Not a bad one, but they leave you a bit shaky, I expect.'

'But I was up yesterday, when my daughter came.'

'You're thinking of Monday. But they'll have you out of bed today, I expect. They don't believe in letting you lie about here. I tell them, I'm waiting to die so that I can get a bit of peace.'

She laughed merrily, but Addie didn't care for that sort of talk. She turned towards her neighbour on the other side. Mrs Bailey said, 'Well, how are you this morning, Adelaide?'

Addie was surprised by the use of her Christian name. It was long since anyone had addressed her as Addie, let alone Adelaide. Well, after all, Mrs Bailey was her contemporary, and a nice woman. She decided she didn't mind.

'I know your name's Adelaide because of the shop. Lots of lovely things I've bought there. I thought you'd remember me. The last thing I had was a coat. My son bought it for me. Mink it was with a Persian lamb collar, lasted me for years. It had a quilted lining and braid trimming on the pockets.'

'I remember it,' said Addie, and she did. Out of all the hundreds of coats she had sold she remembered this one as soon as Mrs Bailey mentioned the braid trimming, but she didn't remember Mrs Bailey, who was still talking.

'My name's Edith,' she said. 'I hope you'll call me by it. Makes you feel a bit more human to be called by your Christian name sometimes. I haven't got many left now. People to call me Edith. When did you lose your husband? I remember him well. Liked a joke, didn't he? I often wondered what he did with himself all day, in a ladies' shop. You had another place in Foreland Bay, didn't you? I expect he used to keep an eye on that. Well, somebody's got to go first, and it's usually the men. Not that there's any joy in being left behind. My Walter and I were never parted, not since the day we were married, except if one of us was in hospital. I don't know what's wrong with them these days, no staying power. As soon as they see someone else they like the look of . . . Of course, we all have our disagreements, but in our day marriage was once and for all . . . '

Addie listened uncomfortably. It had just come to her that she and Ronnie were separated. He'd gone off and lived in his own little flat on the front and left her alone in Witney Gardens. Years and years ago now. And she'd never understood why. They'd really got on alright. If anyone had anything to grumble about, surely it was she, Addie. He ought to have married Bella, she was really more his sort – she'd have been ready to rush off and do stupid things, the way he always wanted to. It wasn't as though she'd jumped at him either. She'd put him off at least twice before finally accepting him. Even when she had at last agreed to name the day, after a year's engagement, it had seemed a pity to put an end to such a pleasant period in her life, for there had still been a family at Jasmine Villa.

Nellie, vigorous as ever, ran the house to a strict yet comfortable routine: clean clothes on Sundays; washday Mondays with a cold dinner; housework on Tuesdays with Mrs Chapman to help; spring cleaning in April; fires started in October; the kettle always on the back of the range; and a dark red plush cloth on the big kitchen table.

That was home, resting your elbows on the velvety surface, drinking tea and talking to Mum. She and Beatrice would close the shop at seven on weekdays, then she would cycle home and go in through the scullery. Straight through into the hall to hang up her things on the hall stand, then back into the kitchen for that lovely cup of tea Mum always had ready. Jay would arrive, engaged to Maud by now, but not yet married and lost, and Bella, full either of gaiety or resentment, for she scarcely ever seemed to be in a normal frame of mind, and greatly exaggerated tales of the staff and customers at the library where she worked. Addie had made it up with Charlie and Winnie at last; that miserable time when he had cut himself off from the family was over; and she saw Holly most days, and little Jimmy and baby Gillian, and there were even music evenings occasionally, though not at Cornwall Lodge because Mrs Kingston had been very ill again and had to have quiet.

Then one evening she'd come in to find Bella weeping and her mother looking worried and upset.

'What's the matter?' she asked anxiously.

Bella turned on her. 'Oh, go away, Addie Clarke. You're always poking your nose in where it's not

wanted. Go upstairs, can't you, I'm talking to
Mum.'

Nellie said, 'She'll have to know sometime, Bell.'

'Why? What's it got to do with her? She won't
understand, she never understands anything. Look
how she treats that poor little Ronnie of hers. Have
you let him kiss you yet? No, I bet you haven't.
You're above all that sort of thing.'

'Bella, be quiet. There's no need for that. It's not
Addie's fault. We're all different, and what you've
done is nothing to be proud of.'

'Why, what's happened? What's she done?'

'You may as well know first as last. She's got to
get married.'

'Got to? Why's she got to?'

'Oh, for Heaven's sake, Mum, what did you want
to go and tell her for?'

Addie sat down at the table, her hat and coat still
on. Bella was twenty-seven, but she was still the
baby of the family, and very young-looking. Her
thick, dark hair was bobbed in the newest style,
and her dress was as fashionable as Addie's. Surely
Bella hadn't done what Holly had done? And here
was Mother, not condemning her, not turning her
out of the house. Did it mean that all that secrecy,
that dread of discovery, the death and horror of the
Terrible Time had been unnecessary? No, of course,
this was different. This was some stupid boy that
Bella had got hold of, while Holly . . . Holly's love
affair had been more guilty.

'Who is it?'

She'd often seen Bella out with youths far

younger than herself, fooling about, giggling too.
But you couldn't really blame her – there were so
few of her own age left, after the war.

'Do you want me to tell her, Bella?'

'What difference does it make? She'll have to
know sometime.'

Addie put her hand on her sister's shoulder. She
hadn't felt so loving towards her in years, not perhaps since she'd been a lovely curly-haired baby
sister in a frilly white dress and bonnet.

'Don't worry, Bell, we'll get you out of it somehow. You don't have to marry him if you don't
want to. We could go away somewhere . . . I've got
some money saved up.'

More than four and ninepence this time, she
thought wryly. In fact it was nearly three hundred
pounds, saved for setting up home with Ronnie.
Well, he'd just have to wait. She saw herself, with
Bella posing as a widow, living in a little cottage in
the country somewhere and bringing up Bella's
child. How it would love its Auntie Addie!

'Of course I'm going to marry him, you idiot.
What else can I do? And if you want to know who
it is, it's Percy Kent.'

'Percy Kent? Percy Kent! Bella, you can't marry
Percy Kent.'

Nellie said, 'Well, he's in quite a good way of
business.'

'A gift shop, down by the harbour.'

'What's wrong with that?'

'Have you seen, have you *seen* some of the things
in his window?' Addie was thinking of some of

the repulsively vulgar 'Presents from Culvergate' on view in his window. And the postcards. She would never have stopped herself, but Ronnie always wanted to look and laugh.

'I'm not marrying his shop window, am I?'

'No, but . . . '

She couldn't say that Percy Kent was as bad as his shop. He was no more than thirty-five, but corpulent, and greasy haired. He lived over the shop with a terrible old mother who wouldn't let him go out with girls, or so the story ran. But he had been out with Bella, or perhaps stayed in with her, though what had they done with the old lady?

'What on earth will the Kingstons think? Have you told Holly?'

'It's me that's got to marry him, not Holly.'

'But, Bell, he's so common, and his awful old mother . . . '

Percy and his mother were a familiar sight on the promenade on Sunday. The old lady wore black, down to the ground in the fashion of her younger days, with a moth-eaten bit of fur round her neck. Ronnie always said you could smell her coming a mile off.

Nellie put Addie's cup of tea on the table and said, 'Go and take your things off.'

In the hall the last rays of sunlight were filtering through the stained glass set in the upper half of the front door. The main feature of the design was a little red boat with white sails on a green sea, under a bright blue sky.

As children, especially when they had first moved

into Jasmine Villa, they had all loved the little boat and noticed how the light altered the colours, making the scene stormy and dull, or full of sunshine, according to the weather. Viewed from outside after dark with the gas lit in the hall, it had a calm sunset look that seemed to symbolize the safe harbour of home. Now they were all so used to it they scarcely saw it, and certainly never remarked on it. Yet at moments of crisis it became, to Addie, suddenly noticeable. Taking off her hat now, she saw how the low setting sun was projecting the colours onto the sleeve of the coat she had just hung on the hall stand. On the dark green cloth they were distorted and sickly, quite unlike the clear brilliance that had showed on the white wall a moment before.

She went back into the kitchen and sat down at the table. Bella was sitting in the Windsor chair by the range, cradling her cup of tea, though the evening was mild.

Addie said, 'I mean it, Bella. You know I've been saving up. We could go to . . . oh, Deal or somewhere, not too far, and I could get a job and we could take some rooms. I can always earn an extra bit, singing. You could go to a nursing home when the time comes, and later on we could always say it was an orphan we'd adopted, or your husband had died.'

Rather sadly, she rejected the cottage in the country. After all, they had to be where she could earn a living.

Nellie said, 'And what about Ronnie? Where does he come into all this?'

'Ronnie,' said Addie vaguely, having by now quite forgotten him.

'Thank you for nothing,' said Bella rudely. 'I'd just as soon be married to Percy and be bossed about by Mrs Kent than have an illegitimate child and be bossed about by you.'

'Ssh,' said Addie and Nellie together. Bella was always too outspoken. Only she would shout 'have an illegitimate child' like that.

Addie was annoyed that neither of them seemed to realize the seriousness of her offer. When she pressed it further her mother just said, 'Oh, don't be so silly. Of course she's got to marry him. After all, she can't dislike him that much, or it would never have happened.'

This was an aspect of the matter that now struck Addie for the first time. She stared at her sister with revulsion and fascination as she remembered what must have taken place to bring Bella to this pass. How could she? Percy Kent was so horribly fat, his face was pale and shiny, and when he went out he wore a cap. A flat tweed cap, not a smart trilby like Ronnie wore. She wouldn't have liked to touch him, let alone . . . At least Ronnie always looked clean and smart, and when people asked her who her fiancé was it was quite nice to tell them that she was engaged to Mr Castle, manager of Pringle's. But Percy, with his mother, was a local laughing stock. You saw them on early closing day, solemnly perambulating along North Street, Percy waiting patiently while his mother looked in shop windows; or if unlucky, you played opposite them at one of the whist drives with which the residents enlivened themselves after the visitors had left. Mrs Kent, severe in her usual unsavoury black, would sneer at poor Percy's inept handling of the cards.

It was true that she herself had felt sorry for him sometimes and thought that if he were slimmer, healthier and cleaner, he would not be too bad. If the old lady were to be so obliging as to die, he might improve; but though believed to be over eighty she looked depressingly strong and full of vitality. Here Addie stopped. Wishing people dead was wicked.

'Well, you can't afford to waste much time,' Nellie was saying. 'I can't think why you didn't tell me before.'

Just for a moment the eyes of the two younger women met, as the same thought occurred to both of them. How extraordinary that Nellie did not understand how difficult the telling must have been for Bella. No wonder she had put it off as long as possible.

'It'll have to be a very quiet wedding.'

'Oh, yes,' said Bella sarcastically. 'No orange blossom for me. I suppose I'd better wear scarlet and be done with it.'

'It's not a joking matter.'

'I didn't damned well think it was.'

Bella's eyes brimmed with tears. The door banged as she rushed out of the room.

They knew that in this mood she was best left

alone, though Addie longed to comfort her. No white dress and veil for pretty Bella, the youngest of the Clarke girls. She would gladly have given up her own grand wedding plans to see her sister a traditional bride.

In the event Bella had quite a nice day and looked charming in beige. Addie was amazed to see that she and Percy seemed quite fond of each other. The old lady was a problem, of course. She looked very strange at the wedding, in a hat she had probably worn to Percy's christening, and an hour after the happy couple had left for a long weekend at Rye, leaving her in charge of Percy's Aunt Lily, she had a fall and broke her leg. She was taken to hospital, but it was not thought necessary to inform the happy couple, as her life was not in danger. However, a day or two after their return she developed pneumonia and died.

Bella was not the kind of woman to pretend a regret she did not feel, but she was concerned for Percy, who was convinced that it was his fault. However, he soon recovered, and smartened up a good deal. He lost a lot of weight too. In the end they had nearly all come round to quite liking Percy. No one remembered that he had been a figure of fun, parading along arm in arm with his mother, wearing his flat cap. He was elected to the council, became Mayor, then a Justice of the Peace, and opened two more gift shops. It was amazing what people forgot, thought Addie. Even Mum and Dad had accepted him, as she never could. He and Bella had finished up quite well-off and were happy together for many years. It didn't seem fair.

Of all the Clarkes, only she had failed to sustain married life to the end. Yet she'd always looked on herself as a pleasant, easygoing kind of person. And so much admired – for her singing, her elegance, her business acumen, and even for her hair. Why then had Ronnie decided he would be happier without her? It would have been understandable if she had been the one to break things up, but he'd simply become more and more irritable and hard to please as the years went by. There'd been no other woman, he just hadn't wanted to live with her any more, though they still ran the business together and often met at Dorothy's and elsewhere. He was always insistent on escorting her home, even coming in for a drink, sometimes. So he wasn't really lost to her. Even now he visited her occasionally.

And surely their life together had been good. That side of things, of course, had been rather a nuisance, but she had put up with it as long as possible. Not many women could do more than that. But enough was enough. She remembered coming downstairs on the first morning of their honeymoon at the Brighton Hotel. It was a sumptuous place. They had agreed that a few days there would be more enjoyable and memorable than two weeks anywhere else. Entering the panelled dining room with Ronnie, having her chair pulled out by the waiter, she felt not only rich, but experienced. Couples at the other tables were not inhabitants of another world, as they had been last night. She knew it all now.

She hadn't been entirely ignorant. Mum had dropped a hint or two, and Holly had been embarrassingly frank, seeming to think it her duty to say a great many things that her sister had no desire to hear. All that part of you was kept covered, safe and private all your life. You didn't even see it yourself; then you got married and everything was different. But still it had been a shock. She knew how men were made, of course, she'd seen her brothers naked often enough when they were all little, but this was different. It was so big, it had hurt, pressing into her, and in the middle of it she had suddenly realized that this was what Nitty Havergal had wanted too, when she was a little girl, and what Bella had done with Percy, when he was still greasy and grubby, in some corner of that smelly flat. And Holly . . . she stopped her train of thought abruptly, as she always did when it threatened to lead her back to the Terrible Time, and returned to the present, in bed, with Ronnie pushing hard into her, bruising, pinching, taking possession, no longer gentle as at the beginning. She tried to tell him to stop, that whatever it was mustn't happen, and suddenly the warm wetness flooded between her legs, and he collapsed shuddering and gasping. In her ignorance she thought he was ill, having a heart attack or a fit there on top of her, but he heaved himself off, murmured something, and was instantly asleep. It was all over.

Quietly, so as not to disturb him, she got out of bed and had a good wash.

In the morning Ronnie had been so happy and pleased, telling her that she was beautiful, that her hair was pure gold, and that he'd admired her from the first moment he'd seen her. She'd felt quite proud of herself for getting through it so well.

When they were dressing he said suddenly, 'Do you love me, Ad?' and she'd said yes, of course. And it struck her that she had been closer to Ronnie than anyone else in the world and that she would have to stick to him now.

He'd asked her then if she was glad they were married, and she'd said 'of course' again. It was true. You didn't want to be Miss Clarke when you were over thirty, and Ronnie, now ready to go down, looked so fresh and smart she would be pleased for people to know he was her husband.

They had succeeded in business too. The war years had been difficult, of course, when they had to close the shop on the coast and move inland to a town where nobody knew them, and they'd had to start all over again. Strictly speaking, they hadn't really had to start the first time. Addie had already built up a good connection when they took over the shop from Miss Jones. There had been a lapse of time when they were first married, and Dorothy had been born. Being at home all day had never suited her, though they had a nice little newish house in Nansen Road, charmingly furnished. No 'front room' for Mr and Mrs Castle: they had a drawing room with a settee and two chairs in dark blue velvet, and a rosewood piano. Addie knew she was lucky. Most young couples in that time of housing shortage had to live in rooms to begin with.

And they had both been delighted with baby Dorothy, though Ronnie had showed a marked aversion to being present when she was anything but perfectly clean and decked out in crisp frills and ribbons.

Before the baby was born Addie had spent most of her time with Holly, or her mother, sometimes even visiting Bella and her little daughter in the flat overlooking the harbour. She was never comfortable there, though. It seemed to her that the place still smelt of old Mrs Kent and also she disliked the way Bella and Percy went on, always hugging and kissing, disgusting, really.

After Dorothy arrived she was forced to spend more of her time at home, alone except for the baby. Then the Terrible Time, awaiting its chance, had leapt at her again; and this time she could not win, no magic worked and it held on, strangling her with guilt and suffocating her with shame for months and months.

Although Dorothy was a good baby who seldom cried in the night and suffered no feeding problems, Addie always felt tired. She worried constantly about the child, bending over the cot to make sure she was still breathing, and hating anyone but herself to touch her. Ronnie, in any ways, was soon rather uninterested. He looked forward to the time when she would be a doll-like little girl with ribbons in her hair, who would go to dancing class like his little nieces in Bromley.

They were hard-up too, with the mortgage to pay, and this did not suit him either. He urged Addie to accept singing engagements when she was offered them, though she was reluctant to leave Dorothy. However, in the end she gave in, dashing to the Winter Gardens or the Grand Hotel in a taxi, and dashing back as soon as her songs were over.

When the second anniversary of their wedding came round Dorothy was eight months old, a happy infant with a beaming smile. Addie, despite her ever present anxiety, was singing somewhere almost every evening. This brought several benefits. First, the money; second, choosing and practising her songs helped to keep her mind occupied during the hours at home; and third, when she had been out singing Ronnie was more ready to accept her excuses of tiredness and headache and would let her sleep in peace on her own side of the big mahogany bed. For this Addie was profoundly thankful.

During this time a leading tenor, Frederick Tarrant, visited the town and heard Addie sing. Impressed, indeed bowled over by the beauty of her voice, he arranged that they should sing some duets. The idea was immensely successful, and they carried out a number of engagements together, after which he suggested they should team up for a professional tour. His excitement was infectious. He was convinced they would soon be nationally famous, and then who knew what would happen? Once again the capital cities of the world were

within reach. Ronnie was enthusiastic. Where
Addie's little local fame had once thrilled him, now
he longed for greater things. And this time it would
be Adelaide Castle, not Clarke on the posters. He
and Frederick Tarrant, with whom he had struck
up an easy friendship, discussed details endlessly.

'But what about the baby?' said Addie.

'Oh, your mother will have her,' said Ronnie.
'She won't notice the difference. I'm the one will
do that!' and he laughed immoderately, looking at
the other man for approval. Addie had no idea what
he meant, but was quite sure it was vulgar.

'I shan't go. I can't leave Dorothy.'

How could she exist away from home, not knowing how the baby fared? That her child should thrive
seemed far more than she deserved, and to leave
her, to betray her trust, that would be to invite
retribution.

In vain Ronnie persuaded and Frederick pleaded.
Then Ronnie bullied and Frederick coaxed. Addie
remained firm and eventually the famous tenor left
the town alone.

Ronnie was disappointed, his hopes of fame and
fortune shattered. When Addie went off to sing
locally he sneered at her for being too timid to go
farther afield. He no longer took any interest in her
choice of songs or asked her how the evening had
gone. If he was in the house while she was practising, he would stay in the little dining room at the
back or go out into the garden, when once he would
have sat listening on the blue velvet settee.

Addie retreated into a proud silence that Ronnie

called sulking. She cared for the baby, took her for walks, visited her mother and Holly and wondered why she had got married. She had been so much happier in Miss Jones's shop, and if it weren't for Dorothy she could quite well go back. Then she would feel guilty, as if the gurgling cheerful baby could read her mind.

She took to staying late at her mother's, arriving home after Ronnie and then taking an hour to deal with Dorothy before coming downstairs to prepare his meal. This being only a light supper – he came home to dinner at midday – he often got it himself. His years as a cook in the navy had made him handy and capable in the kitchen. One evening she left the ingredients for a salad on the kitchen table and came down to find he had created the kind of masterpiece that had been such a success on board the HMS *Yarmouth*. Slices of beetroot and cucumber were arranged in concentric rings on a bed of shredded lettuce, with tinned salmon artistically heaped in the centre. Tomato flowers and whitely gleaming spring onions added to the effect. The table was laid with their best cloth and clean white starched dinner napkins were folded into elaborate water lilies. Flowers from the garden had been arranged in a cut glass vase.

'Oh, Ronnie, how lovely you've made it look!'

'Well sit down and get on with it,' he said gruffly but she ran back upstairs to tidy her hair. Fancy Ronnie doing all that, and when they'd been getting on so badly too. It was only years later that she realized he did this kind of thing for its own sake, for no one's pleasure but his own.

However, on this occasion she was touched, believing he had made an effort to please her, though rather wishing he had not used the best table linen which she reserved for guests. Not that they had any, now that Frederick Tarrant was gone, other than the family or Beatrice. For the first time for weeks they chatted amiably over the meal and afterwards she sang his favourite songs, accompanying herself on the piano. At about ten Dorothy awoke and started crying, so Ronnie was asleep when she got to bed. Just as well, really.

After this they both tried hard to make a success of things. Ronnie carried out various small improvements to the house, putting up shelves and mirrors, even concreting the muddy patch outside the back door.

For these efforts he required a great deal of praise and thanks, which Addie duly accorded him. She arranged to leave Dorothy, asleep in her pram, at Jasmine Villa on some of her singing evenings so that Ronnie could go with her, and now reconciled, or nearly so, to her never becoming world famous, he once more enjoyed basking in her reflected glory, parochial though it was. Addie told herself she had nothing to complain about. A nice home, a pretty little daughter, a hardworking husband, and most of her family nearby – what more did she expect? But these things required peace of mind for their enjoyment and this she did not have.

The Terrible Time, as she still thought of it, con-

tinued to obsess her and most of her mental energy
was spent reliving, justifying and despairing over
her part in it. She longed to confess, but who could
be her confessor? She even thought of going to
Father Christopher, who was after all a professional
in that line, and tried to work out a way of telling
her story without mentioning Holly or her lover by
name, but that did not seem possible.

'Please God, let me think about something else,'
prayed Addie in desperation. And certainly no
kindly God responded, though her prayer was
answered, and soon.

She was in the drawing room, cleaning the windows, when she first saw him. She always worked
very hard at cleaning the house, finding that physical exhaustion sometimes allowed her a spurious
and short-lived mental peace. An oldish man was
shuffling along on the opposite side of the road. At
first she hardly noticed him, but when he passed
her for the third time she thought he might be
looking for a particular house and wondered
whether she ought to help. He looked tired and
pathetic. She went to the front door, opened it, and
was just about to call out when she saw that it was
Nitty Havergal. He had not been about the town
for years, and she had assumed thankfully that he
had been sent away somewhere. Now, older and
even shabbier than before, he was walking towards
her along the pavement. Closing the door and locking it, she sank down on the bottom stair but one,
the little hallway being too small to accommodate a
chair. She felt sick with horror and fear.

After a few moments she looked out of the window and saw that he had gone, but for the rest of the morning she could finish none of the household jobs she had planned to do, because every few minutes she was drawn to the window to make sure he had not returned. She was quite convinced that he had come purposely to find her, and over the next few weeks this fear took total possession of her. She could not tell Ronnie, because this would have involved admitting to her earlier acquaintance with Nitty which she somehow felt was shameful and her own fault. She might have confided in Holly, but by tacit agreement they never reminisced about their childhood, so to talk to her about Nitty Havergal was a hopelessly difficult thing to do.

Twenty times a day she interrupted her work or practice to peer anxiously out of the window, and once or twice a week he would be there, moving slowly along on the other side of the road, or sometimes, and this was much worse, just standing there, staring vaguely round.

It was a punishment, there was no doubt about that. When Ronnie came home at midday and in the evenings, she greeted him eagerly, glad of his protection. He could not understand why, after seeming so pleased to see him, she would so soon withdraw into herself, becoming taciturn and uninterested. He told her she was a misery to live with. Unable to help herself, she knew this was true.

As time went on she became less afraid of her tormentor and more panic-stricken at her own imagined capacity for evil. Supposing she somehow lost control, spoke to him, brought him into the house and invited the fate she felt sure was in store for her? Obscene images crowded her mind, filling her with shame and self-disgust. She stood in the hall with her hands over her face trying to supplant the vision of him, dirty and half-naked on her bed, with some other picture: the garden, the sea, Dorothy, anything.

She lived from day to day, fighting her lonely battle. Sometimes she would dump the baby, hastily dressed, in the pram and push her round the streets for hours, rather than stay in the house alone. She became pale and thin, and Nellie told her she ought to take a tonic.

Every now and then, as the dreary, exhausting weeks passed she would make a determined effort to shake off her obsessions. One morning in the summer of 1926 she washed her hair, now fashionably short, and having rubbed it nearly dry she was arranging it in front of the mirror, standing at her dressing-table in the bay window of the front bedroom, with Dorothy just wakened from her nap, jumping up and down in the cot that stood by the big bed. Trying to ignore the circling images that pressed upon her, she was talking to the child, planning to make her a new dress for her to wear to her aunties,' trying to sound cheerful, telling herself that the bad time was over. Yet irresistibly her eyes were drawn to the window. Just one glance out, to make sure . . . and he was there. Not walking along but standing still on the pavement opposite, and as Addie watched he started across the road towards her. Unkempt, old and dirty, he reached the pavement and lurched towards the wrought iron gate of number forty-seven.

Addie dropped her comb and ignoring Dorothy's startled cries she ran out of the room and down the stairs, through the kitchen and out into the back garden. Surely there had been a shadow visible through the frosted glass panel in the front door? Sobbing, she stumbled up the three steps that led to the tiny lawn, half fell across the vegetable patch and reached the wall at the top of the garden. She pressed herself against it, holding on with both hands.

When Ronnie arrived home at midday she was sitting huddled at the foot of the wall and refused to move. When he tried to drag her away she screamed and fought. She tried to tell him about Nitty Havergal being in the house, but he wouldn't understand. The Browns, Mabel and Ernie, a quiet middle-aged couple who lived next door, came and looked over the fence and asked if they could help. Ronnie must have allowed them to do so, because soon Addie was in a taxi on her way to her mother's, having left by the back gate and the narrow footpath that ran between the two rows of back gardens. She collected her wits sufficiently to say, 'Where's Dorothy?' and Ronnie answered that Mrs Brown had got her.

He sat upright in his corner of the taxi, not touching her, his face cold and angry. He seemed like a

total stranger which no doubt was what he would
have liked to be.

CHAPTER 6

Addie struggled out of her half-sleep and was glad. Glad to see the cheerful ward, the other old women, and the nurses. Glad to be eighty-four and nearly done with it, and to remember that for years she had enjoyed a precarious peace of mind. She could look back upon the self of fifty years ago with pity and impatience – so much of her life wasted in sterile agonising over events and situations she could not change.

During the months following her return to Jasmine Villa she had absolutely refused to go back to her own home and eventually Ronnie moved into Nellie's spare bedroom with her, and their own house had been let furnished. For weeks she had remained trapped in the prison of her own mind, where the only sounds that meant anything were the silent echoes of Holly's long-dead screams and the whisper of the voice that told her what she must do. She would have nothing to do with Dorothy, after the nightmares about the baby began. Sometimes it was Holly's baby, and sometimes it was her own, though Dorothy was now nearly two and full of fun and making delicious attempts to talk. Nitty Havergal was there too, haunting her sleep by night, and her thoughts by day, sickening her with obscene suggestions, telling her he knew her secret. She grew thinner and paler and forgot to brush her hair and Nellie's Iron Tonic did no good at all.

Poor Ronnie must have been miserable. After all, his wife of whom he had been so proud was utterly changed; his smart little home which they had so enjoyed creating was no longer his; he did not much enjoy fatherhood; and the outlook was bleak.

'You're not looking very cheerful, Mrs Castle.'

It was the nurse, the little one with the curly hair and bright smile.

'What would you like to drink? There's Ovaltine or coffee.'

'What's for dinner?' Addie tried to take an interest.

'Goodness, you are in a hurry! You haven't had breakfast yet. It's scrambled egg, or porridge. Both if you like.'

'Scrambled egg, please.'

Addie was furious with herself. She wasn't really muddled like all these old things in the other beds, it was merely that she had been dozing, and thinking of the past.

'I've been thinking of the past,' she said by way of explanation.

'That's right, dear.' The nurse helped her to sit up a little. 'Lovely memories I expect you've got.'

Addie did not answer. The stupid girl was not worth answering. How could anyone live to be eighty-four and not have some memories that were, to say the least of it, mixed? She was glad to have hers interrupted by breakfast. This morning she made a determined, indeed obstinate effort to feed herself, though the nurse was not encouraging. Still, she did manage most of her scrambled egg unaided.

I couldn't have done that yesterday, she thought, or perhaps she said it aloud, because Mrs Bailey in the next bed said, 'They'll be getting you up today, I shouldn't wonder. You keep trying, dear, it's the only way.'

Looking round the ward it was plain to see who had kept trying and who hadn't. Ruth Stanbrook was leaning back against her pillows with her eyes shut and one or two others were being fed by nurses. Miss Dearlove, who had been a headmistress of a girls' public school had thrown back her bedclothes and was feeling for the floor with pale, misshapen feet. They'd soon tell her off about that. No one was allowed to get out of bed on her own. Further down the room Mrs Arden Woolley was loudly demanding a glass of sherry, and a fracas broke out as a very old woman grabbed the nurse by the arm and scratched her face.

'What these girls have to put up with,' said Mrs Bailey. 'I tell them, I wouldn't have their job for all the money in the world.'

Addie resented this statement, feeling vaguely

that by allying herself with the staff her fellow-patient was letting her down.

The young nurse, her cheeks flushed and the long scratch clearly visible, was passing their beds.

'I saw what happened, dear,' said Mrs Bailey. 'It wasn't your fault. You tell Sister to come to me if there's any trouble.'

'She didn't mean it. It's nothing,' said the nurse crossly, and she hurried out of the ward.

Addie's sympathies shifted to her neighbour, who looked crestfallen. 'Are you having visitors today?' she asked kindly, to cheer her up.

'No, I'm not,' and Mrs Bailey turned her back as well as she could with the bed table in the way.

'Well, really,' thought Addie, and made up her mind to repel further conversational overtures, should any be made later in the day. She had called her Adelaide, too. Well, she would continue to address her as Mrs Bailey. That was the trouble with being in the ward. You were stuck with any common person that happened to be in the next bed, though you wouldn't expect to find that sort in such an expensive place. Probably her children were paying. Turning away herself, Addie's eye was caught by the photographs that were arranged on her locker. Dorothy had brought them. Silly, really. She could remember people perfectly well, better, in fact, without silly little pictures of them grinning and looking unnatural. However, she went on looking at them because it saved her looking at Mrs Bailey or anyone else. It was very

depressing among all these old women, though the
nurses did their best, you had to say that.

The poor old things all looked fresh and tidy and
some of them wore make-up, Mrs Arden Woolley
for one. A hairdresser came twice a week, and all of
them, even Ruth, had pretty bed-jackets and cosy,
colourful dressing-gowns for when they got up;
though what was the use of all that when the
flowered, quilted, embroidered and lace-trimmed
garments concealed dried-up, discoloured skin and
bony, wrinkled bodies with rubber tubes coming
out of them, each ending in a plastic bag half-full
of urine on the floor beside the bed or half-concealed
under a chair? Did anyone ever value youth and
health sufficiently when they had it? Not that youth
was any guarantee against illness or other troubles.
Look at poor Charlie, wheezing away most of his
adult life, and look at Ronnie – still bounding about
like a two-year-old, from what Dorothy said, arguing with traffic wardens and parking on double
yellow lines and thinking he was privileged because
he was old and everybody knew him, old Mr Castle
– and she was stuck in here. It wasn't fair but then
of course life never was and never had been. After
all, hadn't she spent years and years suffering for
something that wasn't her fault? Who were these
people in the photographs by her bed? The girl that
looked so like Holly, that wasn't Holly at all really,
but somebody else. Not Dorothy – Dorothy didn't
look like that – no, of course, it was Dorothy's
daughter; she would remember her name soon. A
nice girl, couldn't sing of course, none of them could

sing, only she, Addie. People had said her voice was a divine gift. There was a baby in that picture too, and there was another one of Dorothy and her husband. Family photographs, that was what Dorothy had said when she put them there 'in case you forget what we look like', which she'd meant as a joke. But these people weren't her real family, although they lived at Jasmine Villa. Her real family was Jay and Charlie and Holly and Bella and Mum and Dad, and she didn't need pictures of them, she could see them plainly.

Even after Mum and Dad had both died of cancer, so young, both in their early sixties, they had kept close until the war, the second war that must have been, split them up and spoilt everything. They had visited at weekends, gone for Sunday walks, sat on the sands . . . and the Christmases! Those lovely Christmases. Even when they'd stopped having music at home at other times they'd still sung round the piano at Christmas. She smiled sardonically, thinking of Ronnie with his stiff white collar turned back to front for his customary rendition of 'The Wedding of the Painted Doll'. He didn't mind making a fool of himself and Bella had always encouraged him. She remembered her saying once, 'Ronnie would be quite good fun, if only you'd let him.' What on earth had she meant by that? Probably that he would always have been making vulgar jokes like her Percy. Well, she was wrong there. Ronnie was not in the least like Percy Kent, though of course if he'd been married to someone else he might have developed quite differently. She thought fondly of Jay and Charlie. What lucky women their wives were. Really, they could have had anyone, anyone. And who had they chosen? Maud and Winnie!

She must have spoken aloud, for the doctor was standing by her bed, with Sister beside him, repeating, 'Maud and Winnie. Friends of yours, are they?'

'No,' said Addie, 'sisters-in-law.'

'Who's the pretty girl?' The doctor leaned over to look at the photographs and just at that moment of course she couldn't think who it was, but Sister came to the rescue, saying it was her granddaughter.

The doctor fitted his stethoscope into his ears and listened to her chest for a long time, looking serious, and then asked her how she felt. She said 'Quite well, thank you', which was true, and agreed that she hadn't any real pains and then she said, 'I'm bored stiff. Have been, ever since I retired.'

'Ah yes. You had a shop, didn't you, where the Gas Board is now?'

She turned her head away, feeling a lump in her throat. Her eyes filled with tears. Her life's work. Madame Adelaide Ltd of Culvergate, Foreland Bay and Albury; all the beautiful clothes, the appreciative customers; visit Madame Adelaide's Bridal Salon for that Special Day; you'll find the evening gown of your dreams in our Regency Room – all reduced by this man to a shop where the Gas Board is now. She looked at him with hatred, knowing that he thought her an awkward old woman, and didn't

When he'd gone, and she had heard him tell Sister to keep her in bed, she went on thinking about the shops. What a long story it was. She was convinced that in the first place the business that had become their livelihood had saved her reason. She didn't want to think any more about the weeks she and Ronnie had spent together at Jasmine Villa. She had not wanted him there, and could not understand why he had not remained at home. It had been Nellie who had insisted on his moving in, Nellie who had cared for Dorothy, who had made Addie see the doctor, and who had finally encouraged them to sell their house in Nansen Road and buy the shop from Miss Jones when the opportunity arose. It had happened so quickly.

All in five minutes it had seemed, their furniture was moved into the flat, a girl was found to help look after the child, and Addie was plunged into stocktaking, organizing a sale, redecoration, window-dressing. The business had deteriorated without Addie, and Miss Jones, old and infirm, had let things slide. They wouldn't be making a profit for quite a time, but Ronnie was manager of Pringles and they had his salary coming in. It would be nice and convenient for him, too, living next to his place of work.

As she was forced to think about other things, Addie's guilt and fear began to occupy her less, and the strange feelings of unreality to recede. She had to make herself smart again, and take an interest in her customers. Then she had the company of her old friend Beatrice, who, thoroughly frustrated while working for Miss Jones who was old-fashioned and difficult to please, made an excellent second-in-command. Ronnie began to look at her in the old way, admiring and possessive. There had been setbacks, though. She recalled the evening Ronnie had come in early, before six, though Pringle's didn't close till seven. She'd been busy, tired; there were dresses to pack that hardworking Beatrice had altered, and would deliver on the way home. Addie had just folded a fragile silk dress, only to find it would not fit into the grey box that awaited it. Crossly she started to fold it all over again. What on earth was Ronnie doing home so early? He'd been in for tea at the usual time.

He spoke to Dorothy, who was cuddling her doll on one of the grey painted chairs. 'What are you doing in the shop?' he said sharply. 'Get upstairs to Phyllis.'

'Phyllis has gone home,' said Addie.

'Well, go and play somewhere else. Go out the back.'

Hearing his angry voice, the child began to cry, whereupon he slapped her. She stumbled, sobbing, into the room behind the shop.

'She can't stay there alone.' Addie knew better than to argue with her husband when he was in this mood.

Beatrice stopped her tidying and followed the child out. The screams of 'I want to stay with Mummy' faded as she tactfully closed the door.

'You're making a hash of that.' Impatiently Ronnie took the dress out of his wife's hands, refolded it briskly and laid it in the box, where it looked neat and professional. 'I should have thought you could pack a dress by now.'

'I've usually got more important things to do.'

Ronnie put down the ball of string. 'If you're going to take that attitude . . . ' His bright blue eyes glittered with anger.

Addie decided not to point out that he had started it all. All she said was, 'You're in early.'

'I suppose I can come in any time I like, can't I? It's my shop, isn't it?'

'Half yours,' she wanted to say, but didn't.

In the silence Dorothy's sobs and snuffles became audible. Ronnie opened the door. 'Can't you keep that flaming kid quiet?'

'I'll take her upstairs.' Beatrice's tone was austere, disapproving, despite the fact that Ronnie was her employer. She gathered the red-faced, snivelling child into her arms.

When they had gone Addie said, 'You can't talk to Beatrice like that, she's not a nursemaid. Supposing she gave notice?'

'She won't.'

Addie moved to a glass-fronted case where the evening dresses hung. Georgette, chiffon, crêpe, marocain, pleated, or cut on the cross to cling, most with the new longer skirts, and all of them expensive, some of them selling for as much as five or six guineas. Hanging there, waiting to be bought, they represented a great deal of capital, all originally earned by Addie's singing. Without Ronnie to encourage her to take risks, to trust her own judgement, she would have bought fewer and cheaper gowns. She knew he had been right. Madame Adelaide's was dedicated to the better end of the trade. Now she busied herself with straightening them on their hangers, a soothing occupation, while she waited for Ronnie to speak. He moved away to the glass-panelled door and stared through the fringed net curtain, out into the street. 'I've been sacked.'

'What?'

'Sacked. A month's notice. Old Pringle's closing this branch.'

Addie, shaking, sat down, a thing she almost never did in the shop. 'Why?'

'Not enough business.'

'What can we do? We can't live off this, not yet.' This was true. Madame Adelaide's was barely breaking even.

'You could start singing again.'

Addie was silent. She had not sung in public since her breakdown. She did not think she ever would again. Eventually she said, 'It's not me that's lost my job. It's you.'

'Well, I couldn't help it, could I?'

This time he spoke without anger or bitterness but in a sad, discouraged way that moved his wife to compassion. She had never known her husband require such an emotion of her before.

'No, of course you couldn't. I suppose he wouldn't keep it going if you took a cut in your wages?'

'I've tried that.'

Addie took a deep breath. 'Well,' she said as cheerfully as she could, 'there's plenty for you to do here until something turns up.'

But this was 1930. She knew nothing would turn up. The companionable days with Beatrice were over. And poor little Dorothy! The presence of a young child, however quiet, was to Ronnie quite out of keeping with the atmosphere of expensive sophistication he wished the shop to achieve. She would have to stay upstairs with Phyllis instead of creeping down to be with Addie at every opportunity. Luckily she would soon be starting school.

But what would Ronnie find to do? He was good at dressing the windows, certainly, but apart from that?

She needn't have worried. He found plenty to do. He packed parcels, delivered them, went to the post and the bank and was useful in a dozen ways. When, as occasionally happened, a customer would ask his opinion of a dress or a hat he could assume an air of stunned admiration that often helped to sell an expensive item, though Addie wondered sometimes if he did not go too far. But his favourite occupation was window-dressing. He changed the display twice a week, insisting on a very sparse arrangement, perhaps of a dress, a hat, and a bowl of expensive flowers. He had an eye for colour and design and soon Madame Adelaide's window displays were a byword for elegance. Addie's time was best employed in serving her customers. Her talent lay in selling. Tall and gracious, she made them feel that they were privileged to buy things from her.

They would leave happily, thanking her for her kindness and interest, and for the time being forgetful of the fact that they had spent three times as much as they had planned. She was on her feet all day, rarely having time to drink the cups of tea that Phyllis brought down to her at eleven and four o'clock. Often, sipping thankfully in a spare moment in the room behind the shop, she would be interrupted by Ronnie.

'Beatrice isn't doing any good with Mrs So-and-So,' he would say, or 'that fool Beatrice is showing Mrs Something that cheap voile thing. She's good for ten pounds if you serve her,' and Addie would return to the shop with her professional smile and tactfully take over from her assistant with a casual 'Finding anything you like?' or 'I must show you this, it just came in this morning.' If she ever felt tired or resentful when he kept her nose firmly to the grindstone she tried to remember that he was always willing to wash up, often did the cooking, and always saw to the shopping. Though this last she missed. A breath of fresh air in the mornings would have been pleasant and she could have taken Dorothy. But the business grew: in the winter the residents, the hoteliers and boarding-house keepers; in the summer the well-to-do visitors, who came and took houses for the season, or stayed at the St George's or the Queen's – all patronized Madame Adelaide. Addie developed her flair for knowing what to buy; there was a steady flow of customers, and when after a year or so the corner shop next-door became empty, Ronnie announced that he wanted to extend.

Addie was horrified. The work! She was rushed off her feet already. More staff, said Ronnie. The risk! They had only just become solvent. You can't stand still in business, Ronnie told her. She lay awake night after night while he slept like a log beside her. A deadline was announced. It appeared that the agent had someone else interested in the place. Once more Ronnie fetched the key and took Addie round, explaining yet again where the archway would be made to connect the two shops.

'What about the dust? It will spoil our stock.'

'We'll cover it up.'

'It needs a new sun-blind. The sun pours in that corner window – everything will be faded.'

'We can get a new sun-blind. Look, we'll never do more than just make a living if we don't have more room. We could put the millinery in here, and the coats and costumes, and you'd have more space for the gowns in there. What this place wants is a nice crystal chandelier, and the walls and carpet pearl grey the same right through . . . '

Addie looked round at what had been a café, garishly decorated orange and black with a vague lingering smell of sour milk, and marvelled at his vision and imagination. It was too much to take on; they would go bankrupt and lose everything. Terror overcame her. 'It's no good, Ronnie. We can't. I can't take on any more.'

'It's not just you. I'll be taking it on too.'

'How much more work do you think I can do?'

'You mean I don't pull my weight?'

'Ronnie . . . '

'That's what you mean, isn't it? God Almighty, don't I do enough? I wait on you hand and foot, deliver parcels like a bloody errand boy . . . '

'Don't swear at me.'

'I'll swear if I damned well like. It was what you wanted, wasn't it, coming back into the shop? You wanted it to be in business, didn't you? You didn't like stopping at home. What am I supposed to get out of married life?'

No need to answer that. Her lack of interest in any physical expression of affection had caused arguments enough. She switched to the offensive. 'It's a good job I am in business, if you ask me.'

'What in hell d'you mean by that?'

Addie faced him. Though taller than he, she was frightened of him when he used that tone. 'Well, if I hadn't been, when Pringle's, when you . . . ' she floundered, wishing she hadn't started.

'Alright then. Alright. So that's it. Now we know. Well, if you think you can do better on your own, just try, that's all. Just bloody well try.' He fished the keys out of his pocket, flung them on the floor at her feet and strode out, slamming the shop door so hard she expected the plate-glass to shatter.

She stood silent. She would certainly not go after him. Their rows almost always ended like this. Trembling, she picked up the keys and went home. She locked up behind Beatrice, having wished her goodnight pleasantly, and went up to Dorothy, who was sitting up in bed with a picture book. 'Where's Daddy?'

'Gone for a little walk.'

'When's he coming back?'

'Soon.'

'I don't want him to come back. I don't like him.'

'That's a naughty thing to say. Of course you like him. He's your Daddy.'

'Do you have to like your Daddy?'

'Well, I suppose you don't have to, but it's nicer if you do. Shall I read you a story?'

Dorothy had never been known to refuse a story, so this uncomfortable subject was at least temporarily forgotten. Twenty minutes later Addie kissed her goodnight.

'You'll come if I call you?'

'Of course I will.'

'But you might not hear me.'

'I promise I'll hear you.'

'I wish I had a sister.'

This surprised Addie. Dorothy had never said such a thing before. Was it a new idea, or something she'd been brooding over? 'A sister? Why?'

'Because then I wouldn't be lonely, and I wouldn't miss you so much.' The child's voice was matter-of-fact, devoid of self-pity.

Addie said, sounding shocked even to her own ears, 'I didn't know you were lonely.' Desperately she sought for something comforting to say. 'If you had brothers and sisters you wouldn't be able to go to such a nice school; you'd have to go to St Bede's, in Addington Street.' Dorothy was about to start at a smart private kindergarten.

'I wouldn't mind.'

'You would hate it. It's full of rough, dirty children. And you wouldn't have nearly so many dresses. Or comics and sweets.'

Dorothy looked up at her seriously, her dark blue eyes steady. Suddenly she said, 'It doesn't matter,' and turned onto her side.

Addie kissed her again and said goodnight, feeling ashamed of the silly reasons she had advanced for Dorothy's lack of siblings. With her adored brothers and beloved sisters, how could she have suggested that sweets and comics could be a fair exchange? Of course in their position they could not possibly consider having another child and even if they could there would be a six-year age gap. Sighing, she went into the large, pleasant room over the front of the shop. French windows opened from it onto a narrow balcony, where she stood for a few moments looking down into the street, but there was no glimpse of Ronnie, who might by now be on his way home in a calmer frame of mind.

If only he had more patience with Dorothy, and could discuss things without losing his temper. The way he spoke to her! What on earth would Mum have said? Ted was always polite to Holly. Of course, she wouldn't put it past Percy to swear at Bella, but then he was different. Common. Of course neither Jay nor Charlie would ever swear at their wives, but there weren't many like them. Lucky Winnie. Lucky, lucky Maud.

Ronnie came back about an hour later. She was in the room behind the shop, going through some accounts. Hearing him rattle the door handle, she went through and let him in, then turned away immediately. Neither of them spoke. He followed her up to the little dining room where Phyllis had left their supper on the table. As they ate the cold mutton and beetroot he said, 'I'll take the key back to old Bartlett tomorrow. He'll think we're damn fools, but what does that matter?'

Addie didn't answer. He needn't think he could swear at her and get away with it.

That evening he washed up as usual, making a great deal of clatter in the kitchenette, waking Dorothy. Addie had to sit on her bed and talk to her until she went to sleep, by which time it was ten o'clock and she herself could reasonably retire for the night. Ronnie was sitting reading the local paper in the drawing room, which they had renamed the lounge, to keep up with the times. When he finally came to bed Addie was almost asleep, facing outwards, well on her own side of the bed, and wearing a hair-net to keep her waves in place.

In the morning he brought her a cup of tea and took one in to Dorothy, as he always did. Sipping hers gratefully, Addie said, 'Who shall we get then?'

'What do you mean, who shall we get?'

'Well, Elliot's or James's?'

'What the hell are you talking about?'

'To do the alterations. The archway and all that.'

There was scarcely a pause before Ronnie replied,

'We'll have to get estimates.' After a moment he went on, 'You're sure you want to go ahead with it? You've made up your mind?'

'I suppose you won't be satisfied unless we do.'

'There's no standing still in business. D'you want another cup of tea?'

Addie accepted this offer and peace was, for the time being, sealed. Ronnie put her second cup of tea on the chair beside the bed, laid his arm round her shoulders and kissed her. She bore with him quite kindly, letting him take off her hair-net.

'You're hair's so beautiful. Why do you want to wear that awful thing?' He dropped the pink 'Slumbercap' on the floor.

'You know I've got to keep my waves in.'

'Can't think why you had it cut.'

'That was years ago!'

And it was, though still a source of discontent to Ronnie. At the time of their engagement he had been home for the weekend to see his mother in Bromley, and Addie had taken the opportunity to visit the hairdresser and have her hair off, long hair having gone out of fashion. She had been aware that Ronnie did not want her to have it cut, but was unprepared for the strength of his feelings on the subject.

'But you like me to be in the fashion,' she had protested. She'd met him at the station on the Sunday evening, and they had taken a taxi because of his suitcase. She sat with her hat on her lap and tears in her eyes.

'That's alright for people with ordinary hair.

Yours was different. All that gone, and you never asked me, did you? You didn't care what I thought. I don't know . . . if this is what it's going to be like, you doing as you like behind my back . . . '

'You knew I was going to have it done. I told you.'

'And I said you weren't to.'

Addie took off her pince-nez. Her green eyes could never been seen at their best because the strong lenses made them look small, and without the pince-nez they had an unfocussed look which had once led Charlie to tell her, with a brother's candour, that she had 'dead rabbit's eyes'. But Ronnie softened.

'I don't say it's not smart,' he said grudgingly, as she wiped her tears.

That had been over ten years ago. Now Ronnie was drawing her towards him, saying, 'But it's still beautiful. I've never seen anyone else with hair this colour. That black velvet dress, you must have that.'

'Where would I wear it?'

'We'll go out somewhere, it will be a good advert. Everyone will want to know who you are.'

He began to take off his purple dressing gown, not in order to get dressed, but with the intention of returning to bed.

'Ronnie, it's time to get up.'

'We've got ten minutes. Plenty of time.' He laughed in a way she hated.

'Dorothy will come in.'

'I'll bolt the door.'

'No, Ronnie, there isn't time, and listen, I've got

that pain in my back again. I think I'll have to go to the doctor. Again. He thinks it's my kidneys.'

Crossly Ronnie began to drag on his clothes. 'There's nothing wrong with your kidneys.'

He went off to the bathroom to shave and soon Dorothy appeared at the bedroom door. 'Can I come in with you for a minute?'

'No, it's time to get up.'

'Are we going to buy the shop next-door?'

'I expect so.'

'Where will you be?'

'What do you mean? I'll be here.'

'I mean, in here, or in there?'

'Oh, I see. Well, in both, really, there'll be an archway between the two.'

'Who's going to take me to school today?'

'Oh, Phyllis, I expect.'

'Why can't you?'

'Because I've got a lot to do in the shop. Now do go and dress. Here comes Daddy,' and Dorothy, who had managed to slide in beside her mother, slid rapidly out as Ronnie appeared in the doorway.

'I thought you were in such a hurry. What time's your appointment?'

'What appointment? You're not going to the dentist, are you, Mummy?'

'It's not till afternoon. Your clean socks are on the clothes-horse, darling.'

So that day had started. Not so different from many other days. But it had been an important one. Ronnie had dashed about, seeing solicitors and builders. He'd measured the new frontage with a foot rule, and casually mentioned to interested neighbours that they were extending their premises. He nagged Addie to help him compose an announcement for the local press, informing the public of the more spacious surroundings and increased choice of clothes that would soon be theirs if they were wise enough to shop at Madame Adelaide's. And Addie, in an interval between serving customers, visited the doctor, who said yes, one of her kidneys was in definite danger of becoming displaced, and she must wear a surgical belt to support it. It would have to be specially made; she must come back in two weeks.

In two weeks the builders were in next-door and she returned to the doctor to be told that there were difficulties at the factory where the belt was being made to her measurements. It would take longer than expected, considerably longer. In the meantime she must rest as much as possible, to avoid further displacement of vital organs. As there was no likelihood whatever of being able to rest, Addie simply put this last instruction out of her mind and apparently came to no harm thereby. In fact there was so much to worry about in the shop that if her back pains recurred she scarcely felt them.

She had been right about the dust. In the end they were forced to close for a whole afternoon, but it was very exciting to look through the archway and plan what they would do with the extra space. When the decorations were finally completed and the new fittings moved in, Beatrice and Addie and Ronnie worked till midnight arranging the stock so

that all should be ready for the influx of customers
they hoped for on the following day. How happy
Ronnie had been! He hadn't even reprimanded Dorothy for sidling nervously in long after she should
have been in bed. Holly had come across to see how
they were getting on and taken several hats off
stands on which Beatrice had just placed them, and
tried them on and admired herself. Quite rightly,
because with her full lips, unlike Addie's own
which were shapely but narrow, and her soft brown
eyes which were not obscured by spectacles, any
hat became her. Ronnie entered into the game,
taking hat after hat out of the square cardboard
boxes in which they had arrived by passenger train
and horse-drawn van and placing them on his sister-in-law's head as she sat before the huge new
mirror.

Brims had come in again, and these springtime
creations with their trimmings of flowers were really
charming. Addie picked up an ethereal object in the
shade of green she liked best and put it on. It was
not unsuitable but the pale tortoiseshell frames of
the spectacles that had replaced the pince-nez
looked far too businesslike for the frivolous head-
gear, and the circular lenses gave her an owlish
look. Crossly, she took off the hat and replaced
it on its stand. She could never look pretty, only
smart.

'Aren't you going to finish the windows, Ronnie?'

Ronnie said that he was, and made some flir-
tatious remark to Holly about her interrupting his
work. He soon had Beatrice dashing about, fetching

pins and stands and tissue paper, and it was left to Addie to arrange the flowers.

But she was really no good at it, and told Ronnie that he would have to do it himself, and he said that only his wife could make a bunch of flowers look like a suet pudding and they all laughed. At least, he and Holly and Dorothy laughed, and Addie smiled ruefully, and Beatrice looked severe.

Then Ted came over to find Holly, and Ronnie disappeared up to the flat. He came down with a bottle of sherry and some glasses and they all toasted Madame Adelaide's.

When at last they were preparing for bed he was still happy and excited. He wandered round the bedroom, dropping his clothes here and there, and when he had undressed he started putting them back on again, thinking it was morning. Addie had to laugh. In his striped pyjamas at last, he came across the new surgical belt, finally collected that day. It lay on a chair and had been tactfully concealed by a lace trimmed celanese slip. He looked at it with horror. 'What the devil's this?'

'My belt.'

'Your BELT?'

'My surgical belt for my kidneys.'

'God Almighty, d'you mean you're going to wear that thing from now on? That's going to do a lot for our married life, isn't it?'

'The doctor says I've got to wear it. It's not my idea.'

Ronnie made a noise expressive of doubt and got into bed. Once there, however, he fell asleep immediately, being extremely tired. Addie lay very still, being careful not to disturb him.

She woke quite early and began to think about the shop. They had to find a young girl to employ as a showroom junior, but for the time being she would be the sole representative of the extra staff they hoped to need. Money would be tight anyway, with the higher rent and rates, and with Dorothy starting at a private school. And though Ronnie was so full of enthusiasm and such a help, there was no denying that it all depended on her.

There would be plenty of work. That reminded her of the belt, which Dr Fynne had showed her how to put on, lying flat on her back so that her abdominal organs stayed in their proper places. Turning back the bedclothes carefully, she swung her long, slim legs to the floor, fetched it and returned to bed. Pulling up her pink satin nightdress, she worked it into the right position under her back and proceeded to deal with the complicated fastenings, hoping Ronnie would not wake up.

It was a very strong-looking garment, made of canvas and elastic and rubber, with a great many little straps and buckles and laces. It took her some time to get them all done up, and even then it felt so peculiar she couldn't be sure she had not made some dreadful mistake like putting it on upside-down.

Just as she heaved a sigh and relaxed against her pillow, Ronnie stirred, stretching out a hand. A hand that expected to encounter satin, and found instead, the belt.

He sat up.

'For God's sake, you haven't got that thing on already?'

'I have to put it on lying down. It's nearly time to get up.'

She spoke mildly, hoping to avert his anger. He looked at his watch. 'It's just gone half-past six.' They usually rose at seven.

'There's a lot to do today.' She had intended to sound firm, but the voice she heard was shaky and pleading.

'I didn't know.' Ronnie looked at her.` 'It's time we had this out. You haven't let me touch you for weeks. You never liked it much anyway, did you?'

'Women don't.'

But Holly had liked it, that first time, when she was sixteen. She'd said so.

'That's rubbish. Where did you get that idea from? Perhaps it's me you don't like?'

'You know I like you.'

'It was alright to begin with. When we were in Brighton. You liked it then, didn't you?'

Well, she had tried to, and she had genuinely hoped to get used to it. And she'd wanted a baby, but now the memory of the unalleviated agony of Dorothy's birth, with the doctor delayed and the midwife nearly as anxious and frightened as she had been herself was another reason for reluctance. She avoided his question. 'Well, we couldn't have another baby, now, as things are, could we?'

'But you know I always use something.'

'Yes, yes, I know, but they, they . . . don't . . . always . . . ' Oh, how disgusting it all was, how could he possibly talk about these things?

Giving up, Ronnie got out of bed and started to dress. Normally he turned his back when he took off his pyjama trousers. Today he didn't bother. She felt affronted, insulted almost.

'All I can say is, it's a good thing I'm not the type to go off after other women.'

Addie knew this was true. His father had been a womaniser and a spendthrift who had made his wife miserable and deprived his family of all but necessities. Ronnie had despised him and had always been determined to live his life in a different way, a way that would please his mother. He often talked about her.

There really was plenty of time. Phyllis would arrive at eight and cook the breakfast, then she would take Dorothy to school. Addie slowly prepared for the day, putting on a smart black coat and skirt and pearl stud earrings. A good many of her regular customers would be calling in, not necessarily to buy anything, but to wish them luck. Favoured ones would be invited to toast the new venture with a glass of sherry, which might well lower their resistance to her subtle technique of selling. She began to feel excited. All her business life was to her rather like a challenging game. When she ran her eye expertly down the till roll at the end of the day it was more with a feeling of having scored successfully, than with avaricious thoughts about money. That day she descended to the shop happily anticipating a new round of the game. Though Ronnie was more interested than she in making money and spending it, their enthusiasm for the business and their pride in the charming surroundings in which they ran it united them in spite of everything.

Beatrice, in a new black dress, took off the dust sheets, and Addie dealt with the post. Then Ronnie unlocked both front doors. He crossed to Addie, who was sitting at the little desk, looking every inch Madame Adelaide. He kissed her and because she was happy and felt she had been unfair, and because it was safe, Beatrice being occupied on the other side of the archway, she kissed him back.

'Good luck,' he said.

'Good luck to both of us.'

CHAPTER 7

'Lunch time, Mrs Castle.'
The cheery voice of the nurse broke through her consciousness. Opening her eyes, she saw the row of beds opposite, the long windows, and the woman standing there with her tray.

'I'd better heave you up a bit.' Having put the tray down on the bedside table, she grasped Addie under the arms. What in heaven's name was she doing? Addie pushed her away with as much strength as she could muster. She felt lost and disorientated. She only knew that people did not grab Madame Adelaide and manhandle her. She tried to protest and was surprised to find that only feeble grunts resulted.

'Give her a chance,' said somebody. 'She's not awake yet.'

'You'll sleep your life away,' said the nurse, having achieved her object, and Addie, as she came back to the present said, 'I wasn't sleeping, just having a doze. What else is there to do?'

Really, she was quite sensible and in command of her faculties. They'd no right to treat her like some of the poor old things farther down the room.

'Well, you could have fooled me. When I came with the coffee you were flat out.'

'I didn't want any coffee.'

'Well, eat up now, anyway. I'll come and help you in a minute. You'll need all your strength this afternoon. It's blanket baths.'

'I don't mind. A blanket bath makes you feel fresh.'

Addie was unsmiling, but Mrs Bailey joined in the joke. 'You like torturing us, you girls. Which is it to be today, boiling water, or stone cold?'

'Stone cold if you get cheeky, Mrs B!'

What a way to talk to a patient. Sister Rowles would never go on like that. And Mrs Bailey encouraged it.

The fish pie was easy enough to eat, and made with decent fish and a very nice white sauce, but the spoon soon became heavy in Addie's hand and it seemed a long way to her mouth. After a few spoonfuls she gave up, still hungry; but when the nurse came back to help her as promised she told her she had eaten all she wanted, and firmly refused to open her lips again.

'But you've had so little, Mrs Castle. You've got to keep up your strength.'

Addie wanted to say 'why?' but as this would have necessitated opening her mouth she refrained.

When three-quarters of her meal had been carried away she felt a sense of triumph. She had not been fed, she told herself and tried to forget that she was hungry.

Her pudding, a rather delicious creamy affair in a pretty little glass dish, was brought by the senior nurse, who did not even hand her the spoon. Briskly and efficiently she ladled the stuff into Addie, who swallowed it without protest. It made her victory over the fish pie seem pointless. Still, you had to assert yourself sometimes.

Some of the more lively old ladies apparently found bath-time quite a jolly event. There was a certain amount of ribaldry as ancient breasts and withered shanks were exposed to the light of day. Addie ignored it. On her good days she would converse with her attendant on subjects as far removed from the business in hand as possible. The more private the part of Addie being washed, the more impersonal the tone of the conversation. In this way she kept her dignity.

But this afternoon she didn't feel like talking. She wanted to be left alone as soon as possible so that she could return to her inner world. It was so real, though perhaps that was the worst of it. To feel oneself alive, Madame Adelaide, busy, successful and elegant, and then suddenly to be here, old and helpless, with a burdensome body, and a mind that failed to understand so much of what was said to her – hell couldn't be worse than that, surely?

She mustn't complain. She told herself that she should be grateful she was well cared for and after all, there had been so many good years. And she'd been able . . . almost . . . to forget the Terrible Time . . . And if she had not had that breakdown she might never have gone back into business, and neither she nor Ronnie would have had anything like such interesting lives. Funny to think that if it hadn't been for Nitty Havergal she might have lived all her life at Nansen Road and the house in Witney Gardens would never have been hers. They'd bought it in 1937. Who would have thought they would be able to afford it so soon? Nine hundred and fifty pounds it had been, but of course money was different then.

The first two years after they had taken on the new premises had been quite a struggle. So much so that they had left their flat and moved into the one large room over the corner shop. They soon had a small kitchen and bathroom built on but it had been dreadfully cramped at best. And they had Freda and Jack Stone, who rented the flat, for neighbours. Freda was loud-voiced and cheerful, and Ronnie liked her. Thank goodness Jack was a quiet type. Very soon after moving in they had invited the Castles in for the evening, and taught them to play solo. After that the card-playing sessions took place at least twice a week and then the Stones started wanting to include the Castles in Sunday excursions in their Hillman Minx. It had admittedly been nice for Dorothy because Freda and Jack had a little girl the same age, a pretty child with blonde curls, of whom Ronnie made a great fuss. Addie asked him why, when he was not fond of children in a general way.

'She's a pretty kid. Anyone would want to make a fuss of her.'

'What about Dorothy? She's your own daughter. You never go on like that with her.'

'Well, she's not so lively, is she? Always got her head in a book.'

It was true. Dorothy lived in a dream world, Addie knew, peopled with imaginary sisters, in which she did not have to wear glasses. It made her dull company. But she was intelligent, and won prizes at school, which would endear her to Ronnie for a day or two. Addie wondered whether curly hair would help. Dorothy was nearly old enough to have a perm.

One Sunday morning Ronnie came back to the flat, having been to buy his usual *Sunday Dispatch*.

'I've just seen Jack. They want us to go to Culver Point with them this afternoon. Freda's doing a picnic tea. I told them it would be OK. About half past two.'

Dorothy looked up, pleased. She and Josie could have a good time at Culver Point – there were rocks to climb, and caves.

'But we're going to Jay and Maud for tea,' said Addie.

'You never said anything about it.'

'Yes, I did. I told you last night.'

'I'm blowed if I remember.'

'You don't listen.'

'Well, anyway, I've told Jack we'll go with them.'

'Oh Mummy, do let's. We can go to Culver Point, can't we?'

'No we can't, I've told you. We're going to tea with Uncle Jay and Auntie Maud.'

For once Dorothy and her father were in accord.

'Ad, we were there last week. We don't have to go there every bloody week, do we?'

'We weren't there last week. We went to Holly's.'

'Same thing.'

'It's not the same thing at all.'

'Well, look here, let Dorothy go and tell them we can't come.'

'We can come. We can't go to Culver Point. You'd better go and tell Jack we've already made arrangements.'

'Now look here, I'm fed up with going to your family all the time. Oh, Holly's alright, but I don't want to spend my Sunday afternoon sitting round in that little room with Jay and Maud, trying to think of something to say.'

'You needn't then. I'll tell them you didn't want to come. I'll go on my own and you and Dorothy can go with Freda and Jack.'

'D'you want to have a row about this?'

'I'm not having a row, it's you.'

'You make these arrangements, you don't say a blind word about them and then you make me look like a damn fool.'

'You should have asked me first.'

Perhaps this was not quite what Addie meant to say, or perhaps Ronnie misinterpreted it. There followed a good deal of shouting and swearing and banging of fists on tables before he grabbed his hat and stamped off down the stairs, but in the end they went to Jay and Maud's. Dorothy sulked all the afternoon, and Addie was forced to promise they would go to Culver Point the very next time the Stones offered to take them. She could understand the child's disappointment, and realized that it was boring for her, sitting listening to adult conversation. She was not allowed to take a book because Maud had once said that she and her sisters were not allowed to read when there was company. But still, if they didn't go round on Sundays she would hardly ever see Jay. And Maud was such a funny woman; there was so much she couldn't or wouldn't do. While her fear of crowds kept her and Jay away from the cinema and the theatre, her horror of open spaces sometimes became so acute that it prevented their joining the picnics on the sands. Except for visits to relations, they went out as little as possible, but still she always welcomed Jay's family to their little semi-detached house and prepared an elaborate tea. Addie noticed how Jay watched her anxiously, helping and encouraging.

They had no children and the subject was avoided; though Jay was kind and cheerful with Dorothy and would have made a good father, Addie thought. Was it possible he had come to love this peaky, thin woman with the nervous laugh and bony hands? Poor Beatie had never found a husband, luckily for the shop, perhaps, since she devoted herself to it. Addie sometimes felt guilty about Beatie's lonely Sundays in the tiny terraced house her aunt had left her, but there was no love lost between her and Ronnie. It wouldn't have done to invite her round. Perhaps it would all be easier when they had a house. She hoped it would be soon, so that they could get away from the Stones and their demands. Before they bought 16 Witney Gardens they were able to move back into the larger flat, though Freda and Jack were still too close for comfort, in their new bungalow in the next road.

Still, life had gone on very pleasantly. There had been dinners and dances and civic balls which they attended with Bella and the now almost acceptable Percy, and Holly and Ted. Percy had made money, that was something, and Bella didn't need the discount Addie gave her when she bought clothes in the shop. She treated Holly and Maud and Winnie in the same way and was surprised and hurt if they went to Terry's or anywhere else. Not that they often did. But then there was the wedding.

Addie's niece Gillian married a rather well-to-do young man just before war was declared. That was why they'd rushed it, of course, eighteen was far too young. She had taken it for granted that Gillian would have her cousins as bridesmaids, which would be nice for Dorothy, and Addie intended that the bride should have a gown of surpassing magnificence at cost price. It wouldn't do to let Ronnie know this – he would say the Kingstons had plenty of money, why do all that work for nothing? But she wouldn't dream of making a profit out of a family wedding.

Without waiting for Holly or Gillian to broach the subject, she sent off to her most exclusive supplier for patterns and sketches. Not dead white for Gillian who was pale and dark-haired, but an ivory embossed satin with a cream tulle veil, and the bridesmaids in old gold taffeta that would suit Dorothy. Holly, as bride's mother, must look very special indeed. A two-piece, perhaps, but nothing ordinary. No pastel shades, something rich and striking for this special day in her sister's life. And she'd have something new herself, not in her favourite green because people thought that green was unlucky, nor the black in which she felt at her best, but wine, perhaps, or sapphire blue.

A Kingston wedding was a grand affair. No doubt they would hold the reception at St George's. So her mind ran on the festivities to come for two or three weeks until one day it struck her that July was almost over and Holly and Gillian had not yet visited the shop to state their wishes. Naturally, they could rely on her to have everything ready in time, but they might at least come over so that she could get started. Really, she had not seen Holly to speak to for ages, as she was always rushing off somewhere, and Mrs Kingston was ill again with her mysterious malady; how dreadful if the wedding had to be put off after all, what with the war coming and everything so uncertain.

When the patterns of ivory satin came, with the sketches of elongated, emaciated figures drooping in sculptured folds, Addie decided to waste no more time. She went to the phone.

She heard it ringing for some moments in the spacious hall of Holly's home in the most expensive part of the town, then Gillian's voice answered.

'Hallo, Gillian dear. I've got some lovely patterns for your dress. I think it's time you came in to see about it.'

Gillian said, absurdly, 'What dress?'

'Your wedding dress, of course, dear. Have you forgotten?' She laughed but no answering laugh came from her niece.

'But Auntie Addie . . . '

Her voice broke off. There was an inaudible whispered conversation at the other end of the line, then Holly. 'Addie, look, dear, I think there's been a bit of a misunderstanding. I'll be in to see you as soon as I can. Don't worry about the dress.'

A misunderstanding? What could she mean?

'Holly! Holly, are you there?'

But the receiver at the other end had been replaced. Addie put hers down very slowly. *Don't worry about the dress.* For the next three days the words echoed and re-echoed in her mind. They could mean only one thing. Holly's daughter was going to be married in a dress that came from somewhere other than Madame Adelaide's.

She said nothing to Ronnie. She knew he would make a scene, and his anger frightened her, even when it was not directed at herself or Dorothy. Good as she was at hiding her feelings, both Ronnie and Beatrice knew that something was worrying her but did not guess what it was until the arrival of the wedding invitation forced the truth from her.

It was Ronnie who opened the big square envel-
ope, which was obviously not a business letter.
Those he left to Addie.

'Look at this,' he said in surprise.

'Yes.'

'Well, d'you see what it is?'

'Of course I do. It's an invitation to Gillian's wedding.'

'But d'you see when? It's next month. The 25th.
They haven't been in about the dresses yet, have
they? How can they possibly be ready in time?'

Addie's throat hurt. Something seemed to be
sinking inside her chest. 'I don't think she's going
to get it from us.'

'What d'you mean?'

'What I say. It's easy enough to understand, isn't
it? They're getting the wedding things somewhere
else. Terry's or London, perhaps. I don't know.'

Ronnie was incoherent with rage. It wasn't the
money, he said. He knew what a fool Addie was
where her sisters were concerned, he knew all about
the cost price dresses. Well, it was one thing to give
Winnie a bit of a discount, but Maud was alright
and Holly was rolling in it, all the Kingstons were.
No, it was the look of the thing. Did Holly want to
make them look fools in front of the whole town?
If their own family couldn't trust them to supply a
wedding dress . . . If they thought Dorothy was
going to be bridesmaid in a frock from Terry's they'd
got another think coming; none of them would be
going anywhere near the wedding, nor would they
be sending a present, and so on, and on.

Beatrice disappeared discreetly through the archway into the corner shop. Addie's feelings were
extraordinarily mixed. Even now she could not bear
to hear Holly and her family castigated in this way
by Ronnie. She tried feebly to defend them.

'Holly's always been a very good customer.'

Ronnie made a scoffing noise, evidently thinking
of the discounts.

'I expect Gillian's seen some advertisement or
something. They're free to go where they like, after
all.'

Despite her brave word, tears welled over and
she was forced to remove her glasses, now more
flatteringly shaped and with pale blue rims, to wipe
her eyes. Ronnie went on fuming and though her
residual feeling of loyalty prevented her agreeing
with him, she could not help admiring him a little.
He was so wholehearted, so uncompromising, his
flow of words seemingly unending. He reminded
her of her own past kindnesses to her sister: having
Gillian to stay when Holly and Ted went abroad for
their holidays; giving generous raffle prizes when
Holly helped to organize a church bazaar; helping
to pay for the nurse during Nellie's last illness when
they had so little money to spare, and Holly was
comfortably off; and many other instances. Well, he
would never speak to any of them again. And as
for the wedding . . . He snatched up the embossed
card, tore it across and dropped it into the waste-
paper basket.

That morning he chose to dress the largest of
their shop windows. For hours he worked behind a

lowered blind, arranging the most beautiful and expensive wedding gown they had in stock, meticulously setting in order the folds of white and silver brocade, then going himself to the florist's, where he purchased armfuls of every white flower available, and also caused to be made a most expensive and elaborate bridal bouquet. When he raised the blind on his completed work of art he was gratified to see that it attracted a great deal of interest. He insisted on Addie going out onto the pavement with him to admire it, which she sincerely did.

'That'll show that lot what I think of them,' he said, almost cheerfully, and though she found his reasoning difficult to follow, Addie was relieved that he was in a good temper again.

A few days later Holly called. Not during business hours and not at the shop but at Witney Gardens, where Addie and Ronnie now lived in a comfortable modern semi-detached near the sea. It was the custom of the brothers and sisters to drop in on one another for glasses of sherry or homemade wine on Sundays, either before the midday dinner or, in summer, in the early evening. On the Sunday after the arrival of the invitation Addie did not expect to see her elder sister, though it was the Castles' turn to be 'at home'. Addie was carefully applying lipstick in front of her dressing-table mirror when she heard Phyllis open the front door to the Kingstons. The next moment Holly came into the bedroom.

She was still slim and the silver streak in her dark hair added to her attractiveness, if anything. It was perfectly positioned to look as though it was meant to be there. Just her luck. Even little things like that went right for Holly. She was dressed expensively, and with good taste, though more quietly than Addie, who liked to look striking.

Holly put her head round the door with assumed coyness. 'Am I allowed in?'

'I suppose so.'

'Ad, can you ever forgive me? I know it's an awful thing to have done. If you knew the trouble I had with Jill. Nothing would do but going up to London. We went round Harrods, Selfridges, Derry and Toms, Marshall and Snelgrove, wherever you can think of. I was worn out!'

'I expect you got what you wanted.'

'Oh, yes, I must say I'm pleased. I'm not going to tell you what it's like; you'll just have to wait and see. It's not the kind of thing you'd have suggested, I'm sure. As a matter of fact it isn't even white, it's the palest, palest pink, veil and all. But it's what she wanted and that's what matters. I had to put her first, Ad. You're not to take offence.'

'You bought your own things too, I suppose?'

'Well now, I wasn't going to, dear, honestly I wasn't, then I saw this beautiful beige georgette two-piece. I just had to have it, Jill was so keen on it.'

'You certainly wouldn't have got beige georgette from me. Beige isn't your colour.'

'This suits me very well. It's a sort of pinky beige. I'm sure you'll like it, Ad.'

'You have to be very careful with georgette, it so easily looks . . . dabby.'

'Well, this doesn't. I don't think I shall look in the least dabby, whatever that means. Oh, come on Ad, it's about the only dress I haven't bought from you in the last ten years or more.'

'I'd got a lovely wine moss-crêpe I wanted you to try.'

'I don't like wine. It's old, an old colour, and moss-crêpe isn't special enough.'

'That depends on the style. You don't think I'd let you look old, do you? I know what suits you. I always have.'

'But that's the trouble, isn't it, Ad? I'm not allowed to choose. Oh, I know you've got wonderful taste and all that, but sometimes I want to look awful in my own way. Can't you understand? And I haven't got a hat yet. You'll get me a really lovely hat to go with it, won't you?'

But Addie did not like being fobbed off with a mere hat. 'I can't get a beige hat at this time of the year. There's nothing in beige in the autumn collections. You'll have to go to Terry's, they'll probably have some left from last season.'

'Addie, don't be like this – I'm your sister.'

'That's what you seem to have forgotten. Have you thought what I shall feel like, with everybody coming up and saying what a lovely wedding, and how lucky for you to have a sister to do it all? And I shall have to say . . . you went to Harrods.' Addie seized her swans-down powder-puff and pressed it against her trembling lips.

'Well, there's no law against it, is there? Jill

wanted the thrill of going round the big stores, and I didn't see why she shouldn't have her own way.'

'She always does have her own way. You put her first all the time.'

'Of course I do, she's my daughter. I can't see that we've done anything so dreadful, Ad. The trouble is, you depend on the family too much, it's unhealthy. You've got Ronnie and Dorothy. You could try worrying about them for a change.'

'What do you mean by that? Of course I worry about them . . .'

'I know, I know. Forget I said that. That's the trouble with weddings. Everyone gets nervy. All this because I bought a dress somewhere else! Come on downstairs, dear, they'll be wondering where we are.' She led the way out of the room. Crossing the landing, she said, 'Perhaps you're right about the beige. I suppose I could cancel it. I'll come in tomorrow and have a look at that wine moss-crêpe.'

Addie followed slowly. It was all very well for Holly to minimize her offence, but there was a world of difference between 'doing the wedding' and supplying one gown. Holly could look awful in beige georgette if she wanted to. Dressing the bride's mother would be small consolation. And what about Dorothy? Was she not to be a brides-maid? It appeared that she was not, for in general conversation downstairs Holly revealed that the only attendants were to be the two small nieces of the bridegroom. Gillian being of small stature, there would be no taller girls in the bridal procession. Though Addie was angry all over again, Dorothy

was not particularly upset. She and Gillian, with
four years between them, had never been great
friends.

The wedding went off very well on the whole.
The two child bridesmaids looked charming, and
with Gillian being so small the general effect was
probably rather better than if her two tall cousins
had walked behind her. Dorothy looked almost
pretty in ice blue with a halo hat. Addie wore her
silver fox with a new rust silk two-piece, and Holly
in the event wore the beige georgette, the wine
moss-crêpe having proved slightly tight on the hips.
Addie had ordered a hat to be specially made for
her, and spent three weeks worrying about it.
Would it arrive on time? Would the veiling be
exactly the right shade? Would Holly really like it?
Three times she telephoned the London milliner,
urging haste, and finally, five days before the wedding, she persuaded Ronnie to make a special journey to fetch it, rather than expose it to the dangers
of public transport, unaccompanied.

It was the custom for Madame Adelaide's brides
to be attended in the church porch by Beatrice, or
even, for particularly important weddings, Addie
herself, who would arrange the veil and train with
professional expertise, and see that the bride set off
in perfect order. In Gillian's case this vital office was
left to the clumsy hands of the next-door neighbour,
and Addie sat in the congregation with Ronnie and
Dorothy. So it was a pity that it had rained, and an
even greater pity that Ted, helping his daughter out
of the car, had stepped in a rather muddy puddle.

The bride, her train held carefully clear, had managed to avoid it, but somehow just before they started up the aisle her father planted his muddy shoe in the very middle of the carefully spread pink satin. This black footprint followed the bride to the altar, causing the little bridesmaids to giggle, and Ronnie to nudge his wife and whisper gleefully, 'See that?'

'Shut up!' hissed Addie.

But she had seen. And Holly, as the bride passed her, would see it too and perhaps regret the fact that her sister had not been supervising the procession after all.

The fact that Madame Adelaide had not supplied her own niece's wedding gown would have been an intriguing subject for gossip, but at the beginning of September that year there was more a pressing matter for discussion. It really began to seem that war was inevitable, and Holly was in a state of anxiety until her daughter and new son-in-law had returned from their honeymoon. True they had gone no further than the Isle of Wight, but with everyone believing that air-raids, not to mention invasion, were imminent, even calm, confident women like Holly wanted their families near them.

On the Sunday morning that war was declared they were all together in Bella's house at Westgate. The lounge was a large, comfortable room with a geometric pattern on the fitted carpet and wall lights. It reminded Addie of the foyer of the Regal cinema. There were also ornaments that might have come out of one of Percy's gift shops and quite a lot of very shiny cushions. Bella was wearing trousers and a sun-top made with a triangular scarf, though the weather hardly warranted such an outfit. Neither did Bella's age, for she was well into her forties. Also she was too plump for the trousers, which outlined her rather heavy buttocks closely. What with that, and the fact that, the day being cool, her nipples made firm little bumps in the red-and-white spotted silk, Addie thought she looked a sight. Yet in spite of all this, and her rather frizzy permed hair and her incipient double chin, all the men present seemed to find her irresistibly attractive. Why was this? She had been quite pretty as a girl, but now it was noticeable that her face was too round and her nose too long. Addie decided that it was sex, and thought Bella was making herself cheap.

June looked as if she was going the same way as her mother. A well-developed fifteen-year-old, she was clothed in a two-piece bathing costume, ruched all over with elastic thread. It was one thing, thought Addie, for children to wear bathing suits around the house in the summer, but on a Sunday, with visitors expected . . . and June was obviously not a child any more.

Dorothy was wearing a pretty cotton dress and had curled her hair. She looked fresh and attractive and was happy because Ronnie had been pleasant to her, cracking jokes at which his daughter laughed eagerly. Addie, wearing a rather sombre silk print, well-suited to the occasion, was the only one who really seemed to be worried about the future. The young ones especially seemed more excited than anything.

Freda and Jack were there too. They had arrived that morning, eager to talk about the political situation, just as the Castles were getting into the car. Ronnie had greeted them: 'We're all off to Bella's. Why don't you come too? Bella won't mind. The more the merrier.'

Addie frowned at him from behind Freda.

'Can Josie come in our car?' Dorothy broke in excitedly, making the Stones' acceptance a foregone conclusion.

'It's right over at Westgate,' said Addie. 'Don't let us make you late for your dinner.'

Even to her own ears this sounded ridiculous. They all knew the Stones never ate until two on Sundays. Freda and Jack needed no persuading from Ronnie, and Dorothy and Josie were already chattering together in the back of the car. Addie fumed inwardly for the duration of the short journey. Josie's presence made it impossible for her to tell Ronnie what she thought of him for inviting the Stones like that. It was just the sort of sloppy behaviour she couldn't stand. Treating Freda and Jack, whom they'd known only a few years, as if they were the same as family! And on a day like this, when anything might happen – it might be the last Sunday morning they'd have together for years. Perhaps there would never be another. She wanted to look round the room at them all, at Holly and Jay and Charlie – surely Charlie and Winnie would

be there today – and Bella. At their children, Jimmy
and Gillian and June and the twins, and know that
they were alright and all together. And the others
of course, the outsiders. Ted and Maud and Winnie
and Percy, and Gillian's new husband Roger. They
belonged, after all, and Gillian must be forgiven,
because somehow being at war made forgiveness
possible and necessary.

So she certainly didn't want the Stone family but-
ting in on all this. Freda was a decent sort in many
ways, but the longer you knew her the more bossy
she became, and she and Ronnie seemed to have a
lot to say to one another, which left Addie with
Jack, a quiet little man with whom she had nothing
in common. She wondered sometimes how this so-
called friendship had come about, and how it had
endured. At least there was one consolation: if they
moved away because of the war, which seemed
probable as there was already talk of the town being
evacuated, that would be the end of that.

Addie didn't speak to Ronnie until they were all
in Bella's lounge, drinking sherry, and then she had
to because someone would have noticed. Of course
her sister had been delighted to see Freda and Jack,
whom she knew quite well, and in any case the
Kents prided themselves on their hospitality.

The young ones, who had never experienced a
war, were enjoying the drama of the situation; the
others were varied in their reactions. Percy said in
a rather lordly way that it would hardly do for the
Mayor to think of leaving the town but he would

have to consider sending the girls, meaning his wife
and daughter, away from the coast.

'What, and leave you to your own devices? Not
likely!' said Bella, nudging Freda Stone so that she
almost spilled her sherry. 'Send June away if you
like, but you needn't think you're getting rid of me.'

'We'll have to see about that,' said Percy heavily.

There was one thing to be said for him: he did
look after Bella.

Maud was sitting close to Jay as usual, never
speaking unless she was spoken to. Apart from
going to work at the gas company, Jay almost never
left his wife's side. They had been married for fourteen years, and in that time Addie had scarcely ever
spoken to Jay alone. Even at their parents' funerals,
when as their eldest brother he should have walked
with her, sat with her and comforted her, he had
been totally taken up with Maud. Well, now Maud
would have to manage on her own if the evacuation
was ordered. Jay, of course, in his position, would
have to stay and so would she and Ronnie. They
would make exceptions of business people. How
would it be organized? she wondered. Would there
be enough people left to enable them to make a
living? There must be thin times ahead, no doubt
about that. But still, there could be compensations.
She visualized Jay coming to Sunday dinner every
week, perhaps Charlie too, if Winnie were evacuated with the twins. Her thoughts were interrupted
by an angry shout from Ronnie.

Dorothy had been tearing about the wide lawn
with her younger cousins and now came rushing in

through the French windows, the rest at her heels. Crying 'Daddy, save me!' with a confidence born of their earlier rapport, she flung herself upon Ronnie with all the clumsiness of an excited fourteen-year-old. She looked hot and untidy, the flowery cotton of her dress crumpled and stained green from rolling on the grass, and she knocked Ronnie's glass out of his hand. It fell into the hearth, where it shattered, its contents having already splashed over one of the emerald green cushions.

Ronnie pushed his daughter away roughly. She lost her balance and fell, hitting her knee sharply on the corner of a small table and violently rocking Bella's favourite lamp. This was in the form of a nude girl modelled in misty green glass, supporting an iridescent sphere about nine inches in diameter. Winnie screamed, and Jay, leaping to his feet, expertly fielded the object. No damage was done, unless it were to Dorothy.

Ronnie swore picturesquely. For some reason connected with his war service he always swore in Italian, a habit which irritated and embarrassed his wife. Though of course swearing in English might have been worse. 'Santa Maria,' he shouted. 'San Christi la Madonna.'

Addie put her arm round Dorothy, who flung it off rudely. She was sobbing, scarlet with humiliation.

Ronnie having finished swearing was now concerned with saving face. 'What have I done to have a clumsy fool of a kid like this?' he demanded in a voice rich with false geniality. He turned to Dorothy who was still kneeling on the floor. 'Get up, idiot!' he hissed, then resuming his jovial tone for the benefit of the company he spoke to Jack. 'What about swapping her for your Josie, eh? It's time I had a daughter who didn't let me down. I don't know what I've done to deserve a lump like this.'

Dorothy scrambled to her feet and ran out into the garden, where Addie followed her, to be repulsed once again.

'He doesn't mean it,' she told her, keeping her distance. 'He's just thinking of himself. He can't bear to look a fool.'

'I hate him, I'd like him to die.'

After some minutes, Addie re-entered the house. Percy had refilled all the glasses and the talk was again of war. Dorothy was forgotten and Ronnie was totally unaware of his own cruelty.

Dorothy must be told she was too big to rush around, at least when her father was about. Naturally he was upset at having spoiled Bella's cushion, but still, he needn't have behaved like that. The next time he spoke to Addie she pretended not to hear. Twenty minutes later they drove home, not for the first time in complete silence.

But they soon had to start talking again – there was so much to discuss. Should Dorothy go with her school to Wales? Should they close the corner shop, move back into the flat, install an air-raid shelter? What if the flow of customers dried up completely? Were the good, prosperous days finished for ever? It did seem unfair after the years of being hard up, of ploughing every penny back

into the business. Just as things had become easier
and they had a house and a car, Hitler had come
along to ruin everything.

Round-faced, cheerful Phyllis, so beloved by
Dorothy, who had been with them for over eleven
years, departed to join the ATS and Addie had a
nasty feeling that Beatrice would have gone too if
she had been younger, but she was forty-seven, the
same age as herself. There seemed to be no loyalty
left.

As the weeks passed and France was invaded by
Germany, bringing the war nearer, it began to seem
inevitable that, far from staying in the danger area
to run the shop, they would have to move the business away from the coast if it was to survive. By
this time Beatie was the only assistant left and they
could very easily have done without her services,
so far and few between were their customers. In
the end Addie agreed to premises in Albury, found
by Ronnie on one of several sorties inland. There
was a tiny flat over the Albury shop, which they
would have to occupy. Obviously houses in an
evacuation area were quite unsaleable, so they were
not in a position to buy another elsewhere.

Jay and Maud called to say goodbye on the eve
of their departure. They sat among the dust-sheeted
furniture, drinking the usual sherry. Ronnie was
excited – any change or innovation pleased him.
Maud, strangely enough, seemed almost lively. She
had never for one moment considered going to a
safer place, though Addie had more than once suggested to Jay that it might be wise. She had pointed

out to him how nervy his wife was, how Maud herself had said she had no intention of ever entering an air-raid shelter, and if she wouldn't, then Jay couldn't, but her persuasions had been useless. Now she thought that Maud had never had so much to say as on this last evening.

'What will you do when the air-raid warning goes?' asked Addie.

'Take no notice,' answered Maud.

'You could go into the garden. At least then the house won't fall on you.'

'I might be cooking the dinner.'

Jay laughed. 'It'll take more than a Jerry to ruin our dinner.'

'Jay's joining the LDV,' said Maud proudly. 'If he's going to be standing guard on the front, the least I can do is have a meal ready.'

'She thinks I'm going to save the country single-handed.'

They looked at each other fondly. Addie found them very irritating.

'Of course we wouldn't be going if it weren't for the business,' she said.

'Oh, no. You've got to go, of course,' said Jay. 'When we get fed up with the bombs dropping on us we'll come up for a few days.'

Somehow it had begun to seem as if he and Maud were the privileged ones, staying in the nearly deserted town.

'Charlie's the one who ought to get away somewhere.' Addie voiced another of her worries. 'What about his chest? He can't spend nights in an Anderson shelter. He'll get pneumonia.'

'Oh, didn't you know? They'll be moving in with Winnie's mum and dad. They've got a good cellar in the old place, and Winnie's dad's fixing it up with bunks so that they can all sleep down there if necessary.'

'Go back to that flat, d'you mean? Give up their home?'

'Well, I know Win wants to get back. The old people are really past running the shop now, but it's a good little business. Pity to let it go.'

'Well, I shouldn't think there'll be much doing there while the war lasts. Not that it was ever anything much really.'

'That's what they've decided anyway.' Jay closed the subject firmly.

So that was it. That was why Charlie and Winnie had not come up to say goodbye. Charlie must know how she would feel about this extraordinary decision. It was all Winnie's doing, of course. She'd always been more daughter than wife, dragging him off to her parents every Christmas and Easter, however much Charlie might have wanted to be with his own family. Of course, Charlie would be very useful in that little shop, she could see that. He'd be getting up at five to do the newspapers as soon as Winnie's old father decided he didn't want to do it any more. And he'd be behind the counter every moment of his spare time. She pictured Charlie, getting tired and thin, coughing miserably, lying awake in the cellar all night, shivering with cold on a comfortless makeshift bed.

They should have kept closer. That was the trouble. She had allowed her youngest brother, her little Charlie with his blond curls and chubby face, to drift away. How seldom, when she came to think of it, had he and Winnie joined the summer groups on the sands or the Sunday morning sherry parties. Then it must be admitted that she had not often visited them. Charlie and Winnie had not progressed as the rest of them had, moving from flat to house, bicycle to car, polished linoleum to fitted carpet. She had always felt uncomfortable in their tiny living room, and her praise of Winnie's simple household arrangements fell insincerely on her own ears.

She could not stop herself remarking on the convenience of having the kitchen open directly from the living room and the fortunate, though unavoidable, placing of the cooker so close to the sink.

Once she had replaced a cheap cup, accidentally broken by Dorothy, with a complete, good quality tea-service. Apparently this had offended Winnie, though she could not for the life of her see why. She had not meant to patronize, but why should Charlie drink out of Woolworths china when he had a sister who could afford to provide him with something better? After all, they didn't have to live like all the other council house tenants, did they? Though even the council house was better than living with Winnie's mum and dad. She wondered how she could find an opportunity to speak to Charlie before she and Ronnie left for Albury the next morning. Surely they would come round to say goodbye? But then it was always such a job to get rid of Winnie, even for a moment. She sighed.

'Cheer up, Ad!' Ronnie's voice broke in upon her thoughts. 'Cheer up! It may never happen!'

'It's already happened,' she said sombrely.

'It'll be over by Christmas,' said Jay, meaning the war.

'We said that in 1914.'

'This time it's true. In a year from now you'll be back here as though nothing had happened.'

For once Addie felt irritated with Jay. Did he think she was such a fool? It might well be years before they were able to return. They had decided they were going, and go they must, even though at the moment the likelihood of penury seemed even less reason than the threat of air-raids for leaving her home and the people she loved.

Roused by the clatter of screens being placed round her bed, Addie was glad to remember that this was all in the past. Leaving Culvergate and moving to Albury had been one of the worst times in her life. She was grateful that she was not still in the midst of that period. Really, she had been daydreaming too much recently, living in the past. She must concentrate on the present in which, after all, she had a lot to be thankful for. What day was it? Would Dorothy be coming? And perhaps Angela would bring the baby to wave through the window. She felt clear-headed, proud to remember her granddaughter's name, and of not confusing her with Holly as she knew she sometimes did. Understandable, really, they were very alike, both in appearance and ways. She sighed. Who would have believed that Holly would go out to Australia like that to live with Gillian and Roger, apparently content never to see her family again? Holly's grave was on the other side of the world. The wave of sadness that threatened to sweep over her was fortunately interrupted by the nurse.

'Come along, Mrs Castle.' It was the little one who was kind and never called her dear. 'Time to make you look nice. Let's see if you've got a clean nightie.' She found one in the cupboard beside the bed. 'How pretty,' she said approvingly.

Addie resigned herself to being washed and to sundry other less pleasant ministrations, but still when it was all over, with her hair combed and her face powdered with the puff from the marcasite-studded gold compact that Ronnie had given her, she felt quite a pleasant sense of achievement. She could see in the little mirror that she looked quite nice as old ladies went. Her skin hadn't gone blotchy like Mrs Bailey's, neither did it hang in folds like Miss Brown's, and she didn't look half-witted like poor old Ruth. She felt fresh and clean and she was looking forward to her tea.

'Is it Wednesday?' she asked the nurse.

As she said it she had a nasty feeling that she had only a moment previously asked the same question, but the girl said, quite kindly, 'No, Mrs Castle, it's Thursday.'

Not Wednesday. Thursday. It mattered, though at the moment she could not think why. If she stayed quiet she would remember why, in time. But she didn't feel like staying quiet, she felt for once that she would like a nice little chat. Sister Rowles would be coming on duty before long, she was always ready for a few words when she wasn't too busy.

She mustn't be led into conversation with Mrs Bailey. The woman never knew when to stop. Still, she wished they would come and remove the screens. It wasn't very nice having them left round the bed, and supposing Dorothy walked in? She'd think she was ill. There seemed to be a lot going on in the ward, hurrying footsteps and quick, quiet bursts of speech. The little nurse put her head round the screen. 'Shan't be a minute, Mrs Castle. We're just a bit busy.'

Addie heard her say the same thing to Mrs Bailey then there was the sound of the trolley being wheeled in and Matron's voice.

It was a long time before they took away the screens. Addie thought what a pity it was she could no longer see to read comfortably. Though it was years since she had been able to concentrate sufficiently to enjoy any novels, they had once been a great source of pleasure to her. Ernest Raymond, Sheila Kaye-Smith, A. J. Cronin and the rest – it had been pleasant to have a good read to look forward to on early closing days. Phyllis would go down to Boots library to change her book every week, instructing the librarian, 'Choose something for Mrs

Castle, please.' She nearly always came back with one Addie could enjoy. She'd once heard someone say that most people's lives had the stuff of a good novel in them. Well, hers certainly had.

Tea was brought by a girl in a blue overall who called herself a nurses' aide. Although she placed the bed-table correctly and helped Addie to hold her cup, she was not particularly friendly. Addie, left to get on with her lemon curd sandwich and little segment of sponge cake, felt cheated. It was not often she was in a sociable mood, and strong enough to talk, and now here she was, stuck behind a screen. It was quite obvious that someone was very ill, if not actually dying, but they would all be dead soon anyway. It was what they were there for, so why make such a fuss?

When the ward returned to normal Mrs Bailey said crudely, 'So Janie Barton's hopped off the twig at last. A merciful release if you ask me. She was always saying she was at school with me, you know.'

'Wasn't she?'

'Well, we did go to the same school, but she was one of the big girls when I was in the first form.' Mrs Bailey reached for her bell. 'I'll have to get nurse to draw that curtain, the sun's right in my eyes.'

'It's a pity to shut out the sun,' said Addie, but she did not hear her neighbour's response because her own words awoke an echo.

'A pity to shut out the sun.'

How many times had she said that in the long,

dark High Street shop at Albury? It faced west like
the room where she now lay, so that the afternoon
sun flooded the shop windows and delicate aterials
were in danger of fading. Ronnie kept an eye on
the display and would lower the sun-blind at the
first hint of brightness. Standing in the shop looking
out at the sunny street, Addie would remember
the well-lit corner premises that now stood empty
among other empty buildings in the evacuated coast
town. She had felt depression creep over her at such
moments. The Terrible Time and its related anxieties
had left her alone for years, but often since coming
to Albury she had felt they were waiting to spring.

CHAPTER 8

This new version of Madame Adelaide's had been a bicycle shop, though it was hard to imagine it ever housing anything as glossy as a new bicycle. When she first saw it Addie was appalled. It was in far worse condition than she had imagined from Ronnie's description. She stood in the middle of the room, holding her smart handbag because she could not put it down on the stained wooden counter and looking down at her elegant high-heeled shoes among the dirty bits of paper and nameless rubbish on the grimy floorboards.

'I ought to have come with you. I'd never have agreed to this.'

Ronnie stared round gloomily.

'I told you it needed decorating.'

'Decorating!'

'We've done it all before. Think what the corner place was like before we did it up.'

'I can't face going through all that again.'

'What's the alternative? Sit on your arse and wait for the war to end?'

'Ronnie . . . ' but she spoke wearily, as a matter of form.

'We've got to make a living. I was lucky to find a shop in a reception area. Let's go upstairs.'

The staircase led out of what appeared to be a cupboard at the back of the shop. Shreds of filthy carpet adhered to the treads. Halfway up a draggled mop was propped against the wall. When Ronnie took hold of it the thing stuck disgustingly to the floor, finally coming away with a reluctant tearing sound. A few steps higher Addie stopped.

'I'm not going up. The whole place smells. We'll have to get rid of it.'

She picked her way downstairs, walked the length of the shop, and went out into the dusty summer afternoon. It was early closing day, and the street, narrower than Southdown Road, had a dreary, neglected look. They drove the short distance to the Queen's Hotel, where they had intended to stay until the flat was ready. Their room was at the back, overlooking a yard with dustbins. Addie stood at the window.

'We can't stop here. We'll have to go back. We'll manage somehow. I don't care what we do, but I can't stop here.'

'But the lease . . . we've signed the lease. We can't get rid of it just like that. Now look here, old dear . . .'

'We can resell it, can't we?'

'We're bound to lose money if we do.'

'What a damn fool thing to do, to take on an awful place like that! It wants hundreds spending on it, and it'll never be anything but a poky hole, whatever we do to it.'

'Alright, if that's how you feel.' Ronnie looked round for his hat. 'I'm no good to you, you'd do better on your own. You're right, I am a damn fool; nobody but a damn fool would . . . ' He was at the door.

'Ronnie!'

He banged it behind him. She heard him marching off down the long corridor.

Usually pride prevented her from calling after him, but not today. Not today, with depression hanging like cobwebs in the corners of the dingy room, and the ghost of Nitty Havergal poking in the dustbins below the window.

She ran to the door and flung it open. 'Ronnie!'

He heard her, stood hesitating a moment, and then came back. They went down together and ordered tea.

They hadn't made the mistake of visiting the shop again that night. The truce lasted until after breakfast next day.

Returning from the lavatory along the corridor, Ronnie found his wife replacing in the suitcase the few things they had unpacked the previous evening.

'What the hell are you doing?'

'Packing.'

'What's the point of that? We're here tonight, aren't we?'

'No. We're going back.'

'There's nothing to go back to. It's all gone.'

Nothing? Nothing, when they were all still there, waiting for bombs to drop on them?

'This place is doing well. The streets are full of people already. There's money to be made here.'

How could he think about money, when the Germans were a few miles across the Channel from Culvergate? They all lived with the danger of invasion. It had scarcely worried her before, but now, removed from it by a hundred miles or so, she feared it for the others. 'We'll have to see the solicitor before we go. You'd better ring him up. And get the agent to put it back on the market.'

'I'm not having anything to do with it. Whatever you want to do, you can do yourself. And the van's arriving today – have you forgotten that? Are you going to tell them to turn round and go back again?'

'They'll be doing that anyway.'

'What sort of fools will they take us for?'

'What does that matter?'

But it did matter. She imagined the removal men looking at one another, incredulous, sneering, when they said they had changed their minds.

'Well, they won't be here till twelve at the earliest. We may as well have a drive round.'

'Don't forget we'll need enough petrol to get back.'

In the car Ronnie headed for the countryside. Passing a signpost marked St Mary Winterbourne, he said, 'Know where you are?'

Addie did know. It was the village where she had

stayed with her grandparents for six months when she had first had to wear glasses. She had been so miserable about it that the doctor had suggested a change of scene and air. To begin with she had been desperately homesick – she was only seven and she wanted her mother, felt lonely without Holly and her brothers, even missed Bella, the somewhat whiny baby of the family. Then she had grown used to the village school, and liked it better than the large one at home. A natural tomboy, she soon became a ringleader, the first to walk along a wall, or climb over a five-barred gate into a field.

They parked the car and walked through the village, past some terraced cottages, a shop, a pub, and a deserted-looking little church. Though not especially picturesque, it all had a peaceful, timeless quality that was very soothing.

Addie tried to decide which had been her grandmother's cottage. 'It was that one, I think, at the end. No, it wasn't, it was that one on its own.'

In her fur-trimmed coat and town shoes she felt she was an incongruous figure, and Ronnie in his well-cut dark suit even more so. A woman came towards them, wearing shapeless tweeds, her grey hair curling untidily in contrast to Addie's neat waves. Her complexion was ruddy and healthy-looking. She glanced at them curiously as she passed, then said, 'Good-morning' hastily, as if remembering her manners.

'I believe I knew that woman. Perhaps I went to school with her.' Addie turned, half-inclined to call out, then continued up the lane, more slowly. 'It's hardly changed at all. We used to play in these fields – no one seemed to mind. Arnie Pryke and Dulcie Swetnam! The things we used to get up to! I haven't thought of them for years.'

Ronnie looked at his watch. 'We'd better be getting back.'

Reluctantly Addie returned to the car. The joy of being in a place that held only happy memories! The school, she remembered, was a little farther up the lane. As soon as possible she would come back and see it. As they drove back to the town she wondered how she could have forgotten that innocently happy time.

Once more in Albury, they saw the removal van outside the shop as soon as they turned into the main street. The driver and two other men were standing about on the pavement looking bored. As Ronnie drew up one of them bent down to the car window. 'Wondered where you were,' he said. 'We wanted to get started. Got to go on to Reading, see, and pick up a load for Canterbury.'

Ronnie got out of the car and unlocked the shop door. Addie sat still and watched them taking in her furniture and merchandise. In the face of the men's commitment to another job there was nothing she could do but allow them to unload. It was true that they could probably hire another van quite easily and send everything back to Culvergate, but they wouldn't. The die was cast against her.

In a few weeks the shop was ready to open. Beatrice arrived by train and set to work unpacking the stock even before she had found anywhere to live. The business prospered and they were soon making money again, in spite of the difficulties inherent in a luxury trade in wartime.

Sundays were the worst: waking up in the dreary little bedroom that overlooked a row of backyards, washing in the icy, inconvenient bathroom, and then facing the day, the long, dull day with nothing to do, no family to visit. The towpath along the canal was a poor substitute for the cliff walk at home; in any case the countryside in winter seemed dreary in a way the seashore never had. Ronnie would go along the street to buy a newspaper, staying to gossip with the owner of the shop, or any acquaintance he met on the way, but after the paper had been taken back to the flat and read, he was at a loose end. Addie was restless and bored and could not settle to reading. She took to going down into the shop and doing odd jobs – counting clothing coupons, or bringing the stock-book up to date. When she looked out at the street it seemed all greyness, with almost no one about. Sometimes she would sit at her desk and write to her brothers and sisters, scrupulously starting the letters with 'Dear Holly and Ted' or 'Dear Maud and Jay' and quite often she would receive letters in return that began 'Dear Ad and Ronnie'. She never handed Ronnie these missives to read for himself, though occasionally she passed on scraps of interesting news. Twice a week at least she wrote to Dorothy at school in Wales. Her daughter's letters were depressing. She said that she was cold, and had chilblains, that

everything was horrible and could she leave as soon
as she passed her School Certificate? When Addie
tried to talk to Ronnie about bringing her back and
enrolling her in a local school he would only say
she was better off where she was.

'If she was more like Heather, she could come
and work in the shop,' he added disparagingly.

'I certainly don't want her to be like Heather,
even if you do.' Heather was the junior assistant, a
fluffy little blonde of sixteen whose main preoccu-
pation in life was her own appearance. 'In any case,
I don't think Dorothy's cut out for business. She's
very brainy. I think she should go to university.'

'Waste of time and money,' said Ronnie. 'If she
wants to do something useful, she can go and be a
nurse.'

Addie really wished that Dorothy had been the
sort of daughter Ronnie seemed to want. It would
have made life so much easier. School holidays,
with them all in the tiny flat, were really awful.
Fortunately, Dorothy passed her School Certificate
with flying colours and having by this time settled
into boarding, announced that she wanted to stay
on and take her Higher Schools. She intended to be
a teacher, she said. Ronnie was quite pleased and
made jokes about her becoming headmistress of
Roedean, whereupon Dorothy, at this stage ever
ready to oppose her father, said that she hoped to
teach in a primary school in the East End of London,
where, yes, the children would be poor, and very
probably dirty as well. Ronnie was bad-tempered
for the rest of the day.

Yet apart from Sundays when the only enliven-
ment seemed to consist of arguments about their
only child, Addie and Ronnie began to find life quite
interesting. Customers in Albury were a different
breed from those in Culvergate. In the seaside town
they had dealt with visitors in the summer and local
business people with both time and money to spend
in the winter. If the Mayoress had commanded a
new gown for the Civic Ball they had been hon-
oured and delighted, and when the proprietress of
the St George's Hotel had become a regular customer, they felt they were a success.

In Albury, however, they soon realized that such
people were very small fry. Addie, having sold a
simple cotton dress to a rather dowdy little grey-
haired woman with whom she had been as kind
and patient as usual, was stunned to hear her
announce her name as the Countess of Clere. Glad
to be spared the trouble and danger of a visit to
London, the Countess came again, and brought her
daughter, Lady Pamela. Soon most of the rich and
titled women in the vicinity became regular customers at Madame Adelaide's.

Addie changed her own style of dress to suit the
altered clientele. Instead of dark, formal suits she
wore soft, colourful tweeds that set off her tall slen-
derness. The county ladies felt that she understood
their needs, indeed was almost one of them, so as
far as the business went, life was tolerable, even
pleasant, but still Addie and Ronnie lived for the
day when they would be able to return home. They
had very little social life, neither entertaining nor

being entertained, and because to make the flat really comfortable would have been to face the fact that they would be there for a long time, they left it as it was, dingy and inconvenient.

Addie was often alone at home because Ronnie was on a rota of fire-watchers. As far as anyone could see, this meant no more than the occupation of a certain room in a nearby empty flat for a particular time each week. She never found out what her husband was expected to do in the case of a shower of incendiary bombs, and felt doubtful that he had any clear idea either.

On this Wednesday morning she had sent Heather to change her book at Boots Library. With Ronnie out of the way she would try to have a rest and a quiet read. The novel recommended by the librarian was by an author Addie had not come across before. She looked at it doubtfully.

'The lady at the library said you'd like it, but I'll take it back and get something else if you want me to,' offered Heather, eager for another errand.

'It'll do.' Addie glanced up as a customer came into the shop.

A tall woman had entered. She seemed to be dressed for London in a black cloak and a dashing black sombrero. As she glanced round impatiently, apparently used to places where people hurried to do her bidding, Beatrice stepped forward with her usual 'Can I help you, Madame?'

'I'd like to see Madame Adelaide.' The voice was loud and commanding. 'This is her shop, isn't it?'

Addie rose from her desk with dignity. 'You wished to see me?'

The woman waved Beatrice away, rather as one might brush off a fly. 'I don't suppose you have anything that will do,' she said. 'I want something for a luncheon. The wretched cleaners have ruined my poor old Chanel, and I haven't time to go to town.'

'We might be able to find something.' Addie's cool tone concealed inward rage. She at once produced three garments that the woman grudgingly admitted were not unsuitable. Addie turned to Beatrice. 'Help Madame to try these on,' she told her, with a lofty air that surprised her assistant. Turning back to the customer she added, 'I'll be with you in a moment,' after which she walked briskly to the back of the shop as though important business awaited her. All she did, however, was to tell Ronnie to delay the chops – the week's meat ration – for a while, before returning slowly to the fitting room.

'Oh, there you are,' said the customer crossly, as she surveyed herself in a square-shouldered black silk suit. Looking at her critically, Addie decided it was too short in the waist, and directed Beatrice to replace it with a dress and jacket, also black, but in wool with a velvet collar. This time both the customer and Beatrice pronounced the fit to be perfect, but Addie considered the fabric too clinging, and said so.

'I suppose you are going to let me buy something?'

'I may do, if I have the right thing.'

Smiling coolly, Addie returned to the curtained wall-fitting. Taking down the garment she had borne in mind from the very beginning, she heard the voice say, 'Is she always like this?' and hurried back before Beatrice could make some lamentably unsophisticated reply.

This time Addie stayed in the fitting room. Beatrice helped her client into a beautifully tailored silk dress. It was in deep russet brown with a tiny geometric pattern in black, a daring combination of colours for that time. There was no doubt that it was perfect. The tall woman, with her rather dark skin and brown eyes, was flattered by both the style and colouring. Addie thought she had a Spanish look.

'What's that disgusting brooch doing? It cheapens the whole thing.'

'Yes,' agreed Addie, 'I wish they wouldn't put them on. I suppose it's to indicate how well the dress would set off a really good piece of jewellery.'

She tried to remove the offending object, but the pin stuck and she was forced to look closely at the fastening, then to fiddle with the safety catch, absurdly pretentious on a thing of base metal and imitation pearl.

'I'm so sorry,' she murmured, wondering whether to admit defeat and leave the brooch where it was. The sale was in the balance; if she was forced to leave the wretched thing the customer might be put off the dress. So she persevered. Standing there, feeling the warmth of skin through the fabric, knowing the dark eyes with the penetrating, mocking expression were on her, Addie had a strong sense of having experienced the same incident before. For a split second they seemed to be suspended, out of time. Then Beatrice said, 'Shall I try, Mrs Castle?' and Addie replied, 'No, it's alright,' and the next moment the pin came free and she was able to slide it carefully out of the silk.

The decision was made, and the dress removed and packed by Beatrice, who also made out the bill. Addie rarely concerned herself with anything so vulgar as actually taking money from a customer. Normally she might have put away the unsold garments while her assistant performed these mundane chores, but on this occasion she did not. She merely, out of politeness, draped the black cloak round the woman's shoulders.

'I haven't noticed this shop before. How long have you been here?'

'Nearly six months.'

'As long as that? I never come into Albury nowadays, if I can help it. The place is filled with these awful evacuees.'

There was some truth in this. The streets abounded with Cockney mothers and toddlers, and unaccustomed city children. The exiled women shouted angrily at their wretched offspring, hurling abuse at them for dragging behind, or running ahead, for wanting sweets or needing a lavatory. The schoolchildren hung about on their way to their billets, reluctant to part company. Though Addie herself had frequently complained about the mothers' tend-

ency to gather gossiping in the shop doorway, or
the grubby handprints left by the children on the
plate-glass, she was suddenly angry. Who was this
woman, so rich, secure and arrogant, that she
should grudge space on the pavement to these displaced people? Coldly she said, 'Please be careful
what you say. I also am an evacuee.'

Not the way to speak to a customer. Not the way
to encourage her to return, to recommend the shop
to her wealthy friends. But she didn't care. For the
moment she was one with the London mothers, far
from everything loved and familiar, longing for the
end of the war, so that home, if home still stood,
could receive them again.

'I deserved that. Sorry. One forgets. Where have
you come from then?'

'Culvergate, the south-east coast.'

'Oh, yes, I've been there, I think. Ages ago. How
long is she going to be?' She looked round for
Beatrice who was approaching with the dress in
a smart grey carrier bag, with 'Madame Adelaide'
printed on it in a large, artistic scrawl. 'Oh, I can't
take it like that. You'd better put it in my dressing-
case. I don't see why I should give you a free advertisement.'

'Just as you like, of course,' said Addie. 'Pack it
into Madame's case please, Beatrice.'

At least I haven't spoilt anything, she thought. *If she
won't carry a bag she's hardly likely to tell her friends
about us.*

The repacking done and the bill paid, she
accompanied her client to the door and said good-

bye, rather in the manner of a gracious hostess. To her surprise the woman shook hands and smiled. 'I shall come again. If you can bear it,' and she strode off.

Addie took the cheque and looked at it. The signature was illegible. She turned it over. The back was blank. 'Didn't you ask for her address?'

'She gave me this.'

Beatrice handed her a card. On it were the words:

Lady Josephine Scott-Francis
The Manor House,
Aldeclere,
Berks.

Addie went to tell Ronnie they had a new titled customer.

Later on, alone in the flat, she sat down by the fire with a cup of tea and her library book. She took off her shoes and stretched her toes to the warmth. *Nice legs*, she thought. *Not many women of nearly fifty have legs as nice as mine.*

Only the other day the doctor had told her that her body was remarkably youthful. He had also ordered her to leave off the surgical belt she had worn for so many years. She had never needed it, he said, and it had never done her any good. She must throw it away. He was a forceful man and she obeyed him, surprised to find she felt perfectly alright without it.

She leaned back in her chair, enjoying the feeling

of relaxation, and opened the book. It was called
Time's Fool, and the author's name was Josephine
Ireland.

Another Josephine. One of her favourite names.
They had considered it when deciding on a name
for Dorothy. The only one she had actually known
was Josie, the daughter of Jack and Freda. There
had been a letter from Freda a few weeks ago. She
would have to answer it sometime. But now she
opened the book.

It was not quite the kind of novel she would
have chosen. Though she could not be bothered
with anything she considered highbrow, Addie
despised mere light romances. This did not quite
fall into that category, but it was not very far off.
The lovers in the story were the victims of a con-
suming passion which destroyed their lives, their
homes, and finally, one of them. The writing,
though somewhat florid, was readable and flowing,
and there were some good descriptions of land-
scape both in England and in Greece, where the
protagonists fled. Also the book was redeemed
by an almost brutal honesty that left Addie feeling
that even if these actual events had never taken
place, the emotions that had precipitated them were
real, and endured or enjoyed by real people in real
places.

Addie read on until nine o'clock when she
realized that Ronnie would be home from firewatching in an hour. He would probably return in
a good mood, having spent the time gossiping with

Herbie Cole, the manager of the local men's outfitter's, and Arthur Woods, who was supposed to help his wife in their café.

Thoughtfully she made up the fire. Did most people fall in love like the couple in *Time's Fool*? She did not think it had ever happened to anyone she knew. Surely Bella hadn't been in love with Percy? He'd just been the best she could get. And Holly had put off marrying Ted so long, as she herself had delayed her own wedding. Had she been in love with Ronnie? Certainly she was quite fond of him, especially now that he didn't bother her so much, and with Dorothy away they had less to argue about. Their daughter had been the subject of so many quarrels. He was not a loving father, and though she understood that his way of reprimanding the child in public had sprung more from his own lack of confidence than from any sadistic wish to humiliate her, it was hardly to be expected that Dorothy herself would understand this. Kneeling there on the hearthrug, Addie felt angry at the memory of the scarlet-faced child, eyes brimming with tears behind her glasses, standing staring at the floor while her father drew the attention of assembled relations to her stupidity, clumsiness, and general lack of desirability as a daughter. Ronnie never saw that other people deplored his behaviour, though Holly at least had openly criticized it.

In spite of all this, Dorothy did not seem to be without affection for her father. Addie remembered a winter evening about eight years earlier. There had been a family tea-party in the afternoon, and, tired of waiting to be offered a piece of chocolate Swiss roll, and giving up hope of the conversation dropping to a level where a polite request could be heard, Dorothy had helped herself to a piece without asking, reaching across in front of two aunts and a cousin to do so, and almost knocking over a cup of tea.

She might have known that such a breach of good manners would not go unnoticed by her father. After bearing his castigations for about a minute she had tried to run out of the room, only to be ignominiously hauled back. She was made to sit at the table, forcing lumps of unwanted Swiss roll down her aching throat, while the relations pretended not to notice.

When the guests had gone and Dorothy was in bed, Addie went to say goodnight to her as usual. This was a time they usually enjoyed, a time for plans and confidences and stories of Addie's own childhood. But not tonight. The child lay on her side, pretending to be asleep. Kissing her gently, Addie left the room and went to the bedroom she shared with Ronnie. She was taking off the bedspread in readiness for the night when something made her move Ronnie's pillow. Under it she found a piece of paper torn from an exercise book, folded in four, with the words 'To Daddy. Private' carefully written on the outside. Smoothing the paper she read,

'Undear Daddy,
I think you are the most horrible father in the
world.
All my hate,
Dorothy.'

She must have exclaimed, made some sort of noise
as she stood there with the note in her hand,
because she heard a gulp and saw Dorothy standing
in the doorway in her Vyella pyjamas. She had put
on her spectacles, as she always did before leaving
her bed.

'You're not to read it. You're not to read it.' She
flung herself upon her mother, grabbing the paper
and screwing it up. 'You're not to tell him. If you do
I'll never love you again.' She was sobbing wildly. 'I
wasn't going to leave it there. I felt like that then,
but I don't now. You're not to tell him.'

'Well,' said Addie, 'he wasn't very nice at tea-
time. Perhaps he deserved it.'

'No, he didn't,' screamed Dorothy, 'and you're
not to tell him.'

It was several minutes before Addie, feeling
nearly as confused as her young daughter, returned
downstairs. After that she kept the child away from
her father as much as possible, and tried to make
up for Ronnie's deficiencies by giving her as much
of her own time as a successful businesswoman had
to spare.

No, during Dorothy's childhood her mildly affectionate feelings towards her husband had dwindled
to mere toleration, apart from her appreciation of

him as a business partner. He was always more
daring than she, always had more faith in her than
she had in herself. But in love? No, never with
Ronnie, or with anyone else. She'd liked Dick Kingston, and might have had a more peaceful life with
him, but she'd never been happy about the idea
of marrying a Kingston. Had it been impossible,
though? She had refused him because she thought
she couldn't marry without confessing about the
Terrible Time, but in the end she had never told
Ronnie, never told anyone, perhaps now never
would.

For the first time in her life she began to wonder
if she had missed something really worth having.
She knew what love was, of course. She loved her
sisters and her brothers. She would do anything,
make any sacrifice for Holly, or Jay or Charlie, even
for Bella. Sometimes, when Jay had been in the
army, she'd imagined him bringing home a friend,
remarkably like himself, and they would have fallen
in love and married at once, and Jay would have
come to live with them after the war. How lovely it
would have been. But she couldn't, simply couldn't
imagine ever wanting to give up home and family
like Josephine Ireland's heroine and being content
to live for ever in some tiny far off village, seeing
no one but the beloved. Well, it hadn't happened
to her, and it obviously would not in the future – it
was too late. She went out to the kitchen to prepare
some supper for herself and Ronnie. It was becoming really difficult to provide adequate meals, now
the meat and cheese rations were so small. Fortu-

nately a customer who kept chickens had brought her half a dozen eggs that morning. They would be able to have poached eggs on toast.

The very next morning something happened which focused her thoughts even more on this gap in her experience. Beatrice arrived early and amazed her employers by thrusting out a hand on which reposed a quite respectable diamond ring. Beatrice, at forty-seven, was engaged! Ever since arriving in Albury to join them she had lived in lodgings with an elderly woman and her son, a widower. It was this man, a grocer's assistant, that she was to marry.

Addie had always felt sorry for Beatrice, missing the boat as she had, losing her parents, and then having Jay filched from under her nose by the determined Maud. They had been close friends then, but of late years their relationship had been little more than that of employer and trusted employee. She had even agreed with Ronnie when he complained that Beatrice, however able in dealing with the wishes of boarding-house keepers, seemed unable to assume a manner suitable to attendance on the aristocracy.

Poor Beatie must have been lonely. But still, a man who spent his life slicing bacon and weighing out cheese . . . She sought for the right thing to say. 'It's splendid news, dear, both of you on your own . . . a very sensible thing to do.'

Beatrice interrupted her fiercely. 'It's not like that at all. You make it sound so half-hearted. Edmund and I are in love. I'd go to the ends of the earth for him, and so would he for me!' And she looked like one in love, starry-eyed, with heightened colour, her greying curly hair full of life and spring.

Addie floundered. 'But you never said . . . '

'You don't, do you, about important things?'

'Well, we must have a celebration at lunchtime; we must drink your health.'

'Well, perhaps we could do that tonight. You see, I'm meeting Ed, and we're going out to lunch.'

It was a strange reversal. Always really, without thinking about it, she had felt comfortably superior to Beatrice. Not only in worldly success, but in every other way, and now the tables were turned. She had missed a desirable experience in which this quite commonplace couple were openly wallowing.

Beatrice had evidently forgiven her tactlessness, for she was back in the office a moment later, talking excitedly. 'Oh, I've got something else to tell you. Not nearly so important though. You know that woman who was in late yesterday morning? The tall one with the cloak who was rather rude? Well, she's an authoress, Josephine Ireland. I was telling Ed's mum, and she's read all her books but she said she didn't know whether I ought to read them. I had to laugh! I told Ed he'd better read them as well.'

'How extraordinary! I'm reading one of hers now. Heather got it for me yesterday. I don't think it's the sort of book a man would enjoy.' She couldn't imagine the tall, thin Edmund reading a novel of any kind. In fact she could not imagine him doing anything other than stand behind the counter at David Greig's in a white overall.

'Oh, well now, what a coincidence! I'll have it when you've finished with it. Funny sort of person, wasn't she?'

'I didn't see anything funny about her.'

'I mean, you wouldn't know where you were with her, would you? One minute really charming, and the next quite offhand. I wonder if she'll turn out to be a regular?'

Addie thought a great deal about her new customer that day, veering between irritation at her remembered arrogance and mildly excited anticipation of another visit. After all, she was a titled lady, lived in a house with an imposing name and was a successful novelist. All in all the type that needed good clothes and had the money to buy them. There was of course the little matter of coupons – seven for a dress, twelve for a coat, and only thirty to last the year, including stockings and underwear. They wouldn't see her very often unless she had some extra ones from somewhere. The likelihood was that she would not reappear for some weeks, but strangely she was often in Addie's mind. Several times, thinking she heard the rather loud, clear voice of Josephine Ireland in the shop, she left her desk in the office with a sense of pleasurable anticipation. Once, fearing she might have missed her, she said to Beatrice, with studied casualness, 'We haven't seen any more of Lady Scott-Francis, have we?' and felt irritated when Beatrice replied that people like her probably went to Hartnell or somewhere in the usual way.

Beatrice didn't seem to think it mattered, being

less interested in customers these days, with her
wedding plans to think about. She was becoming
rather tiresome with her constant quoting of her
husband-to-be: 'Edmund doesn't like me staying
late' and 'Edmund thinks a part-time job would suit
me better'. Of course Beatrice was entitled to a life
of her own, but all the same, by flinging herself at
a grocer's assistant she was really letting herself
down.

Addie was surprised when less than a fortnight
later she went through the shop from the workroom
where she had been helping to solve the tricky problem of making a rather small dress with insufficient
to let out on the seams into a fairly large dress, and
saw the tall, black-cloaked figure on the point of
leaving. Very briskly indeed she walked the length
of the showroom, almost if not quite raising her
voice to call, 'Good morning, Lady Scott-Francis.
Can't we help you today?'

'Ah, there you are. Your assistant said you were
engaged. The thing is, I've a black velvet dinner
dress I'd like to have shortened to wear in the daytime, but she tells me you never do customers' alterations.'

Really! Hadn't Beattie any sense at all? 'Well, not
in the ordinary way, perhaps . . . '

'I'd have thought you'd be glad to take on anything in these hard times. Still, I can always pop
into Harrods – the buyer there is very helpful.'

'Our workroom is kept very busy, but still I'm
sure we'd find time. Call Kathleen, if you please,
Beatrice.'

Without a word, but with a look of extreme disapproval, Beatrice went through the back of the
shop to the workroom, and Addie led Lady Scott-
Francis into the fitting room. There she personally
unpacked the velvet gown from the dressing-case
and helped her into it, just as though she were a
bona fide customer. Kathleen, a birdlike little
woman who was a really brilliant alteration hand,
appeared and after consultation the desirable length
for the dress was decided upon. There and then a
large slice was sheared off the bottom of the skirt
so that the hem could be evenly pinned up.

More than competent as she was, Kathleen had
one unfortunate weakness. She was avid for
appreciation, and for this reason liked to make her
task seem difficult, if not impossible, so that when
the perfect result was produced she would then be
the more praised. Sometimes, however, she
demurred too long, so that the customer would
have doubts about her ability to do the work properly.

Now, when there was no going back, she began
to dwell on the difficulty of handling velvet, its
slipperiness and uncontrollability and its readiness
to show up imperfections and marks until Addie
could willingly have kicked her, and Lady Scott-
Francis almost decided to take the mutilated dress
back to Harrods after all. 'What if it's ruined?' she
asked as Kathleen departed to the workroom.

'It will be perfectly alright. She enjoys making
things look difficult, but she's extremely good at her
job.'

'Well, I'd tell her to keep her mouth shut if I were you. She'll lose you customers.'

'My customers are not so easily lost as that,' Addie answered her in the coolly assured voice which she somehow found herself using with this woman.

Perhaps it was simply another manifestation of her business instinct for as Lady Scott-Francis left she said, 'My dear, I don't know how you keep your patience, dealing with tiresome women like me from morning till night.'

'They are not all as bad as you,' said Addie, smiling.

'You don't belong here at all. How did you get involved in all this?' Lady Scott-Francis glanced disparagingly round the shop, with its fitted carpet, brocade curtains, and gilt furniture, of which Addie and Ronnie were so proud.

'I like to have something to do,' said Addie off-handedly. She spoke as if the question of earning a living had never existed, as though Madame Adelaide's was a little sideline that provided her with pocket money, and passed the time. In doing so she felt disloyal, though to what? She didn't know.

'When you feel like getting away from it all you must come and have an afternoon in the country. You can't spend your life cooped up here. The daffodils will be out soon at Aldeclere.'

Addie murmured something vague. Both she and Ronnie believed that social relations with customers were bad policy.

'I warn you, on the first really nice day, I shall come and kidnap you.'

Lady Scott-Francis strode off and Addie returned to the office. As she entered she was struck by its makeshift, shabby air. Really, there was no need for it. What was the point of pretending that this was a temporary arrangement? The war would go on for a long, long time, and they might as well be comfortable. The room had once been a kitchen when the building was a private house, and a rusty, disused kitchen range still occupied one wall. If that were to be removed they could have a big old-fashioned fireplace. She saw the room with a new red carpet, and some good pieces of old oak. After all, customers were likely to see it. Anyone might ask to use the phone.

CHAPTER 9

Addie was looking at some curtains. Long curtains, printed with a bright floral pattern. Not the office curtains, because Ronnie had found some made of beautiful red velvet, second-hand in a saleroom. With an oak table, white walls, wing chairs and a good fire in the new grate the office had become more comfortable to sit in than the room upstairs, and they often spent their evenings there. Addie put her favourite photograph of Dorothy on the desk. It showed her as a chubby two-year-old, standing beside a poster advertising a concert at which Addie was to sing.

No, these were not the office curtains, nor any other curtains that she remembered. And all these people in bed. Then of course she knew. She was in some sort of hospital. How soon would she be able to go home? When would Ronnie come and fetch her? She mustn't be away from the shop any longer than necessary. She decided to get up and began to push back the bedclothes, which seemed rather heavy and firmly tucked in.

A nurse came quickly towards her. 'Now what are you up to, Mrs Castle? Where do you think you're going?'

Addie looked at the woman with distaste. The way they spoke to you these days! 'I have to get back to the shop.'

'And what shop is that?' Quite a kind voice, but how stupid.

'Madame Adelaide's, in the High Street.'

But even as she spoke she was not sure, for there was more than one Madame Adelaide shop. There was Southdown Road, and Foreland Bay. Such a good thing for Dorothy. But Dorothy didn't want shops, didn't want to be in business, didn't know which side her bread was buttered. So perhaps they weren't there any more. Confused, she allowed the nurse to lift her legs back into bed and replace the bedclothes.

Soon they brought trays of food. It must be evening, because some of the bedside lamps were on. Mrs Bailey was sipping a glass of tonic wine, her little treat, she called it. Addie didn't feel hungry. She ate little, and was glad when the nurse made her comfortable and she could feel settled for the night.

Of course she had been thinking about Jo, though she had made up her mind not to think about her again, ever. Memories of Jo were memories of pain and guilt, but there was such pleasure in them too, pleasure that drew her back through the years. Jo had not wanted to use the phone. She had simply followed Addie into the office one day, having asked if she could borrow a pen to write a cheque.

'So this is where you hide yourself.'

She sat down in one of the wing chairs. When the cheque was written she made no move to go. Instead she took out her cigarette case, offered it to Addie, and took one herself, fitting it into an expensive holder.

Leaning back, she glanced round the room curiously. 'Is that your little girl?'

Addie handed her the picture. 'She's nearly sixteen now.'

'And the name on the placard, Adelaide Clarke? That's you, is it?'

'Yes, that's me. I kept my maiden name for singing because people knew me by it.'

'Special engagement of Miss Adelaide Clarke, mezzo-soprano.' Jo stared at the photograph, and then raised her eyes. 'I see! Of course. I knew I'd seen you somewhere before. That marvellous, incredible voice. That was you!'

'You mean you've heard me?'

'Yes! It must have been about this time. I was about . . . oh, twenty-five or so. My mother had pneumonia and afterwards we went down and stayed there at some hotel. A terrible place – they hadn't got a suite and they made another bedroom into a sitting room for us. We went on long, dreary walks along the front every day, and we went to this concert, and there was this girl with the most marvellous voice. A local girl. And it was you! What

in Heaven's name are you doing here in a shop?
Haven't you been abroad? Did you have no proper
training? It's criminal. Criminal . . . !'

'I was told once that I should have toured the
capital cities of the world.'

'Don't you realize that you have wasted a pre-
cious gift? You had no right to do that.'

'It wasn't wasted. I sang for years.'

'Do you mean you have given it up?'

'I'd have given it up by now in any case.'

'Nonsense. You must practise up again. You will
be as good as ever. Listen. I have the most wonderful idea. Next month I'm arranging a concert in our
local church, a charity thing. Felicity Grey's coming
down to read some of my poetry, and Jonathan
Hayes is going to do something. And you must
sing!'

Addie was horrified. She had several times seen
Felicity Grey on the West End stage. And Jonathan
Hayes, the 'cellist! No, she could never have
appeared with stars of that magnitude, even with
her voice at its best. As for even thinking of it now,
when she had not sung in public, and hardly in
private, for over twelve years . . . ! It was impossible. But ten minutes later she had agreed to practise
and see what happened.

Luckily the piano was one of the items they had
brought with them. This was done to enable Dorothy to practise her violin during the school holidays.
Now, as soon as she was alone in the building,
though at first she had so firmly rejected the idea
of taking part in the concert, Addie struck a chord

and sang an arpeggio. Her voice seemed to her thin and quavery. More to prove to herself that the idea of singing in public was ridiculous than for any other reason, she tried again, taking a deep breath, willing the sound to be firmer. It was a great deal better. She persevered, beginning to enjoy herself. An hour later the idea of the concert was, if still impossible, slightly less absurd than it had been. When Ronnie returned she was able to tell him about it without feeling foolish. To her surprise he was enthusiastic. If her voice was not as good as ever, it was still very good. She must practise every evening. Telling her to keep going, he went out into the kitchen to prepare their supper. Doubtfully, yet with increasing pleasure, Addie went back to her scales.

But singing, after a day's work in the shop, was tiring. Sometimes she felt despondent, and Lady Scott-Francis was pressing her for a definite answer which could only be 'yes' since she refused to accept 'no'.

One evening Ronnie entered the rather bleak sitting room with their supper tray to find her sitting listlessly at the piano, doing nothing.

'We must do something about this room,' she said. 'I don't want to sit in the office all next winter.'

'I've been thinking the same,' said Ronnie. 'We may as well empty the house and bring all our stuff up here. Either that, or it will have to go into store. As it is, we're paying rates for nothing, and the furniture's deteriorating'.

'I suppose you're right.'

But Addie's heart sank. It had been a comfort to think of the seaside house waiting for them with Jay popping in to keep an eye on things.

Ronnie banged about cheerfully, setting a small table. There was a rumble of lorries from the street under the windows. 'Convoy going past,' he said. 'Wonder where they're off to?'

Addie thought of her brothers in the last war, fighting in France, when Ronnie had been enjoying a relatively safe tropical cruise on a destroyer.

He came up behind her and took her face in his hands. 'It won't last for ever.' His voice was kind. Tilting her head, he bent to kiss her. She jerked away irritably, but he persisted. 'Want me to do my Ronald Colman act?' he asked.

This was an old joke between them, though not one that Addie had ever thought particularly funny. It was something to do with being a great romantic lover – she could hardly remember what. In any case they were too old for it now.

Crossly she said, 'If you only knew how I loathed it.'

Ronnie straightened up, his pale face flushing. 'What did you say?'

She didn't want to repeat herself.

'I thought you said "If you knew how I loathed it".'

'Yes, that's what I said.'

'I see. Then that's it, isn't it? What a damn fool I've been.' He was often angry and loud-voiced but this was different. He was quiet. He moved to the window, and stood, looking down at the street.

Addie said, 'I didn't say I loathed *you*. It doesn't mean I'm not fond of *you*. I just don't like that sort of thing. That's all. I never have. You know that. It's not the only thing in marriage.'

He turned away from the window, and in an almost normal voice suggested that they get on with their supper. She didn't comment on the fact that he ate little. He suffered a great deal from indigestion. But looking back, she thought that this must have been when he first considered leaving her.

It must also have been around that time that she ordered the twin beds. Was it earlier? No, after that evening, because Ronnie had made so little fuss. At the time she believed he had finally come to agree that they were too old to worry about that sort of thing any more. Yet he must have been hurt. Perhaps she was wrong to choose that particular time to stop sharing his bed, but it had seemed best to act quickly, knowing she was being unkind, and then try to show him that it didn't really matter, rebuilding the affectionate if tempestuous relationship they had always had. After all, he wasn't perfect, was he? By no means. So he must accept her imperfections and make the best of them.

Having reasoned all this out to her own satisfaction she announced that it was time they bought a new mattress. Their own had seen better days. Ronnie agreed. She suggested a visit to Hamshire's, the local department store. With wartime shortages they might have to wait for delivery, and there was unlikely to be much choice, if any.

It was seldom convenient for Addie to leave the

shop during business hours, in fact it was often difficult to find time for her regular weekly visit to the hairdresser. So she was forced to wait several days for the opportunity to arise, and it did so when Ronnie was dressing a window. Heather stood nervously by with pins and tissue paper amid a small glade of chromium-plated stands while Ronnie arranged dresses, hats, jumpers and other garments in an artistically blended colour scheme of olive green and amber. He hoped to buy some early chrysanthemums to complete the picture.

'I thought I'd pop across to Hamshire's. Are you coming?'

'No, I want to get this done. Don't be long.'

'I shan't be.'

She walked briskly along the busy street in the sunshine. Noticing her reflection in a shop window, she approved of herself. Tall and slim in her tailored silk dress, so plain and yet so flattering, she pitied the women around her in their last year's bunchy cottons, and thought how much better they could all look than they did. She was not long in Hamshire's, knowing exactly what she wanted, and as she had expected, there was not much choice.

The next week, on early closing day, the beds were delivered. Ronnie was firewatching. By the time he arrived home she had made them up, using old double sheets which were tiresomely unwieldy, and finishing them with two new eiderdowns. They were covered in rather nasty mauve taffeta, but as they were the only ones to be had, they would have to do.

She followed Ronnie into the bedroom. It was a smallish, dark room whose narrow sash window overlooked the dismal backyard belonging to the next-door shop. By eight o'clock, when Ronnie's period of duty finished, it was sufficiently gloomy to dull the fierce mauve of the eiderdowns. But she was afraid.

He stood aghast, staring. 'What's this, then?'

'I know the colour's awful, but . . . ' She switched on the light, making it more awful still. 'We can get them re-covered sometime . . . '

'Twin beds. Where'd you get that idea?'

'Most people have them nowadays. It's more up to date.'

'Up to date be damned! You mean you want to sleep on your own. Not with me.'

'It's not that. This room's so small. There's more space like this.'

She had pushed the beds right up to the walls with the widest possible space between them.

He gave her a look of contempt. 'You must think I'm a fool.' To her astonishment, he began to fling off his clothes. 'Don't worry,' he said, 'I'm just going to have a bath, that's all. It's hot, stuck in that little room all the afternoon. Don't bother about supper for me, I've got indigestion.'

He stepped out of his underpants, the smart blue silk ones he had worn ever since he had been able to afford them and put on his dressing-gown without fastening it, letting it hang open.

Addie felt affronted.

'If even seeing it's too much for you, you'd better

go. It's a pity the flat's not bigger, or we could have separate rooms.' He stood still for a moment, his hand pressed to his stomach.

'It's time you went to the doctor. There's hardly anything that doesn't give you indigestion these days. D'you want some of that stuff I got you from Boots? I suppose you had some awful bought cake for tea.'

'Some sort of chocolate muck. Old Woods's wife made it. I couldn't very well refuse.'

'Try a drop of hot water. Sit down there a minute.'

Waiting for the kettle to boil, Addie decided she had got off lightly. She was really sorry about his indigestion. She decided to telephone the surgery herself.

The doctor examined Ronnie and gave him a prescription and a diet sheet. The diet, which would have been dull at the best of times, was almost impossible to follow with food rationing in force. Even so, Addie tried hard to see that he kept the rules. At the little reception following Beatie's wedding she warned him against the remarkably rich cake which Edmund's mother had somehow managed to produce, but fruit cake was one of his favourite kinds.

'You only live once,' he said and helped himself to a generous slice. Afterwards he had pains in his stomach.

Beatrice had been married on early closing day so that Ronnie and Addie could attend. Ronnie gave her away. It seemed rather odd when the bride was getting on for fifty, but still, she had looked very attractive in an ice-blue two-piece and a maroon hat, heavily trimmed with veiling.

Addie, one of the dozen or so people in the front pews, looked affectionately at her old friend as she passed by, holding Ronnie's arm. Years ago, Beatie had been 'like a member of her own family. She remembered the Sunday teas at Jasmine Villa. How Beatie had enjoyed them! And she had worked so hard for Madame Adelaide's, though of late years they had seen little of her out of business hours. It was one thing having somebody to tea when you were a member of a big happy family, different when it was just you and your husband and child. It became a bother. If Beatie had found a husband they might have met for games of whist or solo, been friends in the way Jack and Freda were friends. Though admittedly it was quite a relief not to see Freda any more.

She noticed that the bride and bridegroom were holding hands as they stood at the foot of the chancel steps. At their age! How absurdly sentimental! Well, it wasn't likely to last. The novelty would soon wear off and Beatie would be like every other married woman, complaining that 'he' forgot about clean clothes and never wanted to go out in the evening. She'd have security, of course, but then what about his mother? They were all going to live together. She remembered Percy's mother who had providentially died while he and Bella were on their honeymoon. That wasn't likely to happen here. The old lady would still be mistress of the house. She did hope Beatie hadn't made a mistake. But coming down the aisle to the Wedding March, and afterwards under the rain of confetti outside, the bridal couple looked so radiantly happy that you had to be happy with them.

Arriving back at the shop, Addie went straight through to the office. Ronnie followed her. 'What have you got to do here? Aren't you coming up to have a cup of tea?'

'I've got some letters to write. Special orders.'

'Well, I'll bring the tea down here. Shall I light this fire, instead of the one upstairs?'

'No, I'll be alright with the electric here. I'll be up in a minute.'

But there was quite a lot of correspondence to be dealt with. When she went up to the flat Ronnie was asleep and the tea was cold.

It was November then. A busy time in the shop. They had missed Beatrice and been glad to have her back when she returned from her brief holiday. The workroom was busy, and could have been busier still but for the inflexible rule that they never undertook 'customers' alterations' that is, renovations to garments not recently purchased at Madame Adelaide's. Lady Scott-Francis was the one exception to this rule. Beatrice could never understand why Addie repeatedly caused Kathleen and Jenny, her assistant, to renovate and restore the good quality but well-worn clothes that she so frequently brought in.

'My dear, can your clever little woman do something with this for me?' she said, rushing in just before closing time one Wednesday, and producing from her dressing-case a crumpled ball of black chiffon which proved to be a Chanel model, rather out of date, but exquisitely made.

Addie supervised the fitting as usual while Kathleen rather grumpily pinned and measured, making it plain she resented working on a dress so far from new, and as closing time came and went Beatrice tidied the shop noisily, banging drawers and rattling curtains. Locking the door behind Heather, she said goodbye with unnecessary loudness, and would have switched off the lights if she had dared.

When they were alone she took her employer to task. 'You shouldn't have promised that for Saturday. You know Kathleen's got that black lace to let out for Mrs Parker.'

'Oh, she'll fit it in somehow. Jenny can do the unpicking.'

'Why on earth did you take it on? I thought we had a rule about customers' alterations.'

'I make the rules. I suppose I can break them.' Really, Beatie was getting above herself. Now she was married she didn't seem to care what she said.

'I can't think what you see in her.'

'She's a good customer and a friend of mine.'

'I think she's one of those funny women.'

'What do you mean?'

'Like those two next-door.'

Addie felt her face grow hot. 'I don't know what you're talking about, Beatie. I think you'd better be quiet.'

The truth was that Addie hardly did know what Beatrice was talking about. The two in question worked at the chintzy tea-shop called Little Jane's Pantry. Betty was the waitress, young, fluffy-haired and shy, and Elsa was cakemaker. Some years older than Betty, she wore trousers and an Eton crop and called Betty 'darling'. After closing time they could be seen walking away together, hand in hand. Every now and then they would visit Madame Adelaide's and Elsa would buy Betty a dress. For this she would use her own coupons, saying that as long as her current pair of trousers held together she would need none for herself. They seemed devoted.

To Addie this devotion seemed beautiful and spiritual. She liked their wish to please each other, evident in Betty's choice of dresses and Elsa's pleasure in giving. She thought they were probably sisters, until Ronnie, having gossiped with Harry Woods, manager of the china shop, who regularly lunched in Little Jane's Pantry, enlightened her. Even then she didn't really understand. What could women do? The men, it seemed, avoided speaking to Elsa on the rare occasions when she appeared from the kitchen, whilst making a great deal of fuss of Betty. Addie disapproved of the men's behaviour, and made a point of greeting the older girl pleasantly whenever the occasion arose.

Once they entered the shop together and, instead of looking at dresses, they approached the counter where the fancy jewellery was displayed. This was a profitable sideline introduced by Ronnie and regarded as his special responsibility. He enjoyed arranging the paste and gilt trickets on draped and ruched black velvet, and there was a good sale for these pretty, feminine things which could still be bought for mere money, without coupon or permit. It was all imitation, but good quality of its kind.

As the two young women began to comment on the display of rings Ronnie, who was standing near, turned rather pointedly away. Addie, embarrassed at his rudeness, quickly moved towards them, opened the door at the back of the display case and took out several rings that had been scattered on the velvet.

'That's pretty!'

'Try it on, darling.'

Elsa picked up an artificial amethyst set in silver, and Betty fitted it onto the fourth finger of her left hand.

'Amethysts are supposed to be a charm against drunkenness,' said Addie, smiling and chatty.

The girls looked at one another and laughed. 'It's too late for that, I'm afraid,' said Elsa. Betty said nothing, examining the ring with close attention. Elsa became serious. 'It's really one of those I think we wanted, Mrs Castle.'

Those were eternity rings, some set all round with glowing red or blue stones, while others, more expensive, were studded with darkly gleaming marcasite. It was one of the latter sort that Addie placed before them on the fringed velvet mat. 'These are rather nice. Quiet, but very good-looking.'

Betty looked at it doubtfully. 'I like the coloured stones best.'

Addie took out one of each colour. The blue one fitted perfectly. They all admired the effect of the ring on the small, pretty hand.

'This is better quality. It would last for ever.' Addie indicated the marcasite ring, thinking that it was a much more worthwhile sale than the cheaper, colourful one.

Elsa picked it up. 'That's what we want. Try this on, Betsy.'

That too fitted. After some discussion and some more trying on, it was purchased, and Betty left the shop wearing it, though not without a backward glance at the more showy rings still on the counter. Addie felt happy. She had made a sale. They were two nice girls, real friends. She meant to accuse Ronnie of rudeness to customers.

She had replaced the rings behind glass when the door opened and Elsa hurried in.

She wants to change it, thought Addie crossly, disappointed in the nice girl and generous friend, but no. Elsa came quickly up to the counter.

'I'll take the blue one as well,' she said. 'The child does so like pretty things.'

'I see she can wind you round her little finger,' said Addie. She found a little box, too good for the blue ring really, but still, there had been no box needed for the other as Betty had kept it on.

'I'm afraid she can,' Elsa smiled happily.

Liking her, Addie gave her a small discount, saying it was because she worked next-door.

Later she said to Ronnie, 'You were very rude to those two girls. Good job I was there. They bought two rings, one quite good one.'

'Which two girls?'

'You know perfectly well who I mean. From next-door, Little Jane's.'

'Oh, them. You mean one girl and that other awful creature.'

'She's not awful. A bit of a no-nonsense type, but very nice.'

'It ought not to be allowed. Somebody ought to tell that girl's mother.'

Addie was puzzled. 'Whose mother? What?'

'The young one's mother. What kind of ghastly creature has got hold of her.'

'But why ghastly? They work together. They're friends.'

'That older one. She wants to be like a man, in all ways. With that girl. It's disgusting.'

Addie stared at him. At that moment the telephone rang, and thankfully she moved to answer it. Her voice trembled as she said 'Albury two-o-nine.' She was able to continue the conversation until Ronnie left the office, so the subject was not reopened.

Now it had cropped up again, with Beatie. They all seemed to know something she did not. But Beatie had never taken to Jo, even when she had first started coming into the shop. And since the charity concert she had made a number of disparaging remarks, which Addie had ignored. She thought perhaps Beatie was jealous, and forgave her.

'You'd better be getting home to your Edmund,' she said, in a voice that she intended to be kind, but which actually sounded patronising even to her own ears. Beatrice said 'Humph' and left for her half-day without saying goodbye.

It had been a busy morning. Ronnie had made a stew with a very little meat and a lot of vegetables. It was delicious. Addie ate in silence, thinking about Jo, the two girls from the café, and the concert. She had never been able to decide whether or not it had been a success. She had sung her four songs competently, but she knew that her voice was no more than a shadow of what it had been. One or two people had expressed their pleasure in listening to her with a slight air of surprise.

The famous actress had read some of Jo's poetry. Addie had expected to be bored by this. She had not read a poem since leaving school, apart from the odd verse or two in a magazine. She found that she understood and enjoyed it. It recreated for her that season of country childhood when she had stayed with her grandparents at St Mary Winterbourne. These poems were unsentimental and stark. There was little in them about springtime and flowers; instead Addie remembered with sudden clarity the smell of her grandmother's brick-floored cottage kitchen, the rough texture of her grandfather's working jacket, the deep mud in the wintry lane. She recalled, for the first time in years, how she had crawled through a drain from one field to the next, been soaked to the skin, and struggled up on the other side, breathless and triumphant. None of the other girls had performed this feat, and few of the boys. She had won their respect and admiration, but then she had been forced to face the going home, appearing at the scullery door, wondering if it would be wiser to take off her pinafore and somehow lose it. Grandma had certainly scolded her as she took down the zinc bath that hung outside, dragged it in, half-filled it with warm water and scrubbed her all over. Yet afterwards, when she told grandpa, Addie had heard them laughing in their bedroom. Grandpa had teased her, made a joke of it, been nicer than Gran, though of course he hadn't had to wash the pinafore, boil it back to dazzling whiteness, make starch and iron the frills with a flat iron heated on the fire.

She decided she would buy Jo's book of poems as soon as she could. Perhaps there was more than one. The verse and the novels, of which she had now read two or three, seemed to show different aspects of her new friend. Addie thought she preferred the side of her shown in the poems.

The 'cellist, Jonathan Hayes, had failed to materialize, and his place had been taken at the last moment by the vicar, who was a competent organist. She enjoyed listening to him, having scarcely heard a church organ since that girlhood time when she had sung with the choir at St Augustine's with the Kingstons. Her pleasure was somewhat marred by Ronnie's bored fidgeting. He couldn't understand why anyone wanted to hear such slow, dreary stuff and was amusing himself by identifying the local landowners who attended out of a sense of duty, and smiling in the direction of any he knew by sight. She nudged him sharply.

'Don't keep looking round,' she whispered. 'Listen to the music.'

'Eh? Oh,' said Ronnie. He leaned towards Dorothy on his other side. 'Your mother doesn't think I look holy enough.'

She smiled. She always responded to his attempts to be funny. Addie, observing this out of the corner of her eye, deplored it. If anyone had treated her in the way Ronnie treated their only child, she certainly would not have smiled at his jokes, and he had upset the girl just before they came out by wondering aloud why she didn't know how to make the best of herself. Even her mother had to admit that Dorothy had overdone it. She was helping in the shop during the school holidays and spent all her earnings on make-up. Her nails were a repellent shade of puce, and her cyclamen lipstick was almost as ill-chosen. She had a pretty mouth and lovely eyes, but these were diminished by the thick lenses of her pink-framed spectacles. She had tried, and failed, to master a fashionably complicated hair-style.

Beatrice and Edmund were there of course. Afterwards, outside, Beatie had taken her hand and said, surprisingly, kissing her, 'Lovely to hear your voice again, my dear. Like old times.' She had tears in her eyes. They held hands tightly for a moment, both back in the past with the music and friendship of their youth. Then Beatie hurried away with

Edmund, and the performers and their families walked back to the manor for tea.

Addie was used to the beautiful, shabby drawing room, after several practice sessions before the concert, but Ronnie was plainly over-awed. Fairly knowledgeable about antiques and china, he made his interest in the furnishings of the room rather too obvious. Because he was nervous he made silly jokes and laughed too much, then took it out on Dorothy for spilling her tea in her saucer. Addie was glad to go.

Her farewells were made slightly difficult because though for some weeks she had felt that Lady Scott-Francis was too formal a way to address someone who habitually called her Adelaide, she could not quite bring herself to the use of a Christian name in return. She had made the usual clumsy compromise of avoiding the use of names altogether, which she did on this occasion. The next day a parcel was delivered to the shop by the elderly chauffeur-gardener. It was the book of poems: *The Lane*, by Josephine Ireland. There was no card, but on the title page, in a huge, careless scrawl, were the words 'To dearest Adelaide, from her friend Jo, with love.' After that it was quite easy.

At the end of that summer holiday Dorothy had, for the first time, returned to school not merely without protest, but with anticipation. This saddened Addie. She hinted that it might, after all, be possible to transfer her to the local High School, a prospect her daughter viewed with horror.

She had acquired some extremely left-wing opinions from somewhere, and a source of moral courage which enabled her to argue endlessly with her father on the subject of Socialism. Unfortunately she was considerably better informed than he, and her arguments were more cogent. Ronnie told her that if she was not careful she would develop into one of those ghastly political creatures who shouted their heads off with untidy hair and no make-up. Dorothy said she hoped so.

Yet in spite of this she was anxious to acquire a new dress to take back to school for the fortnightly 'social' evenings, when they were allowed to wear what they pleased for an evening of Monopoly and cocoa-drinking. As all her coupons were used up in the purchase of school uniform, this meant that any item of stock she was given represented a loss of coupons to the business, apart from being against the law. Dorothy, her heart set on a too sophisticated green moss-crêpe, wept and pleaded, but her mother was adamant. Who, after all, could see her at school? But the day before she was due to return to Wales Ronnie said, 'Which frock is it she's making all the fuss about?'

Addie nodded towards the subject of the argument, which since the last discussion of its fate had hung on the outside of a showcase.

Ronnie looked at the price ticket. 'She'd better have it,' he said casually, and moved away down the shop. Addie was astonished.

Dorothy was sitting in the office, filling it with the smell of acetone as she rubbed the puce varnish off her nails, ready for school. She was still wearing the violently coloured lipstick. Addie thought that if Ronnie's prophesy came true it might be an improvement.

'I suppose you'd better take that dress.'

'Oh, Mummy, you angel.' Dorothy sprang up and hugged her fiercely.

'It was Daddy's idea,' said Addie, wishing to be honest.

'Oh, but I know it was you really. I'll go and try it on again.'

She rushed off into the shop. Addie, replacing the top on the bottle of nail-varnish remover, told herself that if she'd realized just how much it meant to the child, it certainly would have been her.

After the school term started the air-raids were intensified, and most nights were spent in a make-shift bed on the office floor, which was considered safer than the bedroom upstairs. Everyone was tired and frightened. Ronnie's firewatching duties were increased as men were called up into the forces. His indigestion increased too, and his irritability to match.

Jo's visits were frequent. Sometimes she came to buy clothes, sometimes to have her own clothes altered, and sometimes she simply dropped in, usually towards lunchtime. She and Addie would sit in the office, smoking Players Number Three, drinking sherry, and talking.

Addie looked forward to these occasions and if a week passed without a call she became worried and depressed. Jo spent much of her time in London, driving an ambulance for the Female Auxiliary Nursing Yeomanry, known colloquially as the Fannies. This was an apparently exclusive branch of the women's services, reserved for privileged women like herself. She wore a khaki uniform, very well-cut and smart, which was somehow quite readily distinguishable from that of the ATS, but Addie rarely saw her wearing it. On her rest days she dressed in her usual elegant, shabby country clothes, well-cut suits or trousers.

When she walked in just before one o'clock that Wednesday in December she was wearing her uniform, having come straight from London. Ronnie was away in Kent. The house in Culvergate had been broken into and, though Addie disliked the idea of his making the journey into a danger area and disliked even more the thought of sleeping alone in the flat, he had insisted on going down to ascertain the amount of theft and damage that had taken place. Not that there was much furniture left in the house by then. All their best things were either in store or had been brought to Albury.

Beatrice and Heather were putting on the covers and dismantling the showroom display when the Hillman Minx Jo used in order to save petrol drew up abruptly just outside. Addie opened the door for her as she crossed the pavement. She looked exhausted. There were dark shadows under her eyes, and when she pulled off her cap her hair had lost its spring and clung unbecomingly to her scalp.

She sank down on the pink brocade settee at the

end of the shop as though at the end of her strength.
'For God's sake get me a drink.' Addie moved
towards the door of the office. 'Not that ghastly
sweet sherry,' Jo called after her.

Addie turned. 'That's all I've got,' she said in
surprise. After all, Jo had drunk a great deal of this
same sherry over the past few weeks. She glanced
at Beatrice, wondering whether she could ask her
to run across to the off-licence, and decided she
could not. Luckily there was some brandy, kept for
emergencies. 'I've got some brandy.'

'That'll do.' Jo drank it quickly, then she ran her
fingers through her hair and at once looked better,
more like herself. 'A terrible night,' she said. 'I've
seen . . . dreadful things. I can never forget them,
never.'

'We had the warning here. I thought of you.'

'I can't be alone this afternoon. I shall shoot
myself if I start thinking.'

'Don't be silly.'

'You wouldn't call it silly if you'd been in London
last night.'

'No.'

'Come home with me.'

Addie hesitated. The raw urgency of this made
her afraid.

'I . . . well . . . Ronnie's gone to Culvergate. He
might ring up.'

'What's he doing there?'

'Seeing about our house. You know it was broken
into.'

'Oh, yes. Well there's nothing to stop you then.

You'd better stay the night. You can't stop in this place on your own.'

The shop with the lights out was dark and shadowy, the office silent, the flat upstairs rambling, a place of passages and corners. Jo was right. She could not stay on her own. Ronnie should not have left her. It was true he had suggested getting Beatie to stay, but she had been so funny and moody of late, Addie hadn't felt like asking her. Anyway, she wouldn't have wanted to leave her beloved Edmund.

'Well, if it's no trouble . . . '

'Oh, for God's sake, get your things.'

Jo seemed to have reached breaking point. She looked so strong, sitting there, relaxed, yet full of power. Her legs in the khaki stockings, her flat brown shoes, her shirt and tie and squarely uniformed shoulders gave her a solid, reliable look, but she had had enough.

Addie went upstairs, found a small suitcase, and packed it with a new lace-trimmed nightdress and her blue velour housecoat, scarcely worn because she preferred Ronnie's thick, old, checked dressing-gown. She put in an unopened bottle of scent, Ronnie's Christmas present, nearly a year old, and a dark wool dress in case Jo expected her to change for dinner.

As she did all this she wondered whether she ought to try to get in touch with Ronnie. He could not have arrived yet, but she could phone Holly, with whom he was going to stay, or Bella, because he was bound to see Bella, but she did not want to.

They had parted friends early that morning, indeed her usual brief kiss on his cheek had been not only affectionate but anxious and guilty as well. Anxious because he was going into a danger area and trains were often targets for bombs, and guilty because of the resentment that had been a barrier between them for the last few days.

Ronnie had given up accusing her of sulkiness some time ago and she thought he had begun to understand that it took her longer to get over scenes and quarrels than he, so relations between them had become comparatively peaceful. Then came this new cause for resentment. Not that there had been a quarrel on this ocassion, only one bitter remark from Ronnie – but one that left too much unsaid.

He had entered the office to find her doing the accounts, and had glanced over her shoulder to see Jo's name in the ledger against a substantial sum of money, about which he made a brief approving comment.

For no reason she could ever understand, Addie said, 'Beatie thinks she's one of those funny women.'

'Funny?'

'Like that girl next-door, you know, Elsa, at Little Jane's.'

Ronnie gave a short, unamused laugh. 'She won't get much change out of you, then, will she?'

His tone was callous, detached, and she felt insulted. Worse than insulted, rejected and unloved. He left the office and she rose, pushing back her chair to go after him and demand to know what he meant. But Beatie and Heather were in the shop, customers too, probably, so she stayed where she was, feeling that in those two gossipy sentences she had betrayed people she liked. Why had she said it?

So now she decided after all not to worry about Ronnie. If he phoned and there was no reply he would assume she had gone to Beatie's. If it had just been a matter of staying with Beatie, she would have done so, but to sleep under the same roof with her and her pale, skinny Edmund was too repellent a thought. She was going to Aldeclere Manor, Jo's house, to the panelled drawing room and the willing, if ancient servants.

CHAPTER 10

FRIDAY

She wanted to go to the lavatory. She needed to go straight away. But it was dark and she could not think where she was. In the dim light of the lamp on Sister's table she saw the row of beds facing her and heard a whimpering cry from the far end of the room. The fever hospital! That was it. She and Charlie with scarlet fever, and he was crying, poor little Charlie, and they wouldn't let her go to him. Well, she would manage it somehow, as she had done so many times, waiting till the nurse was out of the ward, busy in some mysterious and frightening way behind a screen. But first she must creep to the lavatory. Never once in all the days and days she had been in hospital had she asked for a bedpan. The mere idea of making such an appallingly embarrassing request made her feel sick with horror, and as for using it, in full view of the ward like the other children! She would sooner have died. She threw back the bedclothes. She must go to the lavatory and she must see Charlie, poor little Charlie who was so much iller than she had been. She would hold his hands and tell him that Addie was there, that Addie would never leave him . . . A nurse was at her side, she would have to pretend to be asleep, wait until it was safe . . .

Sister Rowles's voice. 'You'll get cold doing that, Mrs Castle. Let me just cover you up. Would you like a drink? You're not in pain, are you?'

Not the fever hospital. Not Charlie crying. 'I . . . I must have been dreaming. I thought . . . ' But what had she thought? She couldn't remember.

'I thought for a minute you were trying to get out of bed. You mustn't do that. You'd probably pull the catheter out, for one thing, and you might slip and hurt yourself.'

The catheter. Horrible thing. She wished she could pull it out. It made her uncomfortable and gave her the feeling that she wanted, more or less acutely, to pass water all of the time.

'I hate the thing.'

'I know. They're not very nice, but we do the best we can. There, is that better? I'll just get you a little something to help you get back to sleep.'

But she didn't want to sleep. Sleep was a waste of time. Strange how her mind had gone back to Charlie and the fever hospital. She hadn't thought about that awful place for years. What extremes life held, even for quite ordinary people like herself. The ward full of children, high iron beds covered with red blankets, the smell of disinfectant and being washed by a plain, elderly nurse who let the soap get into your eyes, then the drawing room at Aldeclere Manor, pale green panelled walls, chintz curtains and a leaping fire reflected in the bright brass fender. She would pretend to be asleep and Sister Rowles would go away and leave her in peace to think.

She and Jo had sat in the drawing room that afternoon and Jo had told her in graphic detail about the horrors of the night, unloading it all. The dead child, the woman with the leg blown off, the half-heard cries from the wrecked houses. She had made nine journeys to and fro with her ambulance, taking people to hospital, never expecting to survive the night herself and hardly caring. Just driving.

Once she said, 'I shouldn't tell you all this.'

'Of course you should. You've been through it. If I can help you to forget . . .'

'Forget! How can I ever forget?'

Addie crossed to where Jo sat on the yellow velvet settee, and put her arms round her, and Jo hid her face against Addie's shoulder and wept. Holding her close, as though she were Holly, Addie for some reason remembered another room and herself lying on a couch while Jessie Marion held a glass to her lips.

Well, she had loved Miss Marion, even if she hadn't known it at the time, and she had loved Jo. Loved her and let her down. Jo who had done so much for her, Jo who had needed her, she had run away and left her. But if she had not . . . Ronnie had needed her too then, or so she had thought. And they were married, surely that meant something? What a muddle it had all been. Were all lives as untidy as hers? Did anyone ever make up his or her mind which person they loved and go on loving and living with that person for ever? What about Holly? Had she ever loved Ted? She must have loved Gillian since she had spent the last ten years of her life in Australia with her and Roger.

But she wasn't going to think about Holly. Not yet. She was going to think about Jo, remember everything both lovely and painful as she had scarcely allowed herself to do in all the intervening years.

How had they spent the afternoon? How long had they stayed like that in the drawing room? She thought Jo must have slept, because she had wanted to phone Holly and see if Ronnie had arrived, but she did not like to use the telephone without asking. In any case she knew Jo would receive such a request with irritability, and why not? Her own husband Major Sir Peter Scott-Francis was serving abroad; she could not always be ringing up to make sure he was alright.

She had been glad she had taken her dark green dress and had changed into it for dinner. It set off her cultured pearls. Just enough. Jo wore black trousers and a sort of Chinese jacket, brilliantly embroidered. She looked tired, but appeared to have thrown off her depression and was amusing and charming company. Fellowes, the elderly butler, had laid dinner on a small table in front of the drawing room fire, the dining room being shut up, to save fuel. They had eaten chicken, deliciously cooked in a creamy sauce, and drunk a good deal of dry white wine. Afterwards they again sat together on the huge settee, and talked and talked. And with no effort, no decision made, no wondering what effect it would have on her listener, Addie told Jo about the Terrible Time. Jo had listened, not interrupting, as Addie described finally how the guilt and horror had haunted her all her life, sometimes rising to an obsession, though often sinking to an undercurrent she could ignore. Or almost ignore. And Jo had absolved her. With pity and love and admiration she had taken away the burden of years.

So it was that, lying in the one-time drawing room at Easton Court, an old woman among old women, Addie was able to relive those dreadful days, and know herself forgiven. It all came back so clearly.

Starting at the beginning she could picture every detail of the front room at Jasmine Villa on that mild Sunday in May – the starched lace curtains; the armchairs each side of the fire in pink and white cotton covers; the pot plants in the window and the old-fashioned upright piano with candle sconces on the front. Holly was practising a new piece, irritable because she could not get it right. She had loosened her clothes as much as she dared, and to Addie at least her altered figure was obvious, but Dad was out for a walk with the boys and Mother was ironing in the kitchen. She usually did this on Sunday afternoons, saying 'the better the day, the better the deed'. She had a piece of old blanket, covered by a square of sheeting, spread on the kitchen table, and she heated her two flat irons on top of the range, in turns.

Feeling vaguely impelled to keep an eye on her sister, Addie had taken her book into the front room. For months she had worried and schemed, glimpsing, however modestly Holly undressed at night, the thickening waistline and swelling breasts. Perhaps today Holly would at last divulge her plans, if such existed. She had persistently turned a deaf ear to Addie's repeated 'But Holly, what shall we do?' though she had long since admitted, without actually saying the words, that she was going to have a baby. Tinkling out the complicated runs and trills, stopping and starting, muttering angrily to herself, Holly continued her practice and Addie curled up in the armchair to read. She had found a bound volume of the Quiver, a Victorian weekly paper of strong moral purpose, that had once belonged to her grandmother, and was reading a serial called 'The Tangled Web' that ran through several numbers of the magazine. It was an absorbing story, headed, above each instalment, with the words, 'Oh, what a tangled web we weave, When first we practise to deceive.' Addied envied the heroine, whose deception was innocent compared to hers and Holly's.

The room, facing south, was filled with afternoon sunshine, and Nellie, fearing for her rosewood furniture, came in with the intention of drawing the curtains. Surely this moment, with the house empty

of brothers and father, presented an ideal opportunity for Holly to confess? Addie longed for her to
do so. She looked up, hoping to catch Holly's eye,
thinking perhaps she would leave them together.
But Holly banged a furious discord as Nellie
drew the green plush side curtains over the white
lace.

'Don't do that, Mum. I can't see the music.'

'You've done enough for today. Go and get some
fresh air.'

'I hate fresh air.' Holly's hands dropped to her
lap, but she remained where she was, on the music
stool.

'You're beginning to look as if you do . . . a
proper pasty face. And you're getting quite stout.
Air and exercise, that's what you want. I shouldn't
think Teddy Kingston likes fat girls.'

'Who cares what Teddy Kingston likes?'

'Well, anyway, put your hat on and go out for an
hour, or you'll end up like Auntie Annie.' Nellie's
sister Annie weighed fourteen stone.

'I shan't. You're horrible. You're a horrible
mother.' Holly jumped up, and with a sob, rushed
out of the room.

'Holly! Holly! Come back . . . how dare you . . . ?'

But before the words were out they heard a crash
and a scream as the mat at the foot of the stairs slid
from under Holly's flying feet and she went down
heavily, grabbing at the hall stand which Addie
caught just in time before it fell on top of her. Nellie
tried to help her daughter up.

'Leave me alone! Leave me alone, can't you?'

Holly pushed away her mother's hands, scrambled to her feet unaided and, flushed and tearful, stumbled up stairs.

They picked up the scattered hats and gloves which had fallen from the hall stand then Nellie said, 'I hope she hasn't really hurt herself,' and followed her. Addie stood listening for a moment but her mother had evidently shut the bedroom door for she heard nothing. So she went through the kitchen and scullery, and out into the back garden. It was very quiet, with that special Sunday afternoon feeling. Addie thought that if she went to sleep for a hundred years and woke up on a Sunday afternoon she would immediately know the day and the time.

By means of the water butt and an old stool that stood by it she climbed up onto the garden wall and began to walk along the top. Down to the bottom, round the difficult sharp angle where the elderberry grew, along to the next corner which was hardly a corner at all because the garden was not square like other people's gardens, and so back to the house, where the zinc bath hung outside the scullery door. Would they ever have a real bathroom? Dad was talking about it. He had put baths into several new houses and seemed in favour of the idea. Addie sat down on the wall and slid to the ground by way of the dustbin, then she went into the scullery. She decided not to wash her hands as she had only touched the dustbin with her feet and went straight through to the kitchen where Nellie had gone back to the ironing.

All the way along the wall Addie had been thinking, *Perhaps she's telling her now. At this moment. Please God, let Holly tell her now.*

But when she saw her mother's face she knew that nothing so momentous had taken place. She looked rather tight-lipped, but no more. 'You'd better go up to Holly,' she said. 'She won't have anything to do with me. I don't know what the world's coming to.'

'She didn't like you saying she was fat, that's all.'

Addie ran upstairs. Holly, still weeping, lay on the bed.

'Oh Holly, are you alright?'

'Of course I'm not alright, stupid idiot.'

It was the first time Holly had referred unprompted to her condition since that first confession.

'You must tell her, Holly, you must tell.'

'I'm not going to tell her. I'll die first. I probably shall die. And if you tell her I'll kill you. D'you hear? I'll kill you.'

Such was her ferocity that Addie retreated. She went along the landing to the lavatory. This was quite spacious, with a frosted glass window overlooking the back garden.

There was a willow pattern lavatory pan, inside which the words 'The Burlington' were inscribed in bright-blue curly letters. Addie thought this an impressive name which made the Clarkes' lavatory superior to the Kingstons', which was only the Gosport, though with mauve pansies, but once she had used the Ladies at the Queen's Hotel and noticed with interest that the unusually wide porcelain bowl there bore a picture of sailing ships and was called 'The Westphalia'.

Solitude being hard to achieve at Jasmine Villa, Addie was grateful for the little square room. She pushed up the lower part of the sash window, and stood staring out across the springtime garden. The elder tree had covered itself with its little bunches of white flowers and the vegetable patch was tidy, though in Mother's part there was nothing apart from the sprawling brown leaves of the daffodils.

It would have been nice to have a garden like the one at Cornwall Lodge, with a rockery and a summer house and small pretty trees. You could walk round without being seen all the time and there were little private bits where you could sit down.

But she mustn't think about gardens now. She dragged her mind back to the problem in hand. For the hundredth time she tried to decide on a course of action. She could not tell her mother without Holly's permission. Even with it the telling would be almost impossible. To confide in Dad, who was in some ways more approachable, was out of the question. He was a man. And who else was there? Bridget Kingston? She was supposed to be Holly's best friend. She was bright and lively like Holly, and very grown-up and knew a lot about everything. But she would tell her mother and Auntie May Kingston would tell Nellie and this would be the worst possible thing.

The only solution that came to Addie's mind was

that she and Holly should run away and to this end she had for some weeks been saving every penny of her pocket money and every sixpence she could earn helping her father in the office. On that day she had in her money-box the sum of four shillings and ninepence. Sighing, she pulled the chain unnecessarily and left her refuge. Back in the kitchen, she found her mother preparing the tea, the Sunday tea of bread and butter and jam, with two kinds of cake, sponge sandwich and Dundee. It was comforting to be there, with everything just as usual: the kettle singing on the range; the table laid for seven; and Mother in her Sunday dress of plum-coloured silk, with lace at the neck. And this afternoon, the boys were safe with Dad and would soon be home. If it weren't for Holly, everything would have been perfect.

The following Monday dawned dull and drizzly. Holly shook Addie awake early.

'Go and tell Mother I'm unwell,' she said.

'Holly! How can you be? I thought . . . '

'Do as I say.'

Baffled and ignorant, Addie dressed quickly as far as her flannel petticoat and went downstairs. Could babies disappear? After all this time could Holly be unwell, and then there not be a baby? Addie delivered the message but her mother scarcely listened. She was looking at a telegram.

'It's from Aunt Annie. Grandma's had a bad fall. I shall have to go. I shall have to cross London.'

She sounded as though the prospect alarmed her. Addie, whose knowledge of London was drawn from the more lurid passages of *Oliver Twist*, visual-ized it as a vast slum interspersed with palaces, peopled by pickpockets who would steal her mother's purse, and rich people who would sneer at her clothes. She was in sympathy.

'Oh, Mum, can't Dad go with you? We'll be alright.' And as she spoke she knew that their absence would in some way help Holly.

'We should have to stay the night,' said Nellie. 'Perhaps two. Oh, dear.'

'I'll look after the boys and Bella, and Holly can cook.'

Though she knew that Holly would not be doing any cooking. Her mother was looking into her face, weighing up the situation, wondering if she, Addie, would be sufficiently responsible. Addie gazed back unflinchingly.

'I suppose you could manage. But no going out after school, mind. You're all to come straight home and stay in for the rest of the day. Jay can see to the fire. Now, what about Holly? Is she getting up?'

'I don't think so. She's got a bad pain.'

'Well, I suppose it won't matter for once if she stays at home. You can take a note to Miss Taylor. Your father's already over at the yard. You'd better take this to him.'

While she dragged on her school dress of bottle-green stuff, Addie told Holly the news, then she ran down to take the telegram to her father. As she left by the back door a pleasing sense of her own importance for a moment outweighed her anxiety.

By the time she started for school with the others

her parents were almost ready to leave. They would not reach the village where Nellie's mother lived until afternoon. Addie spent most of the morning staring unseeingly at the blackboard. Miss Bishop rapped her knuckles with a ruler, for inattention. At twelve o'clock she ran all the way home, glad that Jay and Charlie and Bella loitered as usual.

She pushed open the scullery door. The washing up was neatly stacked, but not done. The kitchen was neat and empty, the house silent. A sense of foreboding gripped her even before she heard Holly's cry.

Standing at the foot of the stairs, she listened to the long drawn-out sound that was neither scream nor groan but both at once. Only when it had faded to a low moan could she bring herself to climb the stairs, and then she went slowly, fighting an urge to run, run away anywhere and never come back. Entering the bedroom, she saw her sister hunched in the disordered bed, her face white and sweaty, her eyes full of terror.

'It's coming,' she said.

'I'll go and fetch Nurse Wright,' said Addie.

Hadn't Nurse Wright gone to Mrs Green when Billy's baby sister was born? She felt proud of knowing what to do.

Holly glared at her, no longer frightened, but fierce. 'You will not. You won't tell anyone. I know what to do. I've found out. Get a lot of newspaper, and a bowl of hot water, and get rid of the kids.'

'But . . .'

'Do it,' hissed Holly, as falling back, she yielded to more pain.

Of course there was no dinner ready for the children, who arrived as Addie was hunting for old newspapers in the cupboard under the stairs. She fetched her four and ninepence, shared it between them and told them to buy sweets. They must eat them in the park and return to school. Four and ninepence would buy a lot of sweets. Even Jay did not argue, though he looked suspicious.

'And you're not to tell,' she shouted after them as they ran off. But she knew she was safe. The enormity of what she had told them to do guaranteed that. Then she went back to Holly and stayed with her, giving her sips of water, uncomplaining when she gripped her arm so hard that it hurt, afraid all the time that some neighbour would hear the screams and knock at the door.

No one came. At two o'clock Holly gave birth to her seven months' child. Addie, sick and trembling, looked down at the ugly little human creature that lay between her sister's legs on a dozen thicknesses of newspaper, still joined to its mother by the umbilical cord.

'It's alright,' she said. 'I think it's alive.'

Holly in an exhausted whisper gave her explicit instructions on tying and cutting the cord, which Addie did with tape from her workbox, and her mother's cutting-out scissors.

'Is it breathing?'

'I don't think it is. Oh, Holly, what shall I do?'

Somewhere at the back of her mind, Addie knew

already what must be done. From some half-heard scrap of conversation, from some forbidden book, she knew she had to pick up the baby and smack it. Make it cry. But would this be right? It looked so small and fragile, such a funny colour and so repulsively bloodstained and sticky.

'Holly, what shall I do?'

Holly spoke succinctly. 'Nothing.'

'Nothing?'

'You heard what I said. Leave it alone.'

'But Holly, it will die. It will die.'

And Holly said, 'Good.'

Then there was more pain, and the afterbirth to deal with. Plenty of newspaper. Open up the kitchen fire. The paper caught alight and roared up terrifyingly, but worse than that was the smell. Addie stood by the range, holding down the round lid with the steel handle until the blaze died down.

Back upstairs to the bedroom. Holly had wrapped the tiny body in her pillowcase. Addie, her face greenish-white and shiny, stood by the bed.

'Get my workbox.'

Addie lifted it from the top of the chest.

'Tip everything out into the drawer.'

Addie removed the tray and then emptied the box. The reckless jumble of pins, needles, darning wool, reels of cotton, bits of tape and lace, letters, combs and hairpins seemed to her a measure of their desperation. She took the workbox to the bed. Holly fitted the little body into it, gently, as if it were alive. Then she said, 'Take it, and dig a hole. As deep as you can. In the back garden.'

This, then, was the answer. Carrying the box, Addie left the room without a word.

In the scullery she changed into her outdoor boots, lacing them with clumsy fingers, before going out into the back garden. She chose a site carefully, bearing in mind that it must be a neglected spot that her father did not use for growing vegetables. Behind the elderberry tree in the far corner there was a weed-infested area that had been undisturbed for years. Her mind a careful blank, she placed the workbox on the ground and went to fetch a spade and a fork from the garden shed.

It was hard, backbreaking work. After twenty minutes' labour the hole was not nearly deep or wide enough, while she was hot and exhausted. Dropping the spade, she took up the garden fork, itself an implement too large and heavy for her to use competently. If only she could ask Jay to help. Could she, when he came in from school, pretend there was a doll in the box, for whom she intended to hold a burial service? The risk was too great – she hadn't played with dolls for years, and anyway Bella would ask questions. She put all her weight on the fork, loosening the earth with the iron prongs, then shovelling it away with the spade. At last the hole seemed adequate. Just. So long as no one investigated. Up till that moment she had managed not to think, not to feel, but as she lifted the box and lowered it into the grave tears poured down her face, and she wiped them away, smearing her cheek with dirt. Then she threw back the soil, stamped on it, and with her bare hands drew the

nettles together to hide the place. It was done. The
canary had been given a better funeral.

CHAPTER 11

Three days later Mum and Dad had returned home, and the lies had begun. Holly had been bilious, said Addie, hadn't eaten anything all the time they'd been away. Feverish too, and she had wondered about calling the doctor, but in the end it hadn't been necessary. Mother was upset, vowing she would never leave her family again, whatever the crisis that demanded her presence elsewhere. She bought shin of beef and stewed it for hours to make beef tea, tried to tempt her daughter with nourishing egg custards, and sent Jay to the chemist's for a bottle of iron tonic. Poor Holly, she could not tell her mother that her breasts were agony, and leaning on her pillows with dark shadows under her eyes and her hair lank, she admitted to feeling poorly. But she was lucky, very lucky, for nothing went wrong and in a few weeks she was her old self again.

More lies were necessary when Nellie remarked

on the disappearance of the workbox and Holly said that she had taken it to school. Nellie was surprised to hear that Holly could teach anyone how to sew, and Holly neatly circumvented further questions by saying she didn't want to be a schoolteacher anyway, and why couldn't she give up and do something else? Nellie said they would think about it. They did think about it and eventually Holly went to work in the fancy goods department at Terry's.

It was not until the danger of discovery was more or less over that guilt and horror overwhelmed Addie. At first she tried to talk to Holly but her sister was expert at being busy, leaving rooms and falling asleep quickly, and so she had started on the wretched treadmill that had intermittently exhausted and depressed her ever since.

I did it for Holly. It was not my fault. But I knew it was wrong. And how could Holly know what was right? She was too ill to know anything. I should have made up my own mind. Fetched somebody. We'd have got over it, all of us. But things were different then. I must forget. I must forget.

And no one had ever known. Until now.

'So there it is. That's my guilty secret.'

Jo took her hand. 'And all the time you've gone on loving your sister?'

'Of course.'

'She's a wicked woman. She was a wicked girl.'

'Oh, no. She was in love with this man. And he

was so much older. I don't think she could help herself.'

'For God's sake, I don't mean that. I mean in using you the way she did, and then denying the whole thing.'

'She didn't realize how it had affected me.'

'And you're still defending her. My God, you know what love really means, don't you? I wish somebody loved me like that.'

At that moment, truly at peace for the first time since she was twelve years old, Addie thought Jo the most lovable person in the world.

Later, preparing for bed, in the beautiful though chilly guest room, Addie felt a tremendous surge of joy. She could cope with anything now. She would be more affectionate to Ronnie, more understanding with Dorothy. She would be happy and make everyone else happy. The old-fashioned cheval mirror showed her standing in her lace-trimmed nightdress. The turquoise silk clung to her body. Not bad for nearly fifty. Very good in fact. She decided not to wear her hair-net in case someone brought her tea in the morning. Surely nothing more unbecoming had ever been invented, but it didn't matter when it was only Ronnie.

Her spectacles looked wrong with the pretty nightdress and softly combed hair. She took them off, but then her reflection dissolved into a blueish blur. She was so short-sighted that she could not see herself at all clearly unless her nose was almost touching the mirror. Replacing her glasses, she switched out the centre light and got into the wide, soft bed. On the bedside table were several books. She chose a volume of short stories: *The Ever Fixed Mark, a Collection of Love Stories* by Josephine Ireland. There were other books there that she might have preferred, but somehow it seemed only right to choose one of Jo's when she was staying in her house. And Jo knew! Knew all about the Terrible Time and Holly's little dead baby which she still believed had held the promise of life. She knew it all and had not rejected her.

Addie opened the book, but found she did not feel like reading and put it aside. She wondered if Jo knew what she had done for her, if she appreciated the weight of the burden she had so effortlessly lifted away. She would do anything for Jo now, she thought. In the morning she must make her understand this tremendous sense of gratitude. She imagined them sitting together drinking coffee, and then wondered if Jo would be up early enough. The shop must be opened by nine o'clock, she would have to leave soon after half-past eight. Would Jo ask the chauffeur-gardener to drive her back to the town? Or would she be able to get a taxi? She doubted whether Jo would appreciate the importance of unlocking the door of Madame Adelaide's at nine o'clock sharp. Perhaps it wasn't so important after all. Except that the 'girls' – Beatie and Heather and Kathleen and Jenny – would be waiting on the doorstep. Well, no good worrying about it now. In the morning she would find Fellowes. He would know what to do. She wouldn't disturb Jo, who must still be so tired. Thinking this, Addie wound up her little gold watch, took off her glasses, and was about to switch off the bedside lamp when the door opened quietly.

The dark blur she saw could only be Jo but she reached for her spectacles to make sure. Before she found them, Jo was standing close to the bed, slipping off her navy-blue dressing-gown. Underneath were white silk pyjamas as plain and well fitting as the white undergarments she wore in the daytime.

'I'm coming in beside you, Addie darling.'

Addie moved over. Why not? She had slept with Holly for years. She was as fond of Jo and as close to her now as if she were a sister. Kissing her was not really different from kissing Holly, and Holly, long ago, would sometimes say, 'Let's have a cuddle Ad, it's cold.' But sisters did not do this. Jo was touching her in a way that only Ronnie had ever touched her . . . a way she had always hated. But she wasn't hating it now. She was clinging to Jo and saying her name over and over again. Of course it was wrong. It must be wrong, but she didn't want her to stop. She didn't care about anything so long as Jo did not stop. This was the only thing that mattered.

When she awoke an edge of light defined the door of the adjoining bathroom. She must have forgotten to turn it off. Jo lay beside her, deeply asleep. What had happened? What had she done and what had been done to her? She must be one of those women like Elsa and Betty, that Ronnie called dreadful creatures. But such an amazing, extraordinary feeling. That, of course, was what some women had with their husbands, but not she. Thank Heavens, not she! As if she would ever let Ronnie see her like that. And Jo! How could she ever look at her again, sit drinking coffee with her in the morning? She felt suddenly homesick for the flat. Just to be away from this imposing house, back in her own place with people of her own kind, like Beatie. Beatie. An oddly perceptive woman. She would know something had happened. Beatie must never know she had stayed all night with Jo. A desperate panic seized her. She must get home.

She slipped out of bed and went to the bathroom, gathering up her clothes as she crossed the room. Quickly and as quietly as she could she dressed, struggling into the elastic corselette, doing up all four suspenders, tying the bow of her blouse. At last, she was creeping down the wide stairs, clutching her handbag, thankful for the small torch she kept in it for use in the blackout. At least she was not forced to risk attracting attention by switching on lights, but supposing a servant heard her, supposing she could not open the front door, what could she say?

The key was in the lock, the bolts slid smoothly, the hinges were silent. Conscientiously she relocked the door behind her and slipped the key back underneath it. It had probably gone under the mat but she had done what she could. They would find it sooner or later.

Her footsteps crunched on the gravel drive so she

moved onto the edge of the lawn. It was not far to the huge wrought-iron gates. She glanced round at the house and all the mullioned windows stared back, reflecting the brilliant moon. Would the gates be locked? Surely they would be, but they were not. She walked through them into the dark lane where the trees grew close together and began her four-mile walk.

Though the night was fine, it was very cold and she had not dared to look for her coat. Fortunately her tweed suit was warmer than the green dress – a good thing she had not bothered to hang it in the wardrobe but had left it on the back of a chair. Half running, half walking, shivering and with sobs rising in her throat, she reached the crossroad and turned towards the town. She passed the village school and the church. The gravestones looked eerie in the moonlight, like an old engraving, but Addie's fears were not of anything supernatural. There was a new American Air Force camp to the east of the town and various units of the British Army were stationed round about. Brawls outside public houses were often reported, and occasionally women were molested.

Albury lay in a valley. Addie slowed her pace a little as she began to descend the hill. On her left were large houses set back from the road in their well-established gardens, almost concealed by trees and shrubs. On her right open fields stretched as far as she could see.

Feeling safer near the houses, she walked quickly along close to the wall. But the overhanging trees

made patches of shadow in which anything . . .
anyone . . . might hide, so she crossed into the
moonlight. Here she was exposed, cruelly visible
from all directions, but at least nobody could take
her by surprise. She remembered how unafraid she
had been as a child, walking along the deserted
sands looking for her brothers. Unafraid, that is,
until Nitty Havergal had started following her.
Now, of course, she realized he was more pitiable
than threatening. If only she'd been able to talk to
some adult, her mother for instance, she might have
been saved much anguish. Holly had only made
things worse.

She'd have liked to be the kind of mother Dorothy
could really talk to but she knew she was not. Just
explaining to her about periods had been agon-
izingly embarrassing. Poor Dorothy! It had been a
dreadful five minutes for them both and she had
never been sure Dorothy really understood. Well,
she was almost seventeen, her friends would have
put her right by now.

Her feet began to hurt. The expensive tan leather
court shoes, though entirely suitable with her green
tweed suit, were nevertheless too high-heeled and
light-weight for the rough country road. If only she
could see a light! But there would be none even
when she reached the town, for the blackout was
rigidly enforced. Even if there were people up and
about behind one of the curtained windows among
the trees she would not know. In any case, supposing she knocked on somebody's door, what could

she say? How to explain her presence, out there in the middle of the night?

She'd been nervous of staying alone in the flat, but now it seemed a haven. She longed for the moment when she would open the shop door. She imagined locking it behind her and stepping through the blackout curtains that extended across the front of the shop. She'd switch on the light, sit down on the nearest chair and kick off her shoes. Then she'd go up to the kitchen, heat up some milk, make a hot water bottle and go to bed. In the morning it would all seem like a dream.

She reached the bottom of the hill, but there was still a long way to go. A gust of wind sprang up, rustling the leaves. She thought she saw movements in the shadows on the other side of the road. The corner marked the boundary of the town and she now walked more comfortably on a pavement but her steps sounded loud in the silence, announcing her presence. Now she was passing a row of small terraced houses, with only tiny front gardens to separate her from them. She could bang on a door but what could she say? You could not rouse people in the early hours without an explanation. They might think she was mad or drunk, or they might themselves prove to be a danger. Though that was absurd. These were ordinary little houses where ordinary people lived. She was almost at the end of the row. She must decide. She walked briskly on, across the main road, past the two or three little shops that constituted a suburban shopping centre, and then past the long row of newish semi-detached

houses, finished just before the war. They were not
unlike her own unlived-in home in Culvergate. She
remembered Ronnie, arriving there that afternoon,
and wondered if he had found much damage. The
thought suggested criminals and evil-doers, people
who prowled about at night, broke into buildings,
stole, raped, murdered. Things didn't always
happen just to other people. Her house had been
entered, why should she not be attacked? But she
could scream. Surely someone would hear. Once
more she rehearsed the reasons for and against
knocking on somebody's door and still she hurried
on, intent on reaching her own home. Again she
imagined herself hunting in her bag for her key,
fitting it into the lock. Not until she was in the
kitchen upstairs would she feel really safe. The shop
was always eerie when closed, full of concealed
dustsheeted shapes and inexplicable creaking
sounds. If only they had put a door at the top of
the stairs, so that the flat could be shut off. Anyone
could . . . She checked herself firmly. No good
thinking like that. After all, Ronnie was always
there to protect her. Though a little man, he was
possessed of extraordinary physical courage. One
night, when they'd really thought they heard someone moving about in the shop he had marched
downstairs in his pyjamas clutching the poker, far
too angry to be afraid. If only he were with her
now. What an idiot she was to run away like that!
There was so much she would have to think about
in the morning.

She would soon be in the town centre. Would

that be better or worse? She might meet a policeman or an air-raid warden who would ask what she was doing out alone. Reaching a corner, she crossed the road, and it was then that she heard the footsteps approaching from her left. She did not turn her head, but quickened her step, praying that they might fade away in the opposite direction. After about twenty yards she still could not be sure whether they were nearing her or receding. Then she stepped on a manhole cover that made a loud metallic rattle, and when she heard the same noise repeated she knew they were coming her way. Nearer. Nearer. She started to run.

It was an absurd thing to do. She had not run for years, her shoes made it hopeless and she was out of breath almost at once. Then she caught her heel in a crack and fell headlong. The shoe came off, her ankle was wrenched and stabs of pain went through her knee and shoulder. She did not even try to rise, but lay there sobbing. Addie Clarke, Adelaide Castle, Madame Adelaide lay on the pavement and waited for whatever was going to happen.

'Why, Ma'am, you sure were in a hurry!'

So it was an American. He helped her to her feet. Despairing of escape, of ever reaching home safely, she allowed him to replace her shoe and pick up her handbag. She straightened her glasses, which had luckily not come off in the fall and said, 'Thank you. You're very kind.'

The sky was clouded now, and the moon hidden. Surely day must break soon. Darkest before the dawn. Dark night of the soul. The well-worn phrases drifted across her mind. Her complete hopelessness was somehow steadying. She took a step or two forward but a spasm of pain shot through her ankle and she sank down, feeling sick, on the low wall that bordered the front garden of the nearest house.

'Gee, you're hurt!'

'I'm alright. Please leave me alone.'

'Heck, no! I don't know what you're doing here but you aren't the kinda dame that ought to be around on your own at this time of the night. I guess I'll have to take you home.'

Addie sat on the wall, shivering, her head bent. She felt as though she would never move. The man was standing close in front of her. She realized that he was undoing his coat and memories of Nitty Havergal crowded in. Not again, not twice in one lifetime. What was the evil in her that made this happen?

'Can you stand up?'

What now? Oh, God, what now? Then she saw that he had taken off the coat. She rose unsteadily and he placed it round her shoulders.

'Now, c'mon. How far is it to where you live?'

'In the town, the High Street.'

Slowly they walked on together, he fitting his stride to Addie's painful progress.

'If you put that on properly you could take my arm.'

'It's alright, thank you.'

'Have it your way.'

The coat was warm and heavy. She felt its roughness at her neck as she held it together in front. It smelt of tobacco, and in the clean night air the man beside her was redolent of smoke and alcohol and warm humanity.

'Do you English ladies always wander around in the night?'

'No, of course not.'

'How did you get here?'

'I walked.'

'It's a dangerous thing to do, walk around at night, even in a one-horse place like this, I guess.'

He talked nearly all the time, asking questions and telling her about himself. He came from the Bronx, which sounded like a cowboy place but apparently was not. He told her she should be more friendly. Everyone needed friends, he said and she surely did, or she wouldn't be out alone in the cold and dark. Addie asked herself who were her friends. Ronnie? Jo? Beatie? They'd all played their parts in placing her in this situation.

When at last they turned into the High Street she did not know whether meeting a stray policeman, firewatcher or air-raid warden would be a relief or not. For one thing it might be someone she knew. All the neighbouring shopkeepers took their turn at firewatching. What could she say? 'Could you please tell this man to leave me alone?' But it was barely dawn and she was wearing his coat.

He had been kind, but what lay behind his kindness? With all this talk of being friendly, of men and women needing one another, it hardly seemed

likely that he would leave her at her door with a
polite farewell.

And he did not. Her hands were so cold that she
fumbled with the key and dropped it. He picked it
up, fitted it into the lock, opened the door for her,
and of course followed her through it and into the
shop beyond the blackout curtains. The light. She
must switch on the light. The coat fell to the floor
as she found the switch. He stood there before her,
young, curly-haired, with his uniform hat at a
jaunty angle.

They blinked at one another in the unaccustomed
glare. He looked harmless. Should she, after all,
offer him a cup of tea?

But he was staring at her. He looked surprised,
embarrassed even. 'Why,' he said, 'you're old.
You're an old woman.' Accusing her, almost. 'I
guess . . . you'll be OK now.'

He picked up his coat and found his way out
between the curtains. She heard the door close
behind him.

For some time she sat there in the shop on the
gilded chair, dazed, incapable of movement or
coherent thought.

'You're old . . . an old woman.'

Presently she rose, and pausing on her way
upstairs, stared at herself in the long mirror. She
was bedraggled, her hair limp from the damp night
air, her face colourless, the clear line of her jaw
beginning to sag. But not old. Surely not.

Then like a fountain of joy, she remembered. Jo
had not thought she was old. Slowly, quietly, empty

of thought, she moved about the flat, until eventually she got into bed. As she did so she realized she was not wearing her watch. Was it still on the bedside table at Aldeclere? It didn't seem very important and she was soon asleep.

The telephone was ringing at the entrance to the ward. It was beyond the double doors which once a butler had thrown open to announce guests and meals, and which now, so usefully wide, stood open almost all the time for the passage of trolleys and wheelchairs and hurrying nurses; but still it sounded shrill in the shadowed quiet of the ward.

The night sister went quickly to silence it. An emergency of some kind. And that was strange because it was the telephone ringing on the landing that had roused Addie out of her brief sleep that Thursday morning.

Jo! It must be Jo, who had awakened to find her gone. Addie threw back the bedclothes and tensing herself against the cold air went out and stood in the draught at the top of the stairs to answer it.

It was not Jo. At first she could not think who else it might be.

'Addie? Is that you? My God, you've been ages.'

'I was asleep. Who is it?'

'Holly, of course. Who do you think?'

'Holly!'

'Now, listen, Ad, don't be alarmed . . . '

Alarmed! Of course she was alarmed. 'What is it? Tell me. Are you alright?'

'Yes, of course I'm alright. It's Ronnie.'

Stupid with exhaustion, she tried to grasp the meaning of what Holly was saying. 'Ronnie?' An air-raid. An accident.

'Yes, Ronnie. Do wake up, Addie.'

'What's happened? Is he hurt?'

'He had a haemorrhage. The doctor says it's a perforated gastric ulcer. He's lost a lot of blood, but they're giving him a transfusion.'

'He's alright, then?'

'No, of course he's not alright. He's seriously ill. You'd better come.'

'Today, do you mean?'

'Of course today. Now listen. There's an eleven thirty-five from Victoria. You ought to be able to catch that.'

She'd have to take a taxi from Paddington to Victoria alone, with the possibility of there being an air-raid. She went to London regularly, on buying trips, but then Ronnie was with her. He knew his way around, and how much to tip. He'd worked in London for a few months as a young man, after he left the Navy. She only had to tell him the address of the showroom she wanted to visit and he would be able to find it easily. Once they arrived, he would sit back and encourage her to trust her judgement, to spend hundreds of pounds on stock. He must not be ill, she could not do without him.

Her brain clearing, she told Holly she would be on the train she suggested, the eleven thirty-five from Victoria, sent her love to Ronnie, and rang off. Now she must concentrate. Another suitcase, another nightdress. No dressing-gown unless she took her old one. Well, better than nothing, and not so heavy. Would she ever get her blue one back? Ronnie might ask where it was. But Ronnie was very ill. Anxiety suddenly gripped her. She wanted to speak to Holly again and find out more, but she was afraid, and in any case there was little enough time to prepare for her journey.

Then she thought of Jo, waking up and finding her gone. Jo would think she had been mortally offended, put off, by what had happened, that she had left her for good . . . How hurt she would be, how disappointed. She wanted to tell her that she felt different now. It had just been . . . too much, a shock. How childish, running off like that! But of course, if she had stayed, she would not now be packing to go to Ronnie. The phone would be ringing and ringing in the empty flat, with Holly becoming desperate at the other end. Well, she couldn't stop to think about it now, she would have plenty of time to do that on the train. She became businesslike, found a timetable, ordered a taxi, telephoned Beatie, and even managed to eat a piece of toast.

Her ankle was still painful. She bandaged it tightly and chose her most sensible shoes. The tweed suit she had worn yesterday was perfectly suitable for travelling, and she packed a lighter one for indoors.

Within twenty minutes of receiving her call, Beatie was at the shop door. She was shocked and upset by the news of Ronnie's illness. Surprising, really, when they'd never exactly hit it off.

'Oh, Addie, my dear, how I wish I could come with you!'

Addie wished she could, too, but to leave the shop to Heather and Kathleen was unthinkable.

'He'll come through it, my dear, doctors are really wonderful these days.' Until that moment Addie had not allowed herself to realize that he actually might not come through it. She felt unreasonably annoyed with Beatie. A taxi drew to a halt outside. As she picked up her handbag and suitcase the telephone rang in the office. Beatie ran to answer it, saying, 'Go and get in the taxi . . . '

It might be Holly again. Or it might be Jo. The taxi driver rang the bell and Addie took her suitcase to the shop door. When it was safely stowed away she turned to go back into the shop, but the driver pointed out that time was pressing. She got into the back of the car and wound down the window.   '

Beatie reappeared and came out onto the pavement. 'It's alright,' she said. 'It was only Lady Scott-Francis. I told her you'd been called away, due to illness, but I don't think she believed me. What a nerve! Ringing up before the shop's even open!'

'Beatie. Phone her back and say . . . say I'll . . . oh, never mind.' As the taxi drew away she put her head out of the window and called, 'Don't forget to order those patterns for Mrs Waddington!'

'What?'

'Don't forget . . . ' Giving up, she sank back onto the seat.

'Miss the train if we don't get a move on,' muttered the driver, and Addie, flung sideways as he took the corner too fast, thought that if a road accident was to be next in the sequence of events it would seem merely inevitable. But she reached the station safely and in time.

Then the endless journey. She had dozed fitfully, waking confused and fearful. The train jogged and rumbled, but why was she lying down? She was not on a train, she was in a hospital, being pushed along on a trolley. But it was Ronnie, not her, who was in hospital. He must have died in hospital, and left her alone. But no. He had not died, he had recovered and come back to Albury. Why then was she living alone? She was sure of that, she lived alone in the house in Culvergate. She lived alone there because Ronnie had left her. He still helped her to run the business, the two shops in Culvergate and Foreland Bay after they sold the one in Albury, but when they had returned home after the war he had simply announced his intention of living by himself in a flat. He had found himself a very pleasant one on the sea-front and left her to reinstall herself in the house, to rattle about like a pea on a drum. All he would say by way of explanation was that he thought they would get on better apart. Well, it was true in a way. Too late, now, to remember that afternoon at Aldeclere when she had so lightly dismissed Jo's suggestion that she should leave the shop and Ronnie and go to live with her at the Manor House.

She could see Jo now, speaking slowly, choosing her words. She had told Addie that she did not belong in the vulgar world of business, that all this keeping a shop was degrading and unnecessary. She, Jo, needed someone to come home to, someone who was always there. Addie. As for her husband, they had always led more or less separate lives. After the war, and Heaven knew when that would be, he would go back to the war office and live in their London flat. It wouldn't make any difference. And there was plenty of money.

Of course Addie had not given the idea one moment's consideration. Not at the time, but in later years when Ronnie had dropped her at her gate and gone on in the car to his own place, she sometimes wondered what it would have been like. Of course, it wasn't only Ronnie, or Dorothy. It was Madame Adelaide's. Running a business was the most fascinating game in the world.

As it was she had never seen Jo again. Back in Albury ten days later, leaving Ronnie in Culvergate, weak but improving, she had asked Beatrice if there had been any phone calls, from special customers for instance. People like . . . well, Lady Scott-Francis.

'I wouldn't call her such a marvellous customer,' said Beatie. 'All she does is bring in her old clothes for us to alter.'

'Has she been in or phoned?' Addie kept her voice carefully mild.

'No,' answered Beatie, then added maddeningly, 'not that I remember.'

Obviously there was no more to be learned from Beatie, and as time passed Addie became more and more anxious. On the morning of the day that was to bring Ronnie back to Albury by hired car she picked up the upstairs telephone extension, choosing a time when Beatrice was busy, and asked for Aldeclere two-six.

Fellowes answered. Lady Scott-Francis was not at home. No, she was not expected. She was quite well, as far as he knew. He volunteered nothing, nor did he ask who she was, though she thought he recognized her voice. On the whole, she decided, it was more of a relief than a disappointment. She would not try again.

The sense of movement had ceased. Should she bother to open her eyes? She was in a small, white-. walled room. They had moved her, bed and all, into a side ward. Why?

Nurse was bending over her. 'We thought you'd like a bit of peace and quiet, dear. It's noisy in the ward today.'

Addie wanted to say, 'Thank you,' but no sound came out. Not so well, then. But quite clear in her mind. She hoped they realized that.

'Just relax, Mrs Castle. Everything's fine.'

Fine. How could they say that when Ronnie had left her? Gone away to live by himself? She'd asked him why dozens and dozens of times and he'd never given her a proper answer. Dorothy had seemed to know why, but all she would say was, 'It's the only thing for him, Mum.'

Well, she'd got used to being alone at home except for Dorothy some of the time. After all, she had her family to visit . . . But then she had lost

Holly. She really had thought Holly loved her. Well, she ought to love her – she owed her everything . . .

She had walked into the shop one day, a year or so after they had re-established themselves in the old place. 'Well, Ad. I've made up my mind. I'm off to Australia to Gillian.'

Addie was not very surprised and only slightly dismayed. 'How long will you be away?'

'For good, of course, I'm emigrating.' Then cruelly Holly added, 'There's nothing to keep me now Ted's gone, and Jimmy's in Scotland.'

Holly had never even seen Dorothy's baby – what was her name? Angela. She'd thought Dorothy might have called her Holly, she was so like her – surprising really, when Dorothy had taken after Ronnie's side, though she became more of a Clarke as she got older.

'For good? Don't be silly!'

'What's silly about it?'

'Well, of course you can't go gallivanting off to Australia! What about us, what about your family?'

'Gillian's my family, Ad. I want to be near her and her children. It won't make much difference to Jimmy.'

Addie turned away, vaguely shuffling papers on her desk, so that Holly should not see her stricken face. 'But what about me?'

'You've got Dorothy, and the others aren't far off, and Ronnie wouldn't let you down, even if he doesn't live with you.'

It had to be said. To plead was shameful, but

the debt was there and Holly must acknowledge it. 'After all I did for you . . . '

'What d'you mean? What did you do for me?'

'Holly! All those years ago. At Jasmine Villa. You can't have forgotten.'

Holly moved away. Looked in a mirror. Adjusted her hat. 'Oh, that. You mean when I had the miscarriage.'

'Miscarriage!' Addie was stunned.

'Well of course you were marvellous, dear. I'm sure I couldn't have managed without you.' Her tone implied that she could in fact have managed perfectly well.

'It wasn't a miscarriage. It was a baby. And I . . . ' She could not possibly utter the words, 'buried it in the garden'.

The shop, with its silver-grey carpet, big mirrors and elegantly restrained display of dresses, swam around her. Could this be happening? Two middle-aged, infinitely respectable women – could they be saying these things? Could they possibly be talking like this?

'Oh, my dear, of course it wasn't a baby. It was weeks and weeks premature. It could never have lived for an instant.'

'You don't know how I suffered. For years. And you wouldn't talk about it.'

'I didn't want to talk about it. And I don't now. Some things are best forgotten. I was a silly child. I made a mistake and I paid for it. I certainly wasn't going to let it ruin my life. Anyway, what's all this got to do with me going to Australia? Come on, Ad.

Let's go to lunch at Terry's and I'll tell you all about it.'

So Holly had left her too, though it was for her more than anyone that they had come back to Culvergate. And if they had stayed in Albury she might have seen Jo again. But no, of course, that was ridiculous. Five years of waiting and hoping she might suddenly walk into the shop, five years of never answering the phone without a faint surge of expectation, had been in vain.

Yet they had been good times in Culvergate. Dorothy had come back to live nearby, and she had seen Jay and Maud regularly, and Charlie and Winnie reasonably often, though Bella and Percy only seldom. She had an idea that Ronnie sometimes went there, but nothing was ever said.

She felt dizzy and ill. It must be the train. Long train journeys had never suited her. She was on her way to Ronnie, leaving the shop, leaving Jo, because Ronnie was her husband and must come first. But she seemed to be lying down. Where was she? She could not be going to Ronnie after all because so much had happened since then. At that time, Dorothy had still been at school in Wales, and she knew much more than that about Dorothy. She had left school, served as a VAD nurse, become a teacher. She had married that awful sadistic man and become ill. They had been to see her in hospital, a psychiatric hospital, a frightening place, and she had turned her face away from them and stared at the wall. That had been dreadful. But she was

alright now, happily married to her second husband, though he seemed a dull sort of chap. The
pair of them were continually hard up, both being
teachers without any ambition to become heads of
schools or to progress in any way. Yet they seemed
to think that their way of life was the only right
one.

Still, they had been very kind, having her to live
with them when she couldn't manage alone any
longer, even if they had really spoilt Jasmine Villa,
having walls knocked down and Heaven knows
what. Why had they bought the old family home if
they hadn't wanted to keep it as it was?

She'd always meant to avoid being one of those
old people who went on and on about the old days,
repeating themselves and boring everyone stiff, but
in the end she couldn't help it, because she'd been
so upset when they'd built on the garage. Father
had designed the house himself, so that it was sym-
metrical, because symmetry was pleasing to the eye.
Building on the garage unbalanced it. Dorothy said,
'We know, Mum, we know,' rather wearily and she
realized that she must have said this many times
before.

Of course, she was old. Old people did that kind
of thing. But it didn't seem any time at all since the
childhood days at Jasmine Villa.

And she ought to have seen Jo again – taken the
initiative, made an effort, not just hoped and
waited, because she owed her so much. Because of
her the shame and guilt and horror of the Terrible

Time had never reasserted themselves. She'd even felt glad that Holly had been able to forget, that her sister had chosen to put her debt of gratitude out of her mind. But surely, after that, they must mean more to one another than ordinary sisters? That was why her going to Australia had been such a blow. Ronnie had said, 'You'll be able to go out and stay with her when you retire.'

But she had not retired until she was nearly seventy, and by that time Holly had died. And she'd finished up at Jasmine Villa, only now they called it simply number twenty-two, and most of the garden had been sold off as a building plot, including the bit with the elderberry and the stinging nettles.

She heard Ronnie's voice. He'd come to see her again. Well, that was good of him. He'd been a very difficult man to live with. Irritable and impatient. It would have been understandable if she had left him. Her style was different from his. She couldn't keep arguing and quarrelling, but she could keep quiet. Usually he'd give in, in the end. Once he'd shouted, 'I'm fed up with your bloody sulking,' and he'd raised his arm to hit her. She'd said, 'If you strike me, I shall walk out of here and never come back,' and that had stopped him, of course, because he knew he couldn't manage the business without her.

Somebody was holding her hand. Gripping it.

Would Holly die? Could anyone look like that and not die?

Her pinafore was covered in mud, but she'd done it. Arnie Pryke was pulling her to her feet.

'Coo, Addie, you are a one! What'll your Gran say?'

Outside in the car Ronnie, a thin little old man, but spruce, with a neat moustache, sat with Dorothy, plumpish, middle-aged and untidy.

'I shouldn't have left her,' he said, and blew his nose.

'Never mind, Dad.'

They stayed there for a few minutes, looking out at the rose bushes and the gravel drive, then Dorothy started the car, and they drove away.